❛ The most destructive force in the Universe... ❜

Far out in space, the exploration ship PALOMINO encounters an enormous Black Hole — a vast chasm of all-consuming gravitational pull...

Suspended on its brink hangs the giant research ship CYGNUS, lost without trace twenty years before...

Aboard the CYGNUS, in command of its bizarre crew of robots, is Reinhardt: the man who first devised the ship and has now constructed the force field that keeps it from the edge of destruction.

Has he found the last great secret of the universe or has his genius finally crumbled into an evil insanity...

Starring MAXIMILIAN SCHELL, ANTHONY PERKINS, ROBERT FORSTER, JOSEPH BOTTOMS and YVETTE MIMIEUX and ERNEST BORGNINE
Produced by RON MILLER · Directed by GARY NELSON
Story by JEB ROSEBROOK and BOB BARBASH and RICHARD LANDAU
Screenplay by JEB ROSEBROOK and GERRY DAY
Production Design by PETER ELLENSHAW
From WALT DISNEY PRODUCTIONS

THE BLACK HOLE

Alan Dean Foster

Based on the Screenplay by
Jeb Rosebrook & Gerry Day

NEW ENGLISH LIBRARY/TIMES MIRROR

A New English Library Original Publication, 1979

© 1979 by Walt Disney Productions

First NEL paperback edition November 1979
Reprinted November 1979
Reprinted March 1980

NEL Books are published by
New English Library from
Barnard's Inn, Holborn,
London EC1N 2JR.
Typeset by Parker Typesetting.
Made and printed in Great Britain by
William Collins Sons & Co Ltd, Glasgow

45004569 2

For Unca Walt, who made it all possible,
For Joshua Meador, Bill Tytla and Carl Barks,
For Unca Scrooge, who made it square,
For the Junior Woodchucks of the World and their
guidebook and reservoir of inexhaustible knowledge,
And for their most illustrious threesome; Huey, Dewey
and Louie, who could read microscopic print with the
naked eye and who would have enjoyed this book . . .

'There are more things in Heaven and Earth, Horatio, than are dreamt of in your philosophy.'

Hamlet, Prince of Denmark

'Stars with trains of fire and dews of blood, Disasters in the sun.'

Horatio, Soldier of Denmark

ONE

THE universe bubbled and seethed to overflowing with paradoxes, Harry Booth knew. One of the most ironic was that the mere observation of its wonders made a man feel older than his time, when, instead, it should have made him feel young, filled with the desire for exploration.

Take himself, for example. He was an inhabitant of the years euphemistically called 'middle age'. Mentally the label meant nothing. His body felt as limber and healthy as when he had graduated from the university, though his mind had adopted the outlook of a wizened centenarian – a centenarian who had seen too much.

C'mon, Harry, he admonished himself. Cut it out. That's wishful thinking. You *want* to sound like the all-knowing old sage of space. Your problem is you still have the perception as well as the physical sense of well-being of a university student. Imagine yourself the inheritor of the skills of Swift and Voltaire if you must, but you know darn well you'll never write anything that makes you worthy of sharpening the pencils of such giants. Be satisfied with what you are: a reasonably competent, very lucky journalist.

Lucky indeed, he reminded himself. Half the reporters of Earth would have permanently relinquished use of their thirty favourite invectives for a chance to travel with one of the deep-space life-search ships. How you, Harry Booth, ended up on the *Palomino* when far better men and women languished behind merely to report its departure from Earth orbit was a mystery for the muses. Count your lucky stars.

Glancing out the port of the laboratory cabin he tried to do just that. But there were far too many, and none that could unequivocally be deemed lucky.

Although he had pleasant company in the room he felt sad and lonely. Lonely because he had been away from home too

9

long, sad because their mission had turned up nothing.

He forced himself to stand a little straighter. So you consider yourself a fortunate man. So stop complaining and do what you're designed to do. Report. He raised the tiny, pen-shaped recorder to his lips, continuing to stare out the port as he spoke.

'24 December. Aboard the deep-space research vessel *Palomino*. Harry Booth reporting.

'Ship and personnel are tired and discouraged, but both are still functioning as planned. Man's long search for life in this section of our galaxy is drawing to a close.'

Pausing, he glanced back into the lab to study his companions. A tense, slim man tapped a stylus nervously on a light pad and looked back up at Booth. He wore an expression of perpetual uncertainty and looked much younger than the reporter, though they were not so different in age. The uncertainty and nervousness were mitigated by an occasionally elfin sense of humour, a wry outlook on the cosmos. The man executed a small, condescending bow toward Booth; the corners of his mouth turned up slightly.

Behind him stood a softly beautiful woman whose face and figure were more graphically elfin than the man's sense of humour. Her mind, however, was as complex as the whorls in her hair. Both scientists were more serious than any Booth was used to working with, a touch too dedicated for his taste. He might never truly get to know them, but he had respected them from the first day out. They were cordial toward the lone layman in their midst, and he reciprocated as best he could.

She was feeding information to the lab computer. As always, the sight had an unnerving effect on Booth. It reminded him of a mother feeding her baby. Where Katherine McCrae was concerned, the analogy was not as bizarre as it might have been if applied to another woman. There was a particular reason why one would view her association with machines as unusually intimate.

Booth returned to his dictation. 'Based upon five years of research involving stars holding planets *theoretically* likely to support life by the fair-haired boy of the scientific world, Dr Alex Durant –' the man who had bowed now grinned playfully back at him '– this expedition has concluded eighteen months of extensive exploration and netted, as with all previous expeditions of a similiar nature and purpose, nothing. Not a single alien civilisation, not a vertebrate, nothing higher than a few inconsequential and unremarkable microbes, plus evidence of a few peculiar chemical reactions on several scattered worlds.'

Booth clicked off the recorder and continued staring at Durant. 'That about sum it up, Alex?'

Repeated disappointment had purged Durant of the need to react to such observations defensively. 'Unnecessarily flip, perhaps, but you know I can't argue with the facts, Harry.'

'I'm never *unnecessarily* flip, Alex.' Booth slipped the recorder back into a tunic pocket. 'You know that I'm as disappointed in the results as you are. Probably more so. You can go back with the ship's banks full of valuable data on new worlds, new phenomena, stellar spectra and all kinds of info that'll have the research teams back on Earth singing hosannas to you for years.' He looked glum.

'Sure, we've missed the big prize: finding substantial alien life. But you have your astrophysical esoterica to fall back on. For me and my news service, though, it's eighteen months down a transspatial drain.' He thought a moment, then added, '24 December. Not quite the way we'd expected to celebrate Christmas Eve, is it?' He turned again, looked back out the port.

'We need reindeer and a fat man in a red suit. That would do for a report on extraterrestrial life, wouldn't it?' He grunted. 'Christmas Eve.'

Durant forced a wider smile. 'Beats fighting the mobs of last-minute shoppers. You couldn't order a thing about now. Order channels to the outlets would be saturated.' Nearby, McCrae flipped a control on the computer panel, concluded her programming, then laughed.

'You can both hang your stockings back by the engines. Maybe Santa'll leave you something unexpected.'

Booth eyed her challengingly. 'Can you fit an alien civilisation into a sock?'

'I'd settle for anything non-terran with more backbone than a semi-permeable membrane.' Durant's smile melted his melancholy. 'Or some stick chocolate,' he added cheerfully. 'I never will understand why the galley can't synthesise decent chocolate.'

'I'll threaten it.' McCrae started toward the lab exit.

'Maybe that'll produce results. I'm going back to Power.'

'Be back by Christmas.' Durant watched her depart, glanced down at the calculations he had been doodling with and spoke without looking across at Booth. 'Wonder what Holland would say if I asked him to extend the mission another two months? By widening our return parabola, we could check out two additional systems, according to my figures.'

'I don't think you'll get much sympathy for that idea from our pilot, Alex.' Booth's gaze had returned to the stiff but always fascinating ocean of stars outside the port. 'Privately he'd probably enjoy spending another year exploring. But he wasn't picked to command this expedition because of a penchant to indulge himself in personal pleasures.

'Schedule says we return by such and such a date. He'll move heaven and earths to dock in terran orbit on or before that date. Pizer, now . . . he'd steer us through a star if you could guarantee him a fifty-fifty chance of making the run. But he's only first officer, not commander. He still smells of the audacity of youth. And the foolishness.' Booth looked resigned.

'Life is ruled by such subtleties, Alex. Commander or first officer, experienced or brash and challenging. If there's one thing I've learned in three decades of reporting on developments in science, it's that the actions of people and sub-atomic particles aren't as different as most folks would think.

'If you want my real opinion, I'd rather have V.I.N.Cent in charge than either of them.'

'Me too,' agreed Durant. 'Of course that's impossible. Even though they're supposed to select the best people for each position.'

'True,' said Booth. 'The problem is whether Vincent qualifies as people. He certainly doesn't fit the physical specifications for a command pilot . . .'

At the moment the subject of their conversation was up forward in command with Charles Pizer. V.I.N.Cent's multiple arms were folded neatly back against his hovering, barrel-shaped body. Monitor indicators winked on or off as internal functions directed.

12

His optical scanners were focused on the first officer. Pizer was slumped on one of the pilot lounges, staring at the main screen. He took no notice of V.I.N.Cent. That the robot was not a man was obvious. But the suggestion that he might not qualify as a person was one Pizer would have taken immediate exception to.

Hands manipulated controls. Constellations and other star patterns slid viscously around on the screen. Suns shifted against a background of pale, lambent green, that colour being easier on the eyes – and according to the psychologists, less depressing – than a more realistic black would have been. It was all the same to the robot.

The first officer's thoughts were drifting like the representations of stars and nebulae, though not in harmony with them.

'What does that remind you of, V.I.N.Cent?'

'Presuming you to be referring to the holographic stellar display, Mr Pizer,' the machine responded smoothly, 'I would say that it reminds me strongly of a holographic stellar display.'

'Not me. To me it looks like multipea soup.' Pizer raised up in the lounge, the chair humming as it matched the movement of his body. 'I'm starving . . .'

Lights flashed in sequence on the robot's flanks, visual indication that the machine was preparing to respond. 'What else is new?'

'Mechanical sarcasm is a feature the cyberneticists could damn well have left in the hypothetical stage.' Pizer gave the robot a sharp look. 'Nothing sitting loose in the galley, I expect. What's on the menu for today?'

'Dehydrated turkey. A special treat, Lieutenant, since it's Christmas Eve. Also dehydrated cranberry sauce, dehydrated gravy and giblets, de—'

Pizer cut him off. 'Save me from a full list of the special treats.' The vision of dehydrated giblets had quashed whatever rising surge of hunger he had been experiencing.

'V.I.N.Cent, I envy you.'

'That's not surprising, but why, Lieutenant?'

'No taste buds.' He leaned back into the lounge. Servos whined, adjusting to fit material properly against his back. He slipped his hands behind his head and stared longingly at the ceiling.

'Now if I were home, I'd sit down to a feast. A real one, with the right amount of water already in the food, not waiting to be added. Roast turkey with oyster stuffing, sweet potatoes in orange sauce, vegetables, salad, mince pies . . .' Remembering made him appear even younger than he was.

He drifted happily along on the illusion of caloric ephemera until V.I.N.Cent had to add, '. . . bicarbonate of soda . . .'

Pizer swung out of his chair and moved toward the doorway, shoving the robot with mock belligerence. '*You'll* never know one way or the other. Anyway, I'll be eating the real thing soon enough. Eighteen months. It's the twenty-fourth. Time to start back, as you well know. Back to real turkey and real dressing. Back to real life. Take her home, Heart o' Steel.'

Actually, there was very little steel in V.I.N.Cent's body, the robot having been constructed of far more durable and exotic alloys and metals. But he was still capable of recognising and accepting an affectionate nickname such as the one Pizer had just bestowed on him. He did not offer metallurgical correction as he drifted toward the consoles, plugged the correct armature into the board and began to prepare for the incipient change of course.

'Home for you, Mr Pizer, but out here's the only home I know.' One free limb gestured at the swath of star-speckled blackness that filled the port above the consoles.

Pizer had already left the room.

Kate McCrae made her way down and back to the power centre of the *Palomino*, trying hard to block out the air of disappointment she'd left back in the lab.

Booth's personal pessimism she could dismiss easily enough. His interest in the mission stemmed from cruder needs than hers or Alex's. The reporter would mentally be translating the most significant of their discoveries into credit points with his service, disparaging them by the process which transmuted the advancement of science into monetary terms.

It was in her nature, however, to see the best in everyone. Personal relationships were one area where she neglected to apply scientific method. So she made excuses for Harry

14

Booth. If nothing else, by being less than fervently involved in the problems of science, he kept the journey in proper perspective.

If they were less downcast by their failure to find life than they might have been, it could be attributed to Booth's vision of science only in terms of monumental discoveries. He was a more accurate representative of mankind's hopes and expectations than anyone else on the ship, she reminded herself. As such, his disappointment would fade faster when they returned home. As would that of the general public.

And who was she to condemn Harry Booth's view of the cosmos? Columbus sailed west not to advance science or knowledge as much as to find gold, gems and spices. Da Gama went to India for pepper and nutmeg and cloves, not because he was intensely curious about the Indians.

The motivations of such men did not diminish the magnitude of their discoveries. Maybe the Harry Booths were as necessary to mankind's opening of the universe as were the Alex Durants.

At least the reporter was good company. She had been around many journalists in her career. Others had tried to exploit her peculiar abilities. Not Booth. They could have done a lot worse than the crusty old veteran.

A feeling of power sifted through her as she worked her way around the vast chamber of the centre. Engines snored steadily, shoving them past space – as opposed to through it – at a rapid pace. They were presently travelling at a comparative crawl, having gone sub-light preparatory to changing their course for home.

At one time man had believed faster-than-light travel impossible. She smiled at the thought. If man had learned anything since stepping out past the atmospheric bubble that enclosed his world it was that the only immutability of the universe lay in its infinite bounty of contradictions. On the cosmic docket, the laws of nature seemed perpetually subject to challenge by the scientific court of appeals.

Holland was working in the monitoring complex, his grey uniform blending in with the colours of the tubes and metallic constructions surrounding him. The warmth that coursed through her at the sight was not wholly due to the radiant heat from the engines.

She moved next to him. Though he still didn't look up from his work she knew he had been aware of her presence

15

from the instant she entered the centre.

'Think it'll hold together long enough to get us home?'

He smiled affectionately over at her. 'How can you have any doubts with super-pilot at the controls?'

'Humility is one of your most endearing qualities.'

'After eighteen months, it's nice to see that you've learned some.' He paused, looked momentarily sombre. 'I've been concerned about suggestions of metal fatigue in the propulsion unit's inner chambers. I know they're designed to handle this kind of steady thrust, but eighteen months with only an occasional brief rest is a long time to ask even the densest alloys to function without showing some kind of wear.' The smile returned.

'I think we'll be okay, though.' He adjusted one slide control slightly, watched with satisfaction as two nearby read-outs shifted in response.

'I'll be sorry to see this mission end. It's tough to go home after so long and say the principal reason for making the trip in the first place came up unresolved.'

'You give up too easily. I don't. We'll still have a few systems to study while curving home. And the *Palomino* sweep is only one expedition. There'll be others. And I'll charm the powers-that-be into assigning you and V.I.N.Cent to any team I can get organised.'

'The powers-that-be will have other plans for V.I.N.Cent.'

'Like what?'

'Like taking him apart to study the effects of the voyage on him. He's likely to be outmoded by new models by the time we return. They'll likely take him and . . .'

'They won't do anything of the sort to V.I.N.Cent. I won't let them. He's entitled to remain inta . . . to remain himself, after all he's done for this mission. He's a lot more than a mere machine, to be picked apart at some cyberneticist's whim.'

Holland tried to hide his amusement. 'That's not a very scientific outlook, Dr McCrae. What would you do to prevent such a thing?'

She looked suddenly uncertain. 'I . . . I don't know. But I'd do something. Whatever was necessary. Adopt him, maybe.'

'Be an expensive adoption. V.I.N.Cent doesn't run on bottle formulas and ground-up fruits and vegetables. Fuel-cell pablum's a lot more expensive than the organic variety.'

'Maybe so. But I wouldn't let them take him apart, any more than I'd let them take apart any other close friend.'

'There's just one hitch to your idea. V.I.N.Cent and I've been together a long time. Several missions prior to the *Palomino*. We're a package deal. That goes for any kind of future mission.'

She cocked her head to one side. 'Aren't you a bit long in the tooth for adoption?'

'That wasn't quite the kind of relationship *I* had in mind. How V.I.N.Cent views it is his business.' Holland turned from the controls and embraced her, his arms tightening against her back as he pulled her close against him.

The kiss was interrupted by a voice issuing from the monitoring console's communication's grid. 'I regret the interruption, Captain, but there is something I think you should see. I've put it on the central viewer.'

A little breathless, they separated. McCrae brushed at the hair that had fallen over one eye. 'If you've been together so long and have become so inseparable,' she murmured softly, 'maybe you could do something about that blasted machine's lousy timing.'

'I'll make it a point to mention it to him,' Holland assured her. His smile turned serious. 'V.I.N.Cent wouldn't break in while I was . . . working, unless it was something genuinely important. We'd better go see what he wants . . .'

Pizer, who was closest to the command centre, reached it first. V.I.N.Cent hovered there, blocking out most of the main screen. Wondering what might have prompted the robot to issue the general call, the first officer continued chewing reconstituted turkey as he strolled forward.

'What's up, V.I.N.Cent? Hey, you know, this stuff ain't half bad. Either that or I've been living off it for too long.' When the machine failed to respond with an appropriately sarcastic comment, Pizer dropped his cockiness and moved to look at the screen.

'Something serious?'

'Seriously interesting, seriously fascinating; not seriously dangerous, Mr Pizer. Not at this distance.' V.I.N.Cent moved to one side, allowing the first officer a clear view of the two screens.

What Pizer saw caused him to swallow the last mouthful

of turkey in a rush. One screen displayed stars and other stellar phenomena not according to their output of visible light, but in gravity wave schematics.

In the upper right centre of the screen was a dark oval shape surrounded by increasingly tightly bunched lines like the contour lines on a topographic map. However, instead of designating altitude, these lines represented increasingly powerful regions of gravitational force, the 'depth' of a gravity well of immense proportions.

V.I.N.Cent enlarged the upper right quadrant of the screen, the one containing the dark oval. Instead of moving farther apart as the scale was expanded, as did the lines surrounding nearby stars, those around the dark blotch remained as dense as before. Pizer knew the magnification could be increased a hundred times without any white space ever appearing between the lines immediately encircling the central oval. A secondary screen offered a visual representation of the phenomenon, but it was the g-wave scheme that absorbed Pizer's attention.

The intensity of the gravitational force at the centre of the dark ellipse shape could be measured, if not designated by the lines on the screen. A G2 star floated close by in space, its substance gradually being drawn off by the centre of powerful attraction. By measuring the speed and amount of material being drawn from the star's outer layers, the *Palomino*'s computers could estimate the strength of the invisible point in space.

They had already performed the requisite calculations. The resultant figures were displayed below the g-wave screen. Pizer noted them, let out a low whistle.

'Yes, sir. That is the most powerful black hole I have ever encountered,' said V.I.N.Cent with appropriate solemnity. 'My banks hold no memory of anything stronger. Preliminary scanner results support that assumption.'

'Give me a rough translation of those figures into something someone like Harry could grasp, V.I.N.Cent. He'll be wanting them for his report anyway.'

The robot considered his reply for a moment. 'Assuming a plus or minus ten per cent factor in the wave measurements, Mr Pizer, and a standard composition for the nearby star, I would estimate this black hole contains the remains of anywhere from forty to a hundred stellar masses.'

'That's about what I guessed.' Pizer was nodding slowly in agreement. 'Big mother, ain't it?'

'Only relatively, sir. No pun intended. One stellar mass or a hundred, it's still only a point in space.'

'A good point to stay away from. Let's have a look at it on the holographier.'

The lights in the cockpit softened. A three-dimensional image formed over a projector. Pizer studied it quietly for a while, then thought to speak to a nearby com pickup. 'Hey, Dr Durant, Harry . . . you getting this?'

Durant's voice replied immediately. 'Yes . . . magnificent, isn't it?' He stood on one side of the lab projector, staring at the view suspended in front of him. 'Don't you think so too, Harry?'

Booth, wide-eyed, was leaning almost into the projection. 'Right out of Dante's *Inferno* if you ask me. Maybe you think Hell's beautiful. I don't.'

Durant made an exasperated sound, returned his attention to the projection. In addition to the material being drawn from the surface of the nearby, doomed sun, various extra-solar material in the form of asteroids, meteoric bodies and nebulaic gas was also being sucked into the Pit. As it vanished, crushed out of normal existence by the enormous, incomprehensible gravity, the material signalled its passing by emitting tremendous bursts of X-rays and gamma-rays.

This radiation in turn excited the vast flow of gas pouring into the gravity well to fluorescence, generating a stunning display of visible light in many hues, predominantly reds. It was this magnificent display and not the far more intense lower-spectrum emissions the holographier projector was now revealing to their enthralled sight.

'You have no soul, Harry.'

The journalist wasn't insulted. 'Occupational hazard, Alex. Don't let me put a damper on your party. Enjoy the view.' He heard a sound and turned, saw McCrae entering the lab and, in the corridor, another shape just disappearing.

'Dan going forward?'

She nodded. 'You know Dan. He's comfortable in the cockpit and back in power central. Any place on the ship in between and he feels like a free electron hopelessly trying to regain a lost level.'

Her attention went immediately to the projection and she

19

became quiet.

'The most destructive force in the universe, Harry,' Durant was saying. 'Your hellish analogy is apt, if unflattering to it.'

'I've had several colleagues insist that black holes will eventually devour the entire universe.' McCrae was moving her head, examining the projection from different angles. 'They say that stars, nebulae, people – everything – will eventually end up down a single massive black hole.'

'When you see giant suns sucked in to disappear without a trace, it makes you wonder.' Durant considered. 'Though I've heard some support the theory that beyond a certain point a black hole begins to heat to the point of explosion. Maybe that's how the universe runs, in cycles. From one massive black hole that's swallowed everything. It erupts, the primordial Big Bang, to form new stars and nebulae and worlds, which then are swallowed up again to form another massive black hole, which explodes in its turn, starting the whole creation-collapse cycle all over again.'

'You talking about reversing entropy, Alex?'

'I'm just saying that if we've learned anything about the cosmos, Kate, it's that the only thing that's impossible is for something to be held unequivocally impossible.' He spoke to the nearby com grid. 'Give us some magnification, V.I.N.Cent. Just visual, for now.'

On command, the robot obediently expanded the imaging of the black hole, its attendant vanishing star, and the glowing region of spatial debris funnelling into the abyss. Holland had reached the bridge, joined Pizer in staring at the images on the screens.

'Booth's right,' the first officer said, acknowledging the captain's presence. 'Every time I see one of those things, I expect to spot a guy in red with horns and barbed tail, wielding a pitchfork.'

Holland was now reading the numerical interpretations of the visual magnificence displayed by the screens. 'We've found stranger things. Who knows? This one's a monster, all right.'

'It possesses a certain morbid attraction, sir,' V.I.N.Cent struggled to admit. 'Believe it or not, I have picked up something of still greater interest.'

The robot adjusted controls. The view of the collapsar

leaped out at them, the imager focusing on a small mass far to the left of the most intense gravity. The object was on the opposite side of the spiral of decaying matter from the companion star, relatively close to the *Palomino*.

'Asteroid?' Pizer wondered aloud. 'Nothing remarkable about that, V.I.N.Cent. There are hundreds of similar objects being sucked in by that thing.'

'I think not, sir. Or if it is an asteroid or other sub-planetary body it is a most remarkable one. I've been monitoring it since I first detected evidence of the main gravity well. The thing hasn't moved – not relative to the hole itself or to the nearby sun. I think it safe to say it is not part of this local system. Its stability therefore seems to indicate that it is some kind of independent artifact. In addition to its stability in a zone of intense gravitational disturbance, it possesses a remarkably regular silhouette.'

'A ship?'

'That is what comes to mind, sir,' he told Holland.

The captain spoke hurriedly into the pickup. 'Lab, did you get that last information back there? Do you copy, Alex?'

'We copy, Dan.' Durant's voice reflected Holland's own amazement. 'I copy, but I don't believe it.'

'Neither do I . . . yet.' He turned his attention back to the screens. 'We're near enough to close-image something that size. A ship of those apparent dimensions hasn't been built in years.'

'Assuming it's of human origin, sir,' Pizer pointed out.

'Yes, assuming that.' Holland glanced over at the robot. 'Enlarge again, V.I.N.Cent, and let's try to identify it.' His heart was beating a little faster.

'Yes, sir.' One metal extension reached out from the mechanical's compact body to plug into a receptacle along-side the screen instrumentation.

Back in the lab, Durant and McCrae waited for V.I.N.Cent's actions to produce results. Both were dazed by the apparent discovery. Booth was, for once, beyond words. He stared blankly at the projection.

'How could anybody be out here ahead of us?' Durant mumbled.

'You heard Charlie.'

'What about aliens?'

Durant replied more harshly than he intended, his tone sharpened by months of disappointment. 'Aliens are a myth for story-mongers to toy and tease us with. They're fiction. This trip has been proof enough of that.'

'But it's only been one trip, Alex,' said McCrae. 'It's too early in our history for us to make blanket statements about life in our galaxy. Too early.' She stopped and they both stared at the projection.

On another screen forward, a series of ship silhouettes had begun to appear, overlaid against the distant outline of the mystery object.

'Liberty Seven.' V.I.N.Cent made his announcements in his most business-like tone. 'No mass correlation. No shape correlation.' A second silhouette appeared over the mysterious craft. 'Experimental deep-space station, series five. Reported lost. No mass correlation, no shape correlation.' Another. 'Sahara Module fifty-three.' Still another. 'Pluto four. No mass correlation, no shape correlation.'

Even the most consummate professional can be stirred to excitement. When the next overlay appeared, McCrae was unable to restrain herself. She had more reason than any of them to wish for correlation this time.

'Deep-Space Probe One,' intoned V.I.N.Cent methodically, still unwilling to commit himself. 'Mass correlates, save for minor discrepancies likely due to considerable expenditure of propellants. Shape also matches. Insofar as distance permits, all other details conform.'

With a last, unspoken sigh for the once again fading image of intelligent alien life, Durant said formally to the pickup, 'That's good enough for now, V.I.N.Cent. We'll accept the likelihood of this being an accurate identification until closer inspection proves otherwise. Programme the ship's history and enter it into the tape.'

'Searching records, sir.'

'That won't be necessary.' McCrae kept her voice level, though she was boiling inside at the possibility this identification had raised. 'You know the background of the *Cygnus* as well as any of us, Alex.'

He looked uncomfortable, didn't meet her stare. 'It's a formality, Kate. For the ship's records. We have to enter everything. You know that.'

'I suppose.'

V.I.N.Cent's voice brought her private agony into the open, where everyone had to consider it despite the so far mutual attempt not to. V.I.N.Cent was sensitive for a machine, but he was not human.

'Dr Kate, was that not the ship your father was serving on?'

'The *Cygnus*,' she repeated, as mechanically as V.I.N.Cent might in his less colloquial moments. 'Mission: to survey for potentially habitable worlds and to search for non-terrestrial, extrasolar life. Essentially the same as ours, only on a far more wide-ranging, extensive scale.'

'You mean, "expensive" scale,' said Booth undiplomatically.

No one responded to that sally. Over the intercom they could hear Holland, Pizer and the robot working.

'Signal the ship, V.I.N.Cent,' Holland was saying. 'Try standard communications frequencies first. If they don't respond to any of them, switch to emergency, then military, and then random codes.'

'What about visual display, sir? We may be near enough.'

'If they happen to have a scope pointing in our direction. No, stick with the audio for now. We'll try something more complicated if and when everything else fails.'

'As you say, sir.'

'Activate our long-range sensors, Charlie,' the captain said to his first officer. 'They may be generating all kinds of non-communicative emissions, if their regular broadcast units are disabled.'

'Yes, sir. But it'll be hell trying to pick out anything coherent against that background.'

'Do the best you can. I've seen you make an electron-flow sensor squint.'

No one back in the lab smiled. Both Durant and Booth were watching McCrae, for different reasons. Booth's instincts were heightened by a possible story.

Durant wondered if the journalist had deliberately tried to provoke her with his criticism of her father's ship. He decided Booth wasn't that subtle. He had only been expressing a widely held opinion about the *Cygnus* and its astronomical cost. Objectively, one had to admit that the *Palomino* was performing the same tasks for far less money. The question in Durant's mind was, were they performing

23

them as efficiently? To any space scientist the *Cygnus* was a dream fulfilled. It was difficult to talk about cost-effectiveness in relation to something as awesome as the *Cygnus*. Perhaps now there was a chance to find out who had been right – the men who had built her, or the ones who had paid for her.

'Space Probe and survey ship *Cygnus*,' McCrae was murmuring. 'Recalled to Earth twenty years ago, its mission considered an expensive failure.' She glanced sharply at Booth. He studied the fingers of his right hand.

'How that must have galled Hans Reinhardt,' the reporter said. 'If I remember rightly, he didn't take kindly to criticism. I can imagine how he must've reacted to the recall of his ship and the cancellation of her mission.'

The name from the past Booth had just mentioned was as magical to Durant as that of the *Cygnus*, and was more accessible. He instantly forgot all about the reporter's possible provoking of his colleague.

'Did you actually meet Commander Reinhardt, Harry? I mean, in person. I've heard about him all my life, read his research, studied his theories.'

'Collided with him would be a more accurate description, Alex. You can say one thing about him: he was a scientific genius. Better qualified folks than I said just that – Reinhardt foremost among them.' He grinned.

'Reinhardt was a legend even before he took over supervision of the *Cygnus* project.' Durant tried not to sound as defensive as he felt. He knew he was defending a disgraced man. 'A legend.'

'So *he* believed. Personally, I think he was overwhelmed by the image he had created of himself. You see that sort of thing a lot in my profession. I can't pretend to judge his scientific accomplishments. Only to rate him as a human being. There are all kinds of arrogance, Alex. I don't think Reinhardt considered himself arrogant, but he came off that way to a lot of people who were around him.

'I'll give him this,' Booth conceded, 'he could manipulate people as well as advanced physical theory. Reinhardt had the knack of making his personal ambitions seem a matter of racial pride. "Mankind must conquer the stars" and all that. Talked the International Space Appropriations Committee into funding the costliest debacle of all time. He was certainly the Barnum of interstellar exploration."

'Oh, don't get me wrong. Building and crewing the *Cygnus* was a helluva achievement, one of mankind's proudest moments. Also one of his most impractical. This ship, the *Palomino*, and her sister ships are proof of that.

'But man must have his monuments, right, Alex? The *Cygnus* was the Great Pyramid of our time, and Reinhardt its Cheops. He caused her to be built, staked his reputation on her. So once she existed he was forced to succeed no matter the dictates of logic or reason, no matter the consequences. So he refused to admit failure of his mission and ignored the orders recalling her to Earth.'

'We don't know that for a fact, Harry,' Durant shot back.

'Not yet we don't. No one ever had to communicate across a distance like that, from Earth to the *Cygnus*. Maybe the recall order never got through.'

Unnoticed now, McCrae was standing by the port, staring out into the emptiness that had swallowed her father and the rest of the crew of the *Cygnus*. On the edge of nearby oblivion hovered the answer to one of man's greatest modern mysteries, the silent disappearance of that ship.

She wished she could act more the detached observer, more like the professional she was trained to be. Despite her best efforts, though, all she could think about, all she could consider, was the seemingly absurd but minutely possible chance that her father was still alive.

'I'm going forward,' she muttered. Still busily debating the merits of Dr Hans Reinhardt and the *Cygnus*, Durant and Booth took no notice of her departure.

TWO

PIZER was making no attempt to restrain his own excitement. It stemmed from a similar yet different source from Durant's.

'I've read about the *Cygnus* since I was a kid, Dan,' he was telling Holland, rambling on as disjointedly as the adolescent to whom he had just referred. 'She's sort of the Flying Dutchman of space, the dream ship every explorer imagines himself finding. And we've found her!'

Holland permitted himself a slight smile. 'Get us close enough,' Pizer continued, 'and V.I.N.Cent and I can go aboard her on tethers.'

Surprisingly, the anticipated admonition came not from the man but from the machine. 'To quote Cicero, V.I.N.Cent began, "Rashness is the characteristic of youth, prudence that of mellowed age, and discretion the better part of valour".' The robot regarded the first officer. 'It would be best not to rush headlong into possible danger until we have a better idea of what happened.'

'Yeah. Sure. Of course.' Pizer suddenly frowned, looked up from the control console. 'Cicero who?'

V.I.N.Cent made a noise that passed for mechanical choking. Pizer was rescued from the robot's response by the appearance of McCrae and the sound of Booth speaking through the intercom system.

'We have to go in, Captain,' the reporter was saying. 'No sense leaving the story of a lifetime untold. I'm more afraid of that black hole, that distortion of normal, healthy space, than any of you. But I'd go into Hell itself in search of grist for a story for my listeners.'

'If we get caught by that gravitational field, Harry,' Holland replied, 'that's all we'll be. Grist. Superdense grist. So I happen to think there is a reason for leaving the story of a lifetime untold. It's looking right at us, and vice versa. I'm not going into Hell after a story, nor is anyone else on this ship.'

'But, Captain. . .'

Holland flipped him off, turned to his first officer. 'Picking up anything on the sensors, Charlie? Any response yet to V.I.N.Cent's calls?'

Pizer stared glumly at his read-outs. 'Negative, but with all that electromagnetic turbulence out there the signal might not be getting through. Or it's possible someone on the *Cygnus* is receiving and their reply isn't reaching us. Their signal might be weak if their own broadcast circuitry isn't operating at full efficiency. It could be diluted or scattered by the stuff around us beyond our ability to sort it out. The ether's alive from ten to the twenty-first hertz all the way down through radio. One thing we can assume, though. We have to.'

'What's that?'

'That their radiation shielding's intact. Otherwise anyone left alive aboard would've been cooked as soon as they entered this region, just by the gamma radiation alone.'

'My God,' McCrae finally murmured, breaking her silence and staring at the screen, 'all these years of waiting and wondering, of the authorities being able to do no more than shrug when asked about the fate of the *Cygnus* and her people . . . and there she is. The answer to all those mysteries and rumours.' She looked from the screen to Holland. 'Dan . . .?'

'I know how you must feel, Kate, but that ship's hanging on the edge of a whirlpool to nothingness. We can't take the chance. We can't risk . . .'

'At least check with Alex.' She was pleading, knowing that the physicist's opinion would carry more weight than her own, which Holland was rightly bound to regard as hostage to emotion.

'All right.' He spoke into the com pickup. 'Alex, you've been listening in?'

'Haven't missed a word, Dan,' came the prompt reply.

'Tell me something that'll convince me it's safe for us to take a closer look. Give me a good, solid, non-humanitarian reason for doing so.'

Durant had been busy integrating information from the

Palomino's long-range scanners. 'I can do it with one observation, Dan. According to our instrumentation, the *Cygnus* hasn't moved an iota since we first detected it.'

'You're positive?'

'Absolutely. Its position relative to the nearby star is un-varying. It's not in orbit around either the star or the collapsar. She's just sitting there.'

Holland considered. 'That's crazy, Alex. If it's not orbit-ing the star and its drive isn't functioning – and I can tell that it's not from our read-outs up here – then the ship should be reacting at least marginally to the effect of the gravity well. You sure she hasn't been put in a functional orbit around it?'

'Sorry, Dan.' Durant sounded apologetic. 'She's not orbiting anything. Might as well not be a black hole there for all the effect it seems to be having on her. Or not having on her. It's almost as if she's somehow managed to anchor herself to a point in space. Or found some way to negate gravitational forces other than pushing against them with her drive.

'If it's safe for the *Cygnus* we can assume until shown otherwise that it's safe for the *Palomino*.'

'You're stretching supposition, Alex.'

'Maybe. But I don't have any explanation for her stability. Just the fact that she is.'

'How could a lifeless derelict,' Booth put in, 'defy that kind of steady gravitational pull? If her engines aren't functioning she ought to be sliding down into the well.'

'I don't know how she's doing it, but that's reason enough for investigating her.' Durant directed his voice back to the pickup. 'That's my main reason for advising a closer look, Dan. If the *Cygnus* can somehow negate gravity waves with-out using a drive, it's incumbent on us to try to find out how she's doing it. And, Harry, we don't know that she's lifeless. Not showing her lights or a drive isn't sufficient evidence of lifelessness.'

'Well, she looks lifeless,' Booth harrumphed.

'It could be a natural phenomenon, Alex,' said Holland.

'I know that. That's equally worthy of investigation.'

'No, no. You're missing my point, Alex.' The captain stared indecisively at his instruments. 'The *Cygnus* may not be frozen in space voluntarily. With a sun on one side of her and a massive black hole on the other, there's enough electromagnetic perturbations running through here to do funny things to the fabric of space.'

'Space isn't nylon, Dan.' Durant sounded impatient.

'You know what I'm getting at. If it is a natural phenomenon, we might find ourselves unable to break free of its influence. The *Cygnus* may be sitting where she is because she has no choice. Pull alongside her and the same effect might trap us out here also.'

Durant knew he couldn't just ignore Holland's hypothesis. 'All right, let's do this: as scientific leader of this mission I formally advise carrying out a closer inspection. We'll have all our standard gravwave instrumentation primed to alert us the instant any kind of gravitational abnormality is detected, and I'll programme corollary scanners for backup. At the first hint that anything bizarre is affecting us we'll maximise the drive and move clear.'

Holland's thoughts were still on the side of caution. 'I don't know.' It came down to the fact that ship and crew were his responsibility, even though at such moments he was supposed to follow Durant and McCrae's directives. 'It might be an instantaneous effect. We might not be able to break free no matter how quickly we detect something out of the ordinary.'

'Now you're trying to over-rule me on the basis of an implied dangerous effect for which we have no supporting hard evidence, Dan.

'We're preparing to return home. Let's take this one last risk and then it'll all be over except collecting our back pay. We've been gifted with the chance to answer an awful lot of old questions – about the *Cygnus*, about her mission, and about inconsistencies in gravity-field theory that have plagued physicists since Einstein. There's no telling when another ship might get out this way, and by that time the *Cygnus* may be swallowed up.'

Holland weighed all the evidence and all the arguments. 'My instincts are still against it, Alex.'

'Maybe, but that's hardly sound scientific grounds for not investigating more closely.'

'I know, I know.' Holland grumbled a little, then flipped off the holographier, nudged other controls. 'All right. You get your electronic eyes and ears tuned proper and we'll go in for a closer look. We'll have to go in at an angle or we'll chance being taken by the gravity well. Maybe the *Cygnus* isn't affected by it, but I have to assume the *Palomino* will be. We'll do a tight cometary and get out.' He turned his full attention to the console in front of him, spoke to his first officer without turning.

'Fix a coordinate approach, Charlie. We'll pass as slowly as we can so Alex and Kate can take ample readings, but I want a reasonable margin of thrust programmed in. If we lose too much velocity in passing we won't get a chance to make it up.' He patted his stomach, grinned tightly. 'I'd like to lose a few centimetres off my waistline, but not *that* way.'

'Right, sir.' The captain's cautionary attitude hadn't dampened Pizer's enthusiasm for the investigation, but he was subdued by the seriousness of the attempt. He hadn't been recommended to be first officer of the *Palomino* solely on the basis of his infectiously cheerful personality.

'Coordinate heading three-oh-five x, two-seven-five y, one-seven-seven z.' Pizer's fingers danced over contact switches. 'Computer verifies. That'll give us fifteen per cent extra if we need it.'

'Adequate.' Holland entered the coordinates into the navigation block, activated the necessary instrumentation for attitude adjustment. The *Palomino* shifted silently in space, pointing toward destruction instead of away from it.

'Attitude set.'

'Engines ready,' Pizer replied.

'V.I.N.Cent, give us full power on our sublights.'

'Yes, Captain.' Connected by umbilical armature to the main console, the robot communicated instructions to Power. Useless above light-speed, the ship's powerful conventional thrusters engaged and she began to accelerate forward.

Several minutes passed as they continued to gain speed. Then there was a jolt, expected but still a shock, a physical reminder of the unseen immensity they would have to flirt so carefully with.

McCrae braced herself against the sides of the portal leading into the lab. Durant was adjusting the restraints on his lounge. 'Better strap yourself in. The well will intensify as we near the *Cygnus*. Turbulence could get worse. Nothing's certain in there.'

Booth was already making certain his own restraints were secured. 'I thought the pull would be steady. Growing constantly, and without variance.'

'It does,' Durant explained while securing a last strap over his waist. 'That isn't contradicted by the turbulence. Partly it derives from the huge quantity of gas, solar plasma, and other material being drawn down into the hole. And there are likely to be other effects. Gravity around a black hole, like other things, doesn't act in a manner we're accustomed to.' As if to support his comments, another jolt rocked the ship.

'Think of us as a gnat trying to bell a cat,' McCrae added. 'We're safe from the irresistible strength of the cat, but its snores still affect us.'

'I see.' Booth glanced speculatively out the nearby port. 'The trick is to do the job and slip away without waking it up. Or else . . .'

'We get swallowed,' McCrae finished for him. 'But the *Cygnus* hasn't been swallowed.'

Another unseen hand shoved at the *Palomino*, harder this time. The crew became introspective, each considering the over-riding mystery posed by the *Cygnus*' seeming stability in the face of irresistible forces.

Why hadn't the giant research ship vanished, crushed out of normal space by the strength of the black hole? They would have to employ the full power of the *Palomino* merely to skim the edge of the collapsar's area of influence. The gnat was defying the awakened cat's full strength. It made no sense, no sense at all. But they would somehow have to find the answer, make sense from the information the ship's scanners would provide as they raced past.

Pizer studied the constantly shifting display on the main navigation screen. Lines changed patiently, twisting a cat's cradle around the central, growing image of the motionless *Cygnus*. 'Range two-nine-five-one-six, and closing. Thrusters operating smoothly. No problems.'

'What's your reading on the *Cygnus*' attitude, V.I.N.Cent?' Holland tried to glance around so he could see the robot, but his chair restraints restricted his movement.

'Still holding steady, sir.'

'Position relative to the star?'

'Constant. Most remarkable.'

Holland's stomach seemed to drop half a metre as

external gravity played havoc with the *Palomino*'s internal system. 'Yeah,' he finally replied, regaining his visceral equilibrium, 'most remarkable. I'll find time to admire the situation properly when remarkably we're in the clear again. Gravitational reading?'

'Two-point-four-seven and rising. Rate of rise also increasing, sir.'

The restraints still gave Holland enough freedom of movement to shake his head; he was worried. 'That's not good. With that much additional pull we'll go by too fast to do any good.' He demanded information from the ship's computer, accepted it along with the machine's several suggestions.

'Change course. Put us in an altered escape angle of a hundred seventy-five perpendicular to the axis of maximum attraction. Compensate by cutting thrust two-thirds. We'll still maintain original projected escape velocity at perihelion. But I want constant monitoring of our revised course. If we deviate too much, don't hit it just right, we're going to have a devil of a time breaking clear.'

The *Palomino* continued to arc in toward the amazingly stable *Cygnus*. Turbulence grew worse. The strain was reflected in the faces of the pilots, the buffetting of their ship was matched by emotional turbulence within.

One particularly bad jolt shook them. Pizer felt the impression of his restraints all over his body. 'She's bucking like a bronco,' he mumbled, wishing he were back in Texas NAT dealing with more manageable varieties of turbulence. You could reason with a horse.

'Gravity. Gravity report, Mr Pizer!' Holland repeated sharply when his first officer failed to respond at once. 'No time for daydreaming now.'

'Sorry, sir.' Pizer devoted full attention to the proper read-outs, all thoughts of radical forms of equine displacement forgotten. 'Twenty-point-nine-six and still climbing.'

He wondered how long it would be before the gauge broke. Like the *Palomino*, it was designed to withstand considerable forces. The ship had performed surveys of several jovian-type worlds, handling multiple gravities and methane storms with equal equanimity. The perversion of nature they were teasing now, however, was to the gravity of Jupiter as a pebble was to a mountain.

Holland continued to watch his instruments appre-hensively. If they could count on a steady pull from the black hole, the ship's navigation computer would pull them through without difficulty. But as the turbulence they con-tinued to experience was proving, the region of space they were now passing through was subject to gravitational and electromagnetic variations outside the experiences pro-grammed into the *Palomino*'s brain. They might be forced to manoeuvre suddenly and radically, might have to take risks no machine -- operating solely on logic and a predisposition based on prior navigational experience -- would take.

It was, therefore, time to engage the ship's ultimate navigational programmer, the only one on board that could cope with the unexpected dangers the bizarre distortion of space outside might thrust on them.

'Switching to manual,' Holland said matter-of-factly, touching buttons in sequence on the console in front of him. A metal arm decorated with switches and buttons popped out of the console. He felt unreasonably better now that he was personally in control of the ship's movements, a reaction common to all pilots of all vessels since the dawn of transportation.

'Captain?'

'Yes, V.I.N.Cent?'

'Permit me to elucidate a concern, sir.'

'Go ahead and elucidate.'

'I'm not sure how long the engines will remain operable against this much attractive force when we turn outward again. They are quite capable of producing the thrust neces-sary to carry us clear. But it is their durability under such con-ditions that concerns me. Even a brief loss of power could prove disastrous, and we cannot engage the supralight drive this close to a sun, not to mention what it might do to the *Cygnus*.'

'I know all that, V.I.N.Cent.'

'I merely reiterate it, sir, because of the thought that Dr Alex and Dr Kate will be displeased with anything short of a thorough inspection of the *Cygnus* and whatever strange force is holding it steady in its present location.'

Holland nodded, glanced momentarily at a particular gauge. It read no more than he had thought it would, but he still shook a little inside at the sight of numbers he'd never expected to see behind the transparent face of the read-out.

'Holland here,' he said towards the com pickup. 'The gravity's close to the maxumum we can cope with, Alex. I've tried to slow our speed at perihelion as much as possible. V.I.N.Cent has just expressed concern about the reliability of the engines under this kind of stress. We can afford one pass, but then we have to get the hell out.'

'Isn't it possible,' the scientist's voice intoned over the speaker, 'that we might . . . ?'

'One pass, and that's it. I'll try to give you as much time as I can. Attend to your instruments, Alex. Let's make this one pass worth the effort.'

'Coming up on target and slowing, sir,' Pizer announced.

'Slow us a little more, V.I.N.Cent,' Holland ordered the robot. 'We'll risk passing with a five per cent margin.'

'As you wish, sir. But if I may be allowed to say . . .'

'You may not.'

'Yes, sir.' The robot succeeded in conveying a distinct feeling of disapproval.

'We'll pass below her, sir.' Pizer was dividing his gaze between the foreport and several read-outs.

'Check. Ready on thrusters, V.I.N.Cent.'

'Standing by, sir.'

A vast, dark bulk hove into view. It thoroughly dominated the *Palomino*. The long, roughly rectangular shape bulged at the stern. Each of her eight drive exhausts was large enough to swallow the *Palomino*. She wore her grid-work skeleton externally, like an insect.

She was one of mankind's greatest technological triumphs. Even in the darkness Holland felt a shiver of excitement pass through him at the sight of the enormous vessel. What pilot wouldn't have given an eye to command such a behemoth!

The *Cygnus* had been designed to carry out any imaginable scientific mission deep-space exploration might require. Its research capabilities far outstripped those of a dozen ships the size of the *Palomino*. That those extensive facilities, incorporated into the *Cygnus*' basic design, might never be used was something few gave thought to in the heady days of her planning and construction.

She had been built to be completely self-supporting, able to recycle air and food and water for hundreds of years if necessary, able to travel the length of the galaxy as long as the children's children of her original crew retained the knowledge to man her.

That was a last-scene scenario, however. Her creators expected her to return her original crew to Earth. The concept of a ship capable of carrying on from generation to generation was an appealingly romantic one that served a useful propagandistic purpose, helping to clear the way come appropriations time for vast expenditures of doubtful utility.

She was armed, too – huge sums spent to satisfy an appeal to xenophobic fears that no longer haunted mankind. In subsequent searches through space no intelligent aliens, friendly or otherwise, had been encountered. But such fears had existed at the time of the *Cygnus*' construction. So jingoistic elements had forced the installation on the great ship of the means of extermination as well as of revelation.

Nothing like her had been built before. It was likely nothing like her would be built again. Not when smaller, less costly vessels like the the *Palomino* and her sister ships could do the same work and cover far greater reaches of space for the same expenditure of time and personnel. Nonetheless, she remained a monument to man's mastery of physical engineering and ability. She awed even so stolid a man as Holland by her sheer size and presence.

'Stand by with your scanners, Alex. We're going under her. I'll try to roll us after passage to give every instrument a chance to record, in case of any failures.'

Enormous metal members reached out towards the *Palomino*. They moved nearer, the little ship slipping towards silent supports weighing hundreds of tons on Earth, weighing nothing here . . . and something utterly unexpected happened.

The turbulence ceased.

That was absolutely the last thing Holland would have imagined. Gravitational effects had to have been affected or the *Cygnus* would not have been holding its position as it was. They were more than affected; they no longer were.

He glanced incredulously over at his first officer. As he checked and rechecked the read-outs on the console before him, Pizer displayed a dumbfounded look.

'Zero gravity. Nothing. There's evidence of artificial gravity in use on the *Cygnus*, but nothing from the black hole. According to sensors it's exerting less pull on us now than a toy globe.'

'That's impossible. What about the star?'

'Same thing, meaning nothing,' Pizer told him. 'Gravitationally, they're not there anymore.'

'Reverse thrust.' V.I.N.Cent complied and the *Palomino* slowed to a comparative crawl. 'Stand by. The phenomenon may be temporary.'

It was not. The *Palomino* sat driveless in space under the dark mass of the *Cygnus* like a chick huddled beneath its mother's protective wing. It was coasting now, drifting slowly forward.

'Easy on the thrusters now, V.I.N.Cent. Take us around and upside her, Charlie.' Man and machine moved to comply with the orders. Holland continued to examine his sensor read-outs, still hardly believing what they told him.

'Smooth as glass,' he muttered softly. 'Incredible.' And frightening, he told himself. Anything that could so utterly eliminate the kind of attractive power they had just passed through hinted at knowledge that could prove dangerous as well as benign.

Voices drifted out at him from the speaker. 'It's like the eye of a hurricane.' That was Kate's voice. 'What's happened, Alex? I can't imagine what's causing it.'

'Neither can I,' Durant confessed readily. 'As we suspected, a natural phenomenon or something generated from the *Cygnus*. Not a clue which it is, so far. Look sharp.' Holland could visualise Durant turning his full attention to the information that must be pouring into the lab from the external scanners and sensors.

The *Palomino* drifted around the flank of the immense ship, curved up and started to arc around to pass over it. Everyone was busy at his or her station. They were trying to solve a pair or mysteries: one, the absence of pull from the black hole and, two, the existence of the ghost ship itself.

McCrae was overcome with personal frustration. She left the task of monitoring the incoming statistics to Durant. Slipping free of her chair, she moved to the port and found herself staring fixedly at the metres of metal sliding past behind them. Soon they would reach the end of their turn, come around to pass across the topside of the ship. Her attitude was not very professional just then; it was very human.

Durant addressed the pickup. 'Are you learning anything forward, Charlie? Nothing of a revealing nature has come in back here.'

'And nothing abnormal up here, Alex,' came the first officer's reply. 'Negative. Whatever's cancelling out the gravitational pull hereabouts isn't interfering at all with the rest of the electromagnetic junk that's filling this section of space. It's gravity specific.

'There are a hundred thousand "natural" broadcasts flying around us. I can't punch anything through it, even this close. If there's anyone left on board capable of communicating, which I sincerely doubt, they've got the same problems if they're trying to reach us.'

There has to be someone alive on board, McCrae thought fiercely. There has to be! It . . . it doesn't even have to be dad. Just someone who can tell us what *happened*. To have come this close, actually to have found the long-lost *Cygnus* and not to learn what had happened to her would be intolerable.

She insisted to herself that the reasons for pursuing the investigation further were grounded soundly in science and not personal emotions. But she knew it would be hard, if not impossible, to conceal her feelings from the rest of the crew – especially from Dan Holland. She wasn't at all sure she wanted to make the effort.

The *Palomino* had passed beyond the *Cygnus*, began to curve back towards her. 'Bring us full around, Charlie. We'll try orbiting her forward, then we'll check out the engines.'

'And after that?'

'After that, if there's still no sign of life aboard . . . we'll see.'

'Yes, sir.' Pizer concealed his impatience. 'Bringing her around, sir.'

The *Palomino*'s attitude thrusters fired. A violent tremor ran through the length of the ship, like a sudden chill. Then they were tumbling out of control, away from the *Cygnus*.

A small gauge in front of Holland jumped instantly from zero to eleven, then twelve. It continued rising towards unthinkable levels with terrifying rapidity.

'Gravity approaching maximum, Dan!' Pizer shouted, fighting the panic in his guts.

'My God,' Holland's gaze remained locked on the single, critical read-out, 'it's got us . . .'

THREE

'FULL power on all thrusters. Give me a hundred per cent additional on our roll quads.' Holland was frantically jabbing at controls, eyes darting from one read-out to the next. Each appeared more threatening than its neighbour. On the screen, the *Cygnus* remained peaceful and stable, receding behind them.

Malignant invisibilities smote the tiny vessel. Back near Power, several sensitive monitors ruptured, sending highly compressed gases whistling wildly down corridors and into unsealed rooms.

'What the hell happened?' Pizer demanded of silent fates. 'What *happened*?'

'The zone of null-gee.' Holland spoke rapidly, working at his console. 'Its parameters are variable. I thought we had at least a couple of kilometres of quiet in which to turn, but the radius of the stable zone shifted while we were passing close to the *Cygnus*. It shrank inward.

'My fault,' he was stammering through clenched teeth, 'it was my fault. We should have been monitoring it somehow.'

'Don't blame yourself.' Pizer shifted power from one weakened thruster to another, balanced the propulsive system as best he could given their wild course. 'No one else thought of it. Besides, there's no way we could have monitored it. How can you monitor something you don't understand? We probably don't even have the instruments for it.'

All right, Charlie. You're right. Time for fixing the blame later. A warning light began flashing for attention on the left of his console. V.I.N.Cent noticed it an instant before Holland.

'Air break amidships.' The robot spoke calmly. 'Losing storage pressure.' He studied fresh information, correlated it with what the computer was trying to tell him. 'Regeneration system failure. Seals are forming in the system. Pressure is holding, sir, but cannot do so indefinitely.'

'Do what you can with it, V.I.N.Cent. I haven't got time now. Charlie, give us a full burst at one eighty degrees on my count on the roll quads. If we don't correct our tumble we might as well turn off the engines.'

'Standing by.' Pizer's fingers rested tensely on two separate contact switches.

'Mark. Five, four, three, two, one . . .'

Pizer impressed the switches. The *Palomino* stopped tumbling . . . violently.

The unexpected jolt nearly threw Durant, McCrae and Booth from their positions. Overpressurised beyond design, the air lines running through the lab reacted to the abrupt cessation of spin and the corresponding shift in the ship's artificial gravity by releasing their pent-up force. Compressed air hissed into the room. The *Palomino* was tumbling again, less severely now and in the opposite direction.

McCrae shouted towards the pickup. 'Dan, we've got a line break back here, too.'

Durant was hastily examining the requisite gauges. 'Read-out shows primary and secondary carry lines ruptured. We'll be breathing soup pretty soon and that for only a little while if we don't get them fixed.'

'Then get on it,' was Holland's reply. 'We've stablised enough for you to move around, but watch yourselves. I'm not promising anything.' Including living out the day, he told himself grimly.

McCrae was first out of her chair. She hurried to help Booth unlock his restraints. Their problem now was not a lack of air but a surplus of it. If the pressure in the system dropped too low the regenerators would fail. Emergency supplies would reprime the regenerators, but more than likely they were breathing some emergency atmosphere already.

When that supply was gone they would have only the old air circulating loosely through the ship to breathe. That would turn stale, then unbreathable, all too quickly. Before too long they would suffocate.

All the regular crew had some training in ship maintenance, except Harry Booth. Such diversified expertise was necessary with so small a complement. Kate struggled to recall the schematics of the ship's atmosphere systemology, knowing their lives depended on it. On that, and on Dan and Charlie and V.I.N.Cent halting their plunge.

No use worrying about that possibility, she told herself firmly. If they failed to stop their fall, and soon, she would be flattened before she knew what was happening to her. Concentrate on the regeneration system and let the others worry about keeping them alive long enough to enjoy her repairs.

Pizer adjusted the thrusters yet again, muttered, 'Never rains . . .' The rest was not audible.

'We're doing better, Charlie. But not enough better. Full power on attitude Quads *A* and *B*. We're going in at an angle now, but we're still going in.'

The first officer switched his own instrumentation over to manual control. 'Mark. Five, four, three, two, one . . .'

Again the first officer activated selected external adjusters. Again the *Palomino* reacted. Not as violently this time, and with greater precision.

'If we can just bring her around,' Holland murmured nervously, 'we'll have a fighting chance.' He knew it had to be finished soon. If they fell much further into the grip of that unrelenting gravity they would forever lose all chance of breaking free.

V.I.N.Cent's cautionary remark about the durability of the thrusters under such strain came back to him, but he pushed it from his mind. Either the units would continue to function or they would fail. He had to assume the former because it was fatal to consider the latter.

For a few seconds he toyed with the idea of slamming on the supralight drive, which should be sufficient to pull them clear. *Yeah*, he thought, *in pieces*.

He would leave that for a last resort and pray if he had to do it that the equations were all wrong. The supralight drive operated with wonderful efficiency in a massless environment. Around much mass it displayed a disconcerting tendency to push against the ship instead of against nothing. Under such circumstances it could push a ship apart – also the contents of said ship, which included any crew. Hence the need for powerful sublight engines to shove a starship out into the void where it could function properly and harmlessly.

A new warning light came on. Again, it was V.I.N.Cent who noticed it first. 'Hull breach indication, Captain.'

'Serious?'

'Not immediately. The number four hatch cover just blew outward. The section has been sealed.'

'What's in number four bay?'

A pause while the robot checked inventory, then, 'Miscellaneous supplies, sir. Non-regenerable, some organics.'

'What kind? If it's survey equipment or samples we can forget it.'

'I'm afraid not, sir. Manifest shows pharmaceuticals among the contents.'

'Damn. We can't risk losing that stuff, and we could do just that if we're jolted hard enough, or if the artificial grav goes out. Be just about right for us to break free of this and then die on the way home for lack of the right medicine to treat some otherwise minor infection.'

'I agree, sir.' V.I.N.Cent removed his armature from the console socket and swivelled to depart from the cockpit. 'I'll go outside and secure the hatch.'

'I don't like it, but . . . watch yourself. This is more pull than we've ever had to deal with. If you break loose you won't be sucked in much faster than the ship, but your thrusters might not be enough to boost you back to the hull, and there's no way we could manoeuvre to retrieve you.'

'Yes, sir. I am cognisant of the dangers, sir. Rest assured I will exercise utmost caution.' V.I.N.Cent floated from the cockpit, moving carefully but at high speed back through the corridors.

Scanning the read-outs, Holland's eyes fell again on the still winking lights which reminded him of the damage to their air system. 'Alex, Harry,' he called into the pickup, 'you still okay back there?'

'Rocky, but no injuries, Dan.' Durant sounded tired. 'We're still working on the lines that broke here in the lab.'

'Leave those for Kate. She's faster than either of you. Check out the damage further back, where the initial interruption occurred.'

'Check.' Durant started for the doorway. 'Let's go, Harry. Good luck here, Kate.'

She was already running a diagnostic pen over the multiple tube fracture. 'You fix the first headache, Alex, I'll handle this one.' She waved the pen at him and he smiled back, each grin for the other's benefit and not an expression of humour. Not now.

Apply sealer to the edge of the break, she told herself, trying to see the instruction tape, forcing it to unspool once more inside her head. Place sealant alloy between sealer and

41

far end of break . . . She continued like that, working steadily if slowly, her body tense in expectancy of further jolts and shudders.

Normally V.I.N.Cent would not have bothered with a tether. His internal thrusters provided enough power for him to fly with confidence around any ship. But this was not normal space they were spinning through, and V.I.N.Cent was programmed to be prudent. So he double-checked to make sure the high-strength metalweave cable was attached securely to himself and to the ship. Then he slid back the exterior hatch of the airlock and made his way outside.

The black hole was a dark nothingness resting in the centre of a flowing vortex of radiant gas and larger clumps of matter. It attracted his attention only briefly. He was also programmed to be curious, though less so than humans.

So he ignored the mesmerising view of the stellar maelstrom and turned his optics instead on the various projections extruding from the *Palomino*'s hull. He had to make his way around them so that his extendible magnetic limbs would remain firmly in contact with the ship's skin.

As he moved slowly across the hull back towards the free-floating hatch to be resecured, he was aware of a steady thunder reverberating around him. It was a thunder no human could have heard, a purely electronic thunder, the wail dying matter generated as it was crushed out of existence. It possessed also a certain poignance no human could have appreciated, for in many ways V.I.N.Cent was closer in structure to the meteoric material plunging past him to destruction than he was to the creature known as Man.

Indeed, he mused, *I am the same stuff, differently formed and imbued with intelligence. I am cousin both to meteor and man.*

Then his thoughts turned to more prosaic matters: a loose hatch and the possibility of uncertain footing. *I do wonder why I was programmed to think in so many human metaphors,* he thought. *I have no feet, therefore technically speaking I am incapable of losing my 'footing'.*

Fortunately, his creators and designers had foreseen the possibility of such confusion arising in his electronic mind and had counterprogrammed a restraining, pacifying feature into all such mechanicals: humour.

Holland and Pizer were unaware of V.I.N.Cent's private musings as they struggled to stabilise the ship. But they were very much aware of V.I.N.Cent.

'Give me a check on his progress, Charlie.'

Pizer moved to comply, leaving part of his attention on the still vacillating read-outs before him. 'V.I.N.Cent, do you read? This is Charlie, V.I.N.Cent.'

A loud sizzle like a thousand tons of bacon frying hissed back at him from the speaker. He tried again. 'V.I.N.Cent, do you read? What's it like out there?' Again the sound of the vast cosmic cooking pot.

He looked across to Holland, shook his head. 'No response. You heard what we're getting.'

'I don't like it.' Pizer started to comment, but Holland cut him off. 'Yes, I know I've been saying that a lot lately. Take it easy on me, will you? He may be encountering more difficulty than I thought he would.' He hesitated, then after a moment's consideration, said, 'I hate to bother Kate. It's a strain for her and she's busy enough as it is.'

Pizer said nothing.

Holland finally addressed the com pickup. 'Kate?'

She flashed a last burst with the sealer, set it aside and moved within easy reception range of the com unit. 'I'm here, Dan.'

'How are you coming on with those lines?'

'Getting there. It's easy to work the sealer, but hard to be neat about it. I remember the diagrams pretty well, though, and records are helping me make sure I'm emplacing the new modules properly.'

'You'd better, or we'll find ourselves breathing hydrogen instead of air,' he teased. Then he continued more seriously, 'I don't like to trouble you with this, Kate, but we either have a transmission problem or V.I.N.Cent's receiver is out. In any case, we can't contact him. See if you can esp-link with him. I need to know how he's doing.'

'I understand, Dan.' She sat down in her chair, forced herself to relax. 'I'll give him a call.'

'Appreciate it.'

Kate closed her eyes. Not that it was necessary to the process, but doing so helped her concentrate by eliminating sources of possible distraction. She did not need her eyes to 'see' V.I.N.Cent, any more than he needed his electronic optics to see back at her.

That's what the experts had told her. They had explained everything in detail when they'd inquired if she wished to undergo the operation. That had been ten years ago. Though, in fact, she feared the operation, she had covered her instinctive reaction so professionally, with such naturalness and so convincingly, that no one had thought to test her for truthfulness. The decision had to be a voluntary one. Her intelligence and ability had qualified her without subsidiary tests. So had her psych profile.

She'd known that a scientist able to engage esp-link with a correspondingly equipped mechanical had a tremendous advantage over colleagues in wangling important and interesting assignments. Like thousands of others she had wanted to be selected for deep-space research. In the highly competitive academic free-for-all that surrounded such applications, every advantage one had over one's colleagues was important. Esp-link ability could be critical. It was such a powerful plus because not every operation resulted in the ability to link. Also, not every volunteer came out from under the operation – or sometimes one would emerge into consciousness with parts of his mental self badly confused. Sometimes permanently confused.

Kate McCrae's operation had been one of those that proved completely successful. She well remembered her first and last sight of the esp-link itself, a tiny metal cylinder half the size of the nail on her little finger. It was buried inside her skull now, always ready and able to translate her properly conceived thoughts to a receptive machine unit and to receive impulses in turn from units equipped to broadcast. Sometimes getting it right was more of a strain than anyone imagined, including Holland. But the particular rapport Kate had acquired with mechanicals such as V.I.N.Cent made the risk and strain worthwhile.

Now she adjusted her thoughts as she had been trained to do, letting them flow outward. It pleased her to regard the process as something wonderfully magical rather than the simple transference of wave structures from one point in space to another. -

An alarmingly long time . . . several seconds . . . passed before the robot eventually responded.

'I'm sorry, Dr Kate. I was occupied.'

'You mean *preoccupied*,' she thought back at him.

'No . . . occupied. I am never preoccupied. No one can technically be *preoccupied* as that implies pre . . .'

'Not now, V.I.N.Cent. Save the philosophical homilies for later. You're okay?'

'I am still attached to the ship and functioning as intended, if that's what you mean.'

'You know it is, you disreputable hunk of scrap.'

'Now, doctor . . . no flattery when I'm working. You will distract me.'

'Unlikely. Where are you?'

A brief pause, then, 'Nearly over bay four. I should be able to see the hatch cover soon.'

'Good.' She fought to adjust her brain to create audible words, spoke dreamily towards the com pickup. 'Dan, I've contact with V.I.N.Cent.'

'Fine. He's all right out there?'

'Yes, and nearly in sight of the hatch, he says.'

'Keep us posted.'

She turned her thoughts back inward. 'Any trouble?'

'Electromagmetic effects like I've never experienced. And hope never to experience again. Makes my skin crawl.'

McCrae smiled, eyes still peacefully shut. V.I.N.Cent could sound so human when he wanted to that you had to remind yourself he was a machine, an artificial construct of printed circuits and cold alloy, much like the *Palomino*.

'I am in sight of the hatch now,' he told her, the voice echoing inside her head. 'Over the hatch opening now.' She waited, knowing he was inspecting the damage. His analysis was typically succinct.

'The concussion apparently caused the emergency explosive bolts securing the hatch to misfire. Fortunately, only the bolts on the normally latched side fired, or I'd have no hatch ere to fix. I will make temporary repairs by welding it shut.'

'Good enough.'

She relaxed further, found herself thinking about Dan as V.I.N.Cent worked, about his reaction to her whenever the up-link was brought up. *He knews it's there permanently, inside me. Does he secretly regard me as some kind of mutated freak, part-human, part-machine?* She knew some people reacted that way to those equipped with the links and wondered if that was why Dan was always so kind and gentle with her? Or was it something more, as she'd often

45

hoped? Of course, he had never given any definite indication that he regarded the presence of the link as anything abnormal. But that didn't mean that . . .

V.I.N.Cent was thinking at her again. 'I've inserted vacuum seal around the edges of the hatch and repositioned the cover. Am now activating my sealer.'

She could almost see the robot, visualised the barrel-shaped form secured by line and magnetic lower limbs to the *Palomino*'s hull. One arm would be travelling with great precision over the edge of the hatch, a beam of intense red light emerging from its tip. The vacuum seal would turn molten under the heat of that beam, as would the metal of the hull beneath it. The result, when it cooled, would be a crystalline structure not quite metal, not quite ceramic. It could not be cut away except with the facilities of a zero-gee shipyard.

Hatch four would be useless for the remainder of their journey, but the precious pharmaceuticals stored inside would be in no danger of drifting or being thrown out. Later, the bay could be repressurised and entered safely. The seal V.I.N.Cent was executing would be as airtight as the rest of the hull.

A voice, shatteringly loud and crude, interrupted her musing. 'Kate? How's he coming? You still with him?'

'I'll check, Dan. Right now he's quoting a flight instructor he once knew. "There are old pilots and there are bold pilots, but there are very few old, bold pilots." '

'She's tuned in on V.I.N.Cent, all right,' Pizer murmured

'Let's hope we disprove that maxim. Just a few degree more, Charlie.'

'V.I.N.Cent, how are you coming?' McCrae asked silently

A gratified mechanical responded. 'Finishing the last of it Dr Kate.'

'Dan . . . he's secured the hatch.'

'Good. Let me know when he's back inside.' Hollan turned his attention to his first officer. 'Charlie, we're holdin our own here, but that's not good enough. She's threatenin to destabilise and send us tumbling again. We've got to ge her around. Maximum power on . . .' he checked a brace gauges '. . . quad thrusters E and H, half thrust on A and G

'Working,' replied Pizer, carefully making the requisi adjustments. The ship responded.

Holland switched a second speaker on as the communicator buzzed for attention. He remained in communication with the lab and Kate, added the new call from Power.

'That you, Alex?'

'Check, Dan.' Durant's voice was strained. 'We can only effect temporary repairs back here, and that only to the secondaries. It's a mess. Maybe you and Charlie will get a chance to come back here and refine what Harry and I have done.'

'I doubt we could do much more, Alex. I just pilot 'em, I don't build 'em.'

'That's what we need back here, Dan. A construction engineer. With a full internal plumbing shop. I'm afraid that we'll eventually lose our air supply unless we can replace the critically damaged modules in the main regenerator complex.'

'Damn. You're sure of that?'

'You ought to see what's left of the regenerator's internals and monitors. Looks like a particle beam played through them. You know you can't "fix" any of those microchip links. All you can do is replace them.

'We can seal over and set the larger components back in place, but you know better than I that it'll all be for nothing unless the rest are replaced. And we don't carry any of the necessary replacements.'

Holland thought a moment. 'How about cannibalising the necessary chips from the secondaries?'

'Maybe,' was Durant's reply, 'but I doubt it.'

'Why?'

'Because some of the chips in the secondaries are so weakened from overload they could shatter if we try fooling with their ambient temperatures or voltages. Then we'd lose the secondaries in addition to the main system. But I agree it may come to trying that.'

'Let's hope not, Alex. Let me know when you and Harry have finished. Maybe I can come back and have a look.'

'Will do.'

Holland switched off, knowing the futility of making a personal inspection of the damage. He had added his final comment to placate Durant. If the scientist couldn't fix the system it was because the parts were not available, as he had said. If they didn't have replacements the finest respiratory system technician on Earth couldn't do any better.

V.I.N.Cent shut off the flow of sealant. A moment later he shut off power to his arm and examined his handiwork. The seal was clean, flush to the hull, and appeared tight. No one could tell for certain about the last until bay four could be repressurised and tested for air leak, but he was confident his work would stand that test. He turned his optics away from the hatch preparatory to starting back towards the lock he had used to leave the ship and his confidence was lessened by the sight that greeted him. Neatly severed by age and the wear and tear it had received against the rim of the lock, his cable tether drifted lazily past him.

Calmly he reported the break to McCrae. Her first reaction was concern. 'Are you still secured to the ship, V.I.N.Cent?' She knew as well as Holland that if the robot had somehow slipped free of the hull he was lost.

'Still secure . . . and awaiting instructions, Dr Kate.'

She spoke hurriedly to the pickup. 'Dan, it's V.I.N.Cent. He's finished sealing the hatch, but his cable tether's parted. He's okay for now, but without the tether he has no back up if he loses physical contact with the hull. His thrusters may not be enough to get him back. He wants to know how you want him to proceed.'

Pizer was already half out of his chair. 'Someone has to take him another secured line so he can get back safely. I'll go after him.'

Holland threw him a sharp look. 'Stay put, Charlie. You've plenty to do right here.'

The first officer looked askance at Holland. 'You don't mean that, Dan. What if it were one of us out there?'

'V.I.N.Cent *is* one of us. As to the other, I wouldn't let you go no matter who it was. Stay at your post.'

'What if it was Kate?'

Holland didn't change his expression. 'The same. She knows that. You ought to.' He spoke to the com. 'We can't risk anyone else out there now, Kate. Not till we regain full control. Tell V.I.N.Cent to hang on, to stay at his present location until further notice. I don't want him moving around untethered until we've stabilised our attitude. Too much chance he'll be jarred loose.'

McCrae relayed the information to the waiting robot.

'I concur,' came the prompt reply. 'I don't like sitting out here, but the Captain is right. I believe —'

Transmission stopped. McCrae strained frantically, sweat beading her forehead from the effort of projecting. She knew V.I.N.Cent's human-analog programming did not include breaking off conversation in the middle of a sentence without some kind of explanation.

'V.I.N.Cent. V.I.N.Cent! Report!'

A slight but unexpected jolt had produced exactly the result Holland had feared, despite V.I.N.Cent's dutifully remaining in one place. Flailing metal arms groped for protrusions, missed as the robot began to drift away from the ship, back towards the stern and the distant bottom of the gravity well.

V.I.N.Cent decided not to chance his thrusters unless forced to. There were other methods of remaining in contact with the *Palomino*. The cable he fired from his body had been designed to enable him to pull objects through free space towards him. Now he utilised it to pull himself back to the ship. As he was reeling himself in he was able to respond positively to McCrae's urgent call. 'I am all right, Dr Kate. I momentarily lost my grip, but I am secured again. I will be more conscious now of the forces operating on my body here. I now have physical as well as magnetic adhesion. Please do not worry.'

'Kate?'

She heard the dim voice, took a breath and replied. 'It's okay now, Dan. V.I.N.Cent slipped away for a moment but he's reattached himself. He says he's more secure now than he was before, and that he'll be more careful.'

She gave a brief description of what had happened, relaying the robot's own words.

Pizer listened, then moved as if to leave his chair again.

'Stay at your post, Charlie.'

'What the hell are you made of? He's still stuck out there. Next time he might not be able to get back.'

Holland chose to ignore the question and the challenge behind it. Pizer was operating, like the rest of them, like the ship, under abnormal pressure. As captain, Holland was not permitted the psychological release of insubordination. He would not reprimand Charlie for making use of it, wished only that he, too, had some higher authority to yell at.

Instead of snapping back at his first officer, Holland kept himself under control and spoke quietly to the pickup. 'Kate, tell V.I.N.Cent we're starting to make some progress. We're backtracking to that zero-gee bubble surrounding the

Cygnus. Once we're inside the field again he can hop and skip back to the lock.'

She nodded, though there was no one to see her. The information was relayed to the robot. As she was finishing, Durant and Booth returned to the lab. Both men were mentally flayed, the close mechanical repair work having proven itself as debilitating as any heavy physical labour. They were concentrated out. Neither disturbed McCrae by listing their accomplishments. Durant waited until the wrinkles above her eyes had smoothed out and some of the tenseness had visibly left her body before asking what the esp-link conversation involved.

'Looks like Dan's instincts were right,' she told them. 'We've had trouble.'

'What's wrong, Kate?' Booth asked quickly. 'Problems with the hatch repair?'

'Not exactly,' she murmured. Her eyes were still closed. 'It's V.I.N.Cent. His tether broke. We almost lost him.' Now she did blink, stared wide-eyed at them, stretching the muscles around each orb. 'He's okay now. What about the regenerator?'

Durant shrugged. 'Did the best we could with what we had. But there were still a few items we couldn't find replacements for.' He smiled wanly. 'Just enough of them to cause the entire system to fail before we can get home . . . unless Dan and Charlie can do better, or can find a way to bypass what we haven't got.'

Suddenly, he turned quiet, looked around in confusion. So did Booth. So did McCrae. Something had happened. There was something missing.

They all realised what had happened at the same time. The turbulence, the jostling of the ship, had vanished.

The ship was as still as the inside of a coffin . . .

FOUR

PIZER leaned back in his chair. His muscles ached as if he had just finished a half day's workout in the *Palomino*'s compact gymnasium, though he hadn't moved from his position in all the time they had been playing dice with death.

'Close,' he murmured, 'too close. I want to be buried . . . but not yet.'

As if trying to cover his embarrassment at his outburst over V.I.N.Cent, he spoke reassuringly to Holland. 'Don't blame yourself, Dan. First we stumble into an impossible area of no-gravity around the *Cygnus*. Then we find out it's irregular in outline and uncertain in effect. You can't blame yourself for not foreseeing the instability of an impossibility.'

'Put that way, it makes me feel a little better,' the captain admitted.

'And, Dan?'

'Yeah.'

'I apologise for the way I acted, for what I said. You know.'

'Skip it. That close to a collapsar, everything's stability is a little twisted. Mine too.' He turned, spoke towards the com pickup.

'Kate, we're going to set down on the *Cygnus*. How's V.I.N.Cent doing?'

Her voice came back to him a moment later. 'Still with us and looking for a place to dock. I told him we're going in. He requests permission to remain where he is, for purposes of examination.'

'Permission granted. Tell him to keep his eyes open.' It was an old joke, but he still grinned inwardly. V.I.N.Cent had no eyelids to close with.

'Charlie, you run the lights and scanners. I'll bring us alongside. If you spot anything that looks like an un-damaged shiplock, or at worst a single-entry port, say so. A

51

ship the size of the *Cygnus* should have many. I don't want to waste time hunting through the records for details of her construction. I'm betting we'll find something visually a lot faster.'

'Yes, sir.'

A powerful beam illuminated space between the *Palomino* and the *Cygnus* as the smaller vessel nudged nearer the dark hulk. They cruised slowly across the surface. Pizer played the light over the craft as they searched both visually and with more complex but less decisive instruments.

Quite without warning, they found themselves drifting over a city. A thousand lights winked on below. Their brilliance smothered the single searching beam emanating from the *Palomino*. Ports and domes glowed radiantly. One moment the *Cygnus* had been a dead thing. Now she had shown herself to be alive with energy, if not with organic life. Something had finally reacted to their presence. The great ship had awakened.

'What the devil's going on now?' Durant pressed his face to the lab port. He was straining to see into one or more of the flaring ports below, wishing for the use of a powerful portable scope.

'Someone's alive down there!' McCrae's first reaction was more emotional than analytical. It was also infectious. Behind her and Durant, Booth was fumbling to set up his recorders. Then he began speaking into one in low, hurried tones.

'Like the tree on Christmas morning.' Pizer's attention shifted regularly from console to port and back again. 'Funny. Until now I'd only thought of her as impressive. But she's pretty, too.'

'Pretty or not,' Holland said tightly, 'we'd better set our warheads in firing position.'

'Hold on, Dan.' Pizer sounded surprised at the captain's caution. 'They've got to be friendly. I remember how she was armed. They readied her to do battle with imaginary alien hordes that never materialised. She carries a thousand times more firepower than we do. If her internal lights are functioning we have to assume that her weapons systems are too. She could have blasted us into plasma if she or anyone aboard had such an inclination and done so on our first pass, without revealing that she is operational. She hasn't done so.'

Holland hesitated before replying. 'All right. We'll assume the intentions of whoever or whatever's running her now are friendly. Since you're quite right about our being ridiculously overmatched, I guess we might as well proceed optimistically. I just don't like going in naked.'

He checked the main viewscreen, punched for and received several different views of the *Cygnus* before settling on a particular one.

'There's the command tower. Whoever turned on the lights is likely to be giving directions from up there. There's a subsidiary structure nearby that's likely to be a docking tower.'

The *Palomino* swung around, moving toward the large conical shape near the front of the great research vessel. As they passed close, a large viewport set in the *Cygnus*' upper section came into clear sight.

'Your side, Dan,' McCrae was shouting at the pickup.

Holland twisted to stare out the port nearby. It seemed as if he could make out shapes moving slowly within the translucent area. Then the *Palomino* changed attitude and the momentary glimpse vanished.

'You getting a better view back there, Kate? All I saw were suggestions of movement.'

McCrae and Durant were already repeating computer-view tapes provided by the ship's scanners. Even after enhancement they remained maddeningly inconclusive.

That didn't slow McCrae's enthusiasm. 'There are people aboard, Dan!'

'Just shadows.' The man standing next to her tried not to sound too critical. He knew she must still be imagining an unlikely reunion with her father, but couldn't bear bludgeoning her with reason. Not now.

Besides, hadn't they already survived a host of highly improbable events? First the discovery of the *Cygnus* herself, then the inexplicable zero-gravity field enveloping the ghost ship like some supraphysical amniotic fluid. Who could predict what might reveal itself next? It was only slightly more incredible to expect that her father might be on board and alive after twenty years.

He wouldn't be the one to put a damper on her hopes. Let Holland do that. It was *his* job.

'They appear to be moving shapes,' he added in a more

hopeful tone, 'but we can't resolve them. Neither can the computer.'

'They're people, Alex.' Hope made her more beautiful than ever, he thought. 'I know it. I feel it.'

'I hope you're right.' He smiled back down at her, her inner radiance eclipsing that of the *Cygnus*. He was very much afraid her hopes were groundless.

The *Palomino* slid nearer to the command tower, instrument antennae radiating from her upper sections like the spines of an alloyed sea-urchin.

Pizer's attention was riveted on the less spectacular structure closer at hand. 'It's a docking tower, for sure.' He gestured at it. 'See? There are two extensible walkways.

'Wonder why they didn't roll out the red carpet earlier? Since everything else on board seems functional, I don't see how they could have missed our orbiting them. For that matter I think our calls should have made it through the interference. We were close enough.' He looked puzzled. 'Wonder what's up?'

'I don't know.' Still wishing they were properly armed, Holland tried to study the docking tower they were closing on and the imagined location of possible weapons' ports. And I don't like it. I don't like any of it, but they're calling the shots. We're outgunned and hurting and we've got to repair our air system. Maybe they have the necessary replacement modules and maybe they don't. We've no choice except to try and find out. Either that or pull off a miracle of microtechnology repair.'

Holland sighed. 'Me, I'm tired of surprises. But I'm also fresh out of miracles.'

'Don't look at me, Dan. I'm just your average well-meaning, hot-tempered ço-pilot. I'd want to go aboard even if we didn't have to.'

'Don't get me wrong, Charlie. I'm curious to get inside that grand old mystery myself.' He stared down at the enormous length of the *Cygnus*. 'If there is anyone left alive on board and if they feel like talking, they'll have a helluva tale to tell.'

'That's no lie.' Pizer grinned. 'I can hear Booth drooling over his recorder without using the intercom.'

They eased in tight, main engines silent, using attitude quads to manoeuvre the *Palomino* next to the waiting connector umbilical that protruded invitingly from the docking tower.

Holland's frustration showed as they adjusted and re-adjusted their position, striving to line up the ship's main airlock with the umbilical. 'They should be giving us some help,' he grumbled.

'Maybe someone wants to see what kind of pilot we've got aboard?'

'Pilots,' Holland corrected him. 'Pay attention to your own end. Let's locktight right the first time.'

Temporarily forgotten, the *Palomino*'s advance landing party of one was already active. V.I.N.Cent released his grip on the ship's hull. Using his built-in manoeuvring unit he scudded the few metres remaining to the end of the connector arm. Armature lasers ready, he upended and peered into the yawning maw of the umbilical. It looked deserted. Taking note of the artificial gravity functioning inside the tube, he adjusted accordingly and moved inside.

Holland touched one control, then its mate. Four lights blinked in sequence on the main console – bright yellow stars. He fingered two additional controls. Pizer did likewise on his console. Immediately the four lights in front of Holland turned bright green. They stayed that way as a buzzer whooped once, became silent. He leaned back from the console. 'We're here . . . come what may.'

Holland spoke towards the com. 'Alex, Kate, Harry – we're linked now. I know I can't expect any of you to lie abed and wait for reports. We'll go aboard together . . . but I want everyone armed.'

'Dan, do you really think . . . ?' Kate began.

'Everyone, Kate. That's an order. A pistol doesn't weigh much. I'm not saying I expect we'll have to use them, but we'll be awfully embarrassed if the need arises and our weapons are all resting innocently back here on the ship. You too, Harry, if you think you can handle one.'

Booth sounded mildly perturbed. 'I've had occasion to defend my neck, Captain. I'd rather point my recorders at anything we might meet, but I know which end of a pistol is for business.'

'Good. Assemble at the main lock.'

When they had gathered inside, Holland nodded to Pizer. The first officer performed the final check on the external read-outs. 'Gravity's point seven normal. That's about right for an umbilical link. It should be standard one within the ship itself. Atmospheric pressure's about six and a half kilos per, where it belongs, and a little high in oxygen. Nothing wrong with their biosystem.' He hefted his pistol firmly, glanced over at Holland. The captain nodded again.

Pizer thumbed the last switch. The lock door slid aside silently. They heard a slight *whooshing* as air from within the *Palomino* mingled with the atmosphere of the *Cygnus*.

A blocky, blinking shape was waiting to greet them.

'Nice work, V.I.N.Cent.' Holland gave the familiar metal flank an affectionate pat. He did not bother to ask if the rest of the connector was safe. V.I.N.Cent would have informed Kate if there'd been any danger.

'Out of the frying pan,' the robot quipped, blithely ignoring the fact that he was a nearer relative of said pan than anything liable to be cooking in it. 'Hopefully not into the proverbial fire.'

McCrae moved alongside, eyed the machine critically. 'You sure you're all right?'

'I was banged around a bit when I lost my grip on the hull. Nothing a hammer and a little metal polish can't fix, thank you. It is fortunate that my heart depends on the steady flow of electrons and not corpuscles and cells, or I might have had an attack when I was floating away from the ship. I am glad my body is not subject to such fragile organic fluxations as thromboses.'

'Stick it in your lubricatory orifice,' advised Pizer with a smile. 'One of these days you'll suffer a severe oil blockage and then we'll see who has the laugh. I'll take flesh and blood over cold molybdenoy any day.'

'And you may have it,' V.I.N.Cent shot back, giving a passable version of a metallic shudder.

'Easy now,' said Holland, interrupting the banter. He pointed down the umbilical. 'Company's coming.'

A bright oval of light had appeared at the far end of the connector link. They waited tensely. When the silence and inaction became unbearable, Holland finally yelled out.

'Hey! This is Daniel Holland commanding the *S.S. Palomino*! We've had some trouble with our regulator system and we could use some help.'

His plea for assistance produced no more response from

the opened end of the umbilical than had Holland's self-identification. No one appeared to call back to them.

'Looks like we'll have to go to them.' McCrae's grip on her pistol loosened. 'Funny sort of greeting. First they ignore us. They they turn on every light on the ship, and extend an umbilical for us. And now they're ignoring us again.'

Holland nodded. 'This changes things some. Charlie, you stay with the *Palomino*. We'll use channel C for communication. Linked that way, we ought to be able to stay in touch.'

Pizer started to argue with him, visibly disappointed. 'You're going to need . . .'

'That's an order, Charlie. You or I have to stay with the ship.'

'And since you have rank . . .' Pizer began tactlessly.

'And since it's my place to go and since that's what the regulations say, I'm going and you're staying.'

Pizer slumped, looked resigned. 'Yes, sir. You're right, of course. Sorry for the backtalk.'

'Talk back, Charlie. After eighteen months together you ought to know you can't offend me.'

The first officer's mood lightened some.

'We have each other to depend on,' Holland added, indicating the others surrounding him, 'but we all have to depend on you. Keep the ship's eyes and ears open and see what you can find out. It's liable to be more than we will.'

'That's true.' Pizer managed a smart salute.

'Don't worry, Mr Pizer.' V.I.N.Cent had pivoted to face him. 'They also serve who only stand and wait.'

'V.I.N.Cent, sometimes I think they switched your programming with that of a literary robot. Or were you programmed especially to bug me?'

'No, sir, to educate you.'

McCrae laughed, a little nervously. Beneath V.I.N.Cent's easy humour and his very human sense of camaraderie was the unavoidable fact that he contained far more in the way of factual knowledge than any human brain. But this was the first time she'd ever heard him even hint at his mental superiority. Her reaction, she told herself, was more a reflection of her own hidden, foolish fears than of anything the robot had said. The fact was she had more reason to fear any human than she did V.I.N.Cent.

The comment had no effect on Pizer. 'When I volunteered

for this mission,' he said ruefully, 'I never thought I'd end up playing straight man to a tin can.'

'What is a *tin can*, sir?' V.I.N.Cent asked, revealing (deliberately, McCrae wondered?) a gap in his vast store of facts.

'Antique construction for storage,' Pizer informed him. 'Wasteful of energy and metal. Remind me to refer you to the correct history tape some time.'

'All right.' Holland smiling to himself, had to force himself to sound half-serious. 'End of the lessons all around. Keep your pistols in mind if not in hand, and don't shoot until you see the green of their eyes.'

Holland and McCrae led the way down the umbilical corridor, V.I.N.Cent in the middle, with Durant and Booth bringing up the rear.

Pizer watched them depart, feeling a little better for Holland's words but still deeply disappointed. His gaze moved up, then down to stare through the transparent material of the tube. Around him, the floating city that was the *Cygnus* lay gleaming but still devoid of any sign of life. Silence and light. Well, that was an improvement after eighteen months of silence and darkness. Pizer turned and hurried back inside the *Palomino* . . .

As they neared the end of the corridor, V.I.N.Cent moved slightly in front of McCrae, taking a more prominent position near the forefront of the little expedition. The movement was not born of some mysterious form of mechanical bravery, though V.I.N.Cent could have been counted on to supply that necessary intangible in whatever amount might be required. It was a bit of simple logic, one which noted that his metal body was less susceptible to laser fire than human flesh.

Holland edged close to the end of the umbilical and peered cautiously into the craft. It opened onto a large, well-lit chamber. Lavish compared to the energy-conserving dimmer illumination of the *Palomino*, the bright light made him blink despite his determination not to.

Furniture two decades out of style filled the room. Lounges and chairs were scattered about, and free-form glass ports gave the occupants varying views of deep space. There were decorative plants, some real, some artificial *objets d'art*, and tape viewers for casual reading placed throughout the area.

A large curving desk faced the umbilical Holland now stepped clear of. Its top was bare save for several professional pieces of recording equipment. Holland recognised an already obsolete form of play-back bank, an ident scanner thirty per cent larger than current models, and several other devices – all designed to serve in some fashion to record information or provide it. The fact that this chamber was located on a small artificial world made the function of the reception room no less familiar. No one sat behind the desk.

That was the only expected item missing from the room: a receptionist. The chamber was devoid of official greeters, human or mechanical, but compensated with a feeling they all felt, something sensed but not visible. In a moment Holland realised what it was. There was an aura of petrification about the entire chamber, from the farthest chair to the simple tape viewers.

'Looks like the place hasn't been used in years,' he muttered. 'I get the feeling we may be the first official visitors since the *Cygnus* left Earth orbit.'

McCrae and the others had fanned out into the spacious room. 'Eerie,' she said. 'I don't want to sound melodramatic, but . . .'

'Go ahead,' Booth urged her. 'The situation almost demands it.'

'I feel like not a few but a thousand eyes are watching us.' She was turning in a slow circle, eying the walls. 'If so, where are they? *Something* on this ship turned on the lights, sent out an umbilical and filled at least this section with breathable air.'

Something closed the door to the connector corridor with a plastic *snap*, sealing them off from the *Palomino*. Cracking noises came from places in the walls and ceiling. Holland's pistol was neatly vaporised. So were the others. Suddenly V.I.N.Cent was knocked backwards, his own weapons similarly disabled by the flash of precision laser fire.

'V.I.N.Cent!' McCrae noted that the others were all right, an to check on the metal body that was lurching unsteadily erect.

'Down, but never for the full count, Dr Kate.' His external ights gradually returned to full strength, resumed pulsing in roper sequence. 'Something of a shock. Oh, I don't mean

59

the effects of the beams or their presence. It was the speed and efficiency with which they engaged us. And the accuracy of their aim. Only our weapons were damaged.' His optics began sweeping the room.

'There is at least one major class mechanical or competent class human mind functioning on board the *Cygnus*.'

'Maybe,' she said, looking around nervously now and wishing she possessed the robot's methods of perception, 'it's the *Cygnus*' mind. Maybe that's what turned on the lights and sent out the connector for us.'

'I would consider that hypothesis, Dr Kate, save for one obvious discrepancy.'

'I don't follow you.'

'From our initial circling of the *Cygnus* to this moment,' V.I.N.Cent observed, 'our presence here has been treated with uncertainty. Something or someone is improvising our greeting, acting one step at a time. Machines never act so erratically, only in pre-planned sequence. First we are ignored, then welcomed, then fired upon and disarmed, all without our greeter revealing himself. Very unmachine like. So I am inclined to believe there is a non-mechanical mind functioning in control of or in conjunction with any mechanical consciousnesses that might be inhabiting this vessel.'

'The . . . non-mechanical mind. Have you learned enough to surmise whether it's human or not?'

'Insufficient data thus far to proffer a reasoned opinion, Dr Kate.'

Holland had his communicator out, was speaking to the tiny grid. 'Charlie, this is Dan. Do you read?'

'Loud and clear,' came Pizer's response. 'Something on the *Cygnus* together with the ship's bulk is screening out the majority of the noise around us. You sound like you're standing behind me.'

'I'm beginning to wish I was.'

Pizer's concern was immediate. 'Trouble?'

'Weapons destroyed by laser fire, but no injuries. The intent was clearly just to disarm us, not injure.'

'I'll be there in . . .'

'Hold your position.'

'But what about the . . . ?'

'No!' Holland interrupted him more sharply this time. 'I told you, we're okay. I don't want to tempt whoever's monitoring us into incapacitating the *Palomino* by a further display of arms. Maybe they're just nervous. Such a reception area weapons' system conforms with what we know about this ship. It may operate independently of other functions, to prevent possible belligerents from coming aboard armed.'

'All right. But watch yourselves.' Pizer clicked off.

Booth leaned over to whisper something to Durant. 'So much for the friendship theory. I'd say describing the condition of whoever's got eyes on us as *nervous* is understating it some.'

'Holland's right, though,' the scientist argued. 'They could already have killed us if that was their intent. Or simply denied us entry to the ship. They may want us aboard defenceless, but it's indisputable that they want us aboard.'

'Yeah, well, I can't say I care for their taste in *hors d'oeuvres*. Or for their manners.' Booth was staring uncomfortably at the walls. The weapons which had just destroyed their own pistols were still hidden behind them. No doubt they were primed to fire at any time. He could imagine half a dozen stubby, high-intensity generators aimed straight at his belly.

A door slid aside at the far end of the reception room. They headed for it, striving to appear confident, succeeding only in looking tense.

A high corridor stretched nearly a kilometre into the distance. It was impressively wide. Holland didn't try to conceal his reaction at the sight; he was awed yet again. Intricate yet slim arches of metal supported the ceiling. The corridor was silent and bare, quite sterile-looking after the homey atmosphere of the reception chamber.

This time he was expecting it when the door closed behind them, locking them in the corridor. There was still no reason to panic, though it did place one more barrier between them and the safety of the *Palomino*.

A second, smaller door moved aside on their right. An internal transport vehicle waited there, humming like a tuned dragonfly.

'Looks like we're not expected to walk.' McCrae moved to the air car. 'Maybe someone's suddenly remembered his manners.'

She might not have voiced the thought if she could have

61

seen the ranks of unbeautiful, but formidable-looking mechanicals that now filed into the sealed-off reception room. They emerged from behind wall panels, assembling with a silence broken only by the scrape of metal on metal. It did not take an education in cybernetics to see at a glance that the function of these machines was not to comfort but to disassemble. Ungently, if need be. Without a word passing between them, verbal or electronic, they began to move in unison towards the now open umbilical leading to the *Palomino*.

The air car sped the group silently along the cylindrical passageway. The walls were largely transparent, giving them a spectacular view of surrounding space. It was easy to imagine they were travelling outside the *Cygnus*, tunnelling through the void, instead of speeding down a fully pressurised tube of plastic and metal.

To one side was a vast, swirling whirlpool of energy, the visual dying gasps of matter being drawn down into the collapsar. Elsewhere the distant pricks of light that were other suns blended into the body of light that was the *Cygnus*. They reached the far end of the tube. Their vehicle slowed, came to a halt. A doorway ahead was closed, but opened for them when the air car reached a complete stop.

Holland stepped out of the car, looked around. Behind them stretched the long, empty transport tube they had just traversed. The tube itself showed no other egress. Even if there had been a hatch, it would have opened directly into empty space. They could only continue on ahead, as some one clearly intended they should.

'I'm getting tired of being bounced around like a ball in box,' Booth murmured irritably.

'Calm down, Harry.' Holland grinned. 'Just think of th story this is leading up to.'

'I'm looking forward to it.' Booth relaxed a little, smile back at him. 'Just impatient at the delays, that's all.'

'I don't think any of us will have much longer to wai McCrae said, walking towards the now open door befo them. It led into another empty, though much smalle corridor.

'Slow up, Kate.' Holland hurried to join her and s

waited for the others to catch up. She was staring upwards, towards a wide, illuminated port set high up in the side of the command tower whose base they had reached.

'I know I shouldn't get my hopes up, but it's hard not to,' she told him.

He put a hand on her shoulder, pressed gently. It was a pitifully inadequate gesture under the circumstances, considering what the *Cygnus* itself and now the nearby tower represented to her, but it was the best he could think of. He was better with a ship.

'I know, Kate. We're all hoping along with you.'

She glanced at his face, then down at the floor, then back up at him. 'It helps . . . some.'

The personnel corridor was short. Eventually they reached a section which widened considerably. In the middle of the floor a thick cylinder rose into the ceiling. Several doors were set into its sides. One was open and waiting, the green light above it shining steadily.

'Not much doubt where that goes.' Booth spoke as he checked his recorders, making sure each of the disposable units was fully charged. 'I think we're finally going to meet our hosts.'

'All of you remember one thing,' Holland paused, blocking the elevator doorway, 'the *Cygnus* seems stable, but it's too close to that black hole to take any chances. We've already learned that the field holding it motionless here against the gravity pull is subject to variation. We still don't know if the field is artificially generated or if it's a natural phenomenon. If natural, it could shift radically or even fail at any time.

'We don't know how long the *Cygnus* has been stabilised here. It may have been defying the pull for a decade or more, or it could have become trapped here a day ago. My point is that we know practically nothing for certain about the forces operation in this section of space. Not those active around the black hole nor those keeping the *Cygnus* clear of it. Ignorance is the most dangerous form of instability, and I don't care if you're talking personality or physics.

'The sooner we repair the *Palomino* and leave here, the better for all of us.' This last was spoken while he was staring directly at McCrae. She didn't argue with him and her expression remained unchanged. Good, he thought.

63

Emotionally hyper as she was, she was still functioning realistically. He could still depend on her if an emergency arose to do that which was right rather than that which might be attractive.

And what if her father *was* aboard, and alive? He pushed that possibility aside. Take events as they came.

'Indeed, the sooner we are away, the better I will like it.' V.I.N.Cent nudged his way into the elevator. 'Several of my robotic colleagues were victims of black holes. I personally was acquainted with two. They were transferred to drone probes and trained, like myself, in human-machine esp-link techniques. The theory was that they could then send messages back from beyond the return limits of the gravity wells of such objects as black holes. A grand experiment, the scientists thought. Sadly, it did not work.'

'Ancient history, V.I.N.Cent,' said the reporter.

'Not to me, Mr Booth. For one thing, the project designers had not considered the effects dissolution of their metallic partners under great stress would have on the human end of the esp-links. Several people collapsed mentally under the strain, much as their mechanical mind-partners did physically under pressure of a different kind.

'For another, nothing is ancient that is so close. The heat generated in such regions would melt me before the pressure rendered me dysfunctional. I have sufficient imagination to convince me it is a process I will do all in my power to avoid experiencing.'

The elevator door slid quietly shut behind them. They rose in silence, casual conversation seeming suddenly indecent.

FIVE

BEFORE long the lift stopped. All eyes were trained on the door. Thoughts and circulation raced. The door slid back. Some of the tenseness drained out of them when it became clear there was no one waiting there either to greet them or destroy them.

Cautiously they moved out into the vast domed upper chamber of the command tower. Bare floors made the place seem even larger than it was. The *Palomino*'s compact control cockpit would have been lost here. Above the transparent dome and outside floor to ceiling ports, the stars pressed close.

Indicators of steady electronic heartbeat, lights winked on the ranks of instruments lining the walls. Two storeys of uninterrupted, unrelieved instrumentation. Scopes for staring through or offering other varieties of long-range perception pierced the dome to bring closer the immensity beyond.

Holland tried to imagine the great room as it must have been, filled with busy technicians and general crew, scientists conversing over the results of this or that research project, comparing notes and ideas and dreams while the *Cygnus* swam through the sea of darkness. Now the only sounds came from muffled relays and hidden servos.

Above, a pair of spectrographic displays filled dissimilar screens, reducing stars and nebulae to coded colours and numbers. A larger screen showed a complex pattern of roughly concentric lines and colours, shifting even as he watched it. It had to be monitoring the black hole and the halo of destruction surrounding it, he guessed. Another huge screen showed the collapsar region in magnificent colour and size.

As did everything else about the *Cygnus*, the marvels of the tower impressed Holland. But he kept his perspective.

Man's greatest machines could make mere numbers and equations of the universe, but he had not yet discovered an equation to summarise its magnificence, nor a series of numbers denoting its beauty. *Reductio ad absurdum.*

Some of his companions were less restrained in their reactions. 'Stupendous!' Durant was repeating, wide-eyed as a kid locked in a candy store over a holiday. 'Those scopes . . . bigger than anything we've got on the *Palomino*, bigger than those on non-mobile orbiting stations. And the detail on those screens . . . it's incredible!'

'It ought to be,' Booth commented drily. 'It cost the taxpayers enough.'

Durant turned on him. 'You can't put a price on something like this, Harry. You can't evaluate the possibility of great discoveries in terms of credits.'

'I didn't say I could,' replied the reporter, unmoved. 'I said the taxpayers could. And they did. That's why there'll never be another ship like this one. We've already agreed that ships like the *Palomino* are nearly as efficient and much less costly.'

'Agreed.' Durant's gaze was roving the banks of instrumentation. 'As efficient, maybe. As meaningful, no.'

'That's a tough concept to try and sell the people who have to pay for such projects, Alex.' But Durant's thoughts were now elsewhere. He had moved away and did not hear.

McCrae had walked out into the room. Lights from the instruments and consoles illuminated dim shapes that seemed a part of the machinery across the chamber, yet were not.

'Hello? Can you hear us?'

The maybe-figures did not respond. If they were human they must have been afflicted with universal deafness. Or else they were ignoring her with a studiousness that bordered on the maniacal.

'This is Katherine McCrae, of the *S.S. Palomino*. The ship that's just docked with you. Is . . . officer Frank McCrae aboard? If he is aboard, how may I contact him?'

Still no response. A metal shape moved to hover at her side.

'They appear to be some form of robot, Dr Kate.' V.I.N.Cent sounded puzzled. 'They are unique to my experience. One would imagine at least one or two would have broadcast capability, yet I cannot contact any of them.'

'You've been trying?'

'I have been attempting for several minutes now,' the robot answered. 'They do not respond to any of the standard mechanical languages, on any frequency. It is remotely possible this variety has absolutely no electronic communication capability beyond individual programming. That is difficult to believe, but not without precedent. I have heard tales of other machines similarly restricted in their ability to converse. But I never actually expected to encounter such inhibited mechanicals. It is a terrifying concept to a fully conversant machine such as myself.'

'You make them sound like mechanical cripples.'

'If so, it is unintentional. I presume their designers had their reasons for making them mute.' But she could sense his continued disgust.

Holland had passed them, heading towards the centre of the tower. To the far side, large ports provided views not only of space outside but of the immense length of the *Cygnus* herself. He carefully skirted the charged generation projector set into the floor.

Near the far end of the room was a series of large consoles that had to have functioned as the command station. Lights sparkled more intensely there than elsewhere. Additional dark forms operated the instruments on two levels, some standing, others seated. They remained oddly indistinct despite the bright lighting.

Holland edged carefully around another projecting device, then called for his companion's attention.

'Look over here. This is my guess as to where everything's run from.'

Durant hurried to join him, shaking his head in still unmoderated wonder. 'I've never seen anything to equal this. Never.'

The shadowy figures working at the consoles continued to fascinate McCrae. This close, the humanness of their structure was intensified, but their awkward, stiff movements and lack of response to her questions belied that. And, too, V.I.N.Cent seemed to think they were mechanicals.

She started towards one with the intention of questioning him face to face, found herself being held back by a hand on her arm.

'Hold it, Kate.'

'What's wrong, Dan?'

'I think . . . there's something else here.'

She turned, as did the others. Flashing rapidly, a new sequence of lights travelled across V.I.N.Cent's front, the robotic equivalent of facial expression.

'What is it?' Durant was straining to see what had alarmed Holland.

The dim shapes working behind them did not pause, but rather continued at their work. They were not what had unnerved Holland.

Turning ponderously, a section of the far instrumentation detached itself and began to move towards them. It drifted in uncanny silence for something so massive. It was a mechanical of a size and suggestive power Holland had seen at work only in heavy industry. None of those machines was equipped with more than rudimentary programming. Yet the way this one came towards them hinted at considerably more advanced mental abilities. Freely mobile robots of such obvious strength were forbidden on Earth. Response-time problems and inertial mechanics made them too dangerous to be allowed.

Someone aboard the *Cygnus* had evidently chosen to ignore such laws. Despite his lack of knowledge about the make-up of the great ship, Holland knew that no machine of such power and mobility would have been included among its normal stores. There was no need. Robots of the V.I.N.Cent series were the largest free-floaters permitted on Earth. Someone on the *Cygnus* had gone far beyond those limits in the manufacture of the dark red thing trundling towards them.

It had a single crescent optic slashing the tapered head. The visualiser glowed a deep red. It gave no indication of slowing its progression or of addressing them. V.I.N.Cent appeared to be but a toy in comparison.

Holland had his communicator out. 'Charlie? We've got trouble here.'

There was no answer. Taking no notice of Holland's words or actions, the huge mechanical continued its now decidedly threatening progress towards them.

They started to back away, moving for the elevator shaft near the centre of the tower. If the lift refused to function for them, they would have to try and short the controls somehow.

Meanwhile Holland was frantically hunting for anything

that could serve as a weapon. He found nothing, saw no tool locker or supply cabinet. Everything in the tower chamber was flush, sealed, or functional. Seamed metal ran into the transparencies of the ports. Even the controls on the console were mostly smooth-mounted touch-sensors.

'Do you read me?' he continued to call worriedly into the pickup. 'Charlie, come in, Charlie . . .'

A familiar barrel-shape inserted itself between the slowly retreating humans and their armoured tracker: V.I.N.Cent. Barely a metre away from its much smaller counterpart, the massive red machine slowed, hovered motionless. It did not speak, but anyone could see that the behemoth was considering the implied challenge of its tiny cousin.

V.I.N.Cent did not move, his own armoured upper casement sinking down into the cylindrical body to protect the optics. Since his own weapons had been incapacitated by the hidden lasers in the reception room he was making a possibly fatal gesture. But he remained oblivious to any danger, daring the larger machine to attack or to continue its hitherto inexorable march onwards.

'Here's a story to end all stories, Harry,' Durant was whispering to the reporter. Booth held his recorder stiffly in front of him, like a cobra at arm's length. In a way, it was the weapon he was most comfortable with, though it was unlikely the maroon monster towering over them would be dissuaded from any bellicose gesture by the implied power of the press.

'A ghost ship of robots and computers,' Durant went on, 'with this thing in charge.'

Surprisingly, the colossus reacted to his statement. The head swivelled on the shoulders to stare at the speaker and the nervous reporter next to him.

'Not quite, Dr Durant. A logical supposition, given your present situation and lack of true knowledge about what has occurred here.'

'It talks after all,' Booth mumbled.

'No.' Holland was peering around the hovering mechanial. 'I'm sure that voice didn't come from this machine.'

'Maximillian and my robots only run this ship the way *I* wish it run,' the voice went on. Holland walked around the monster, which did not move to intercept him. The others followed. 'They possess little in the way of programmed initiative, beyond what I chose to bestow on them. Only I command the *Cygnus*.'

The source of the voice was a darkened section of the chamber. Something, a large circular console, rotated to face them. A figure sat inside it, cloaked in shadow.

Durant squinted at it. 'How do you know my name?'

'You have been constantly monitored ever since the *Cygnus*' sensors first detected your approach from deep space. Though we were hardly expecting visitors, I make it a point always to be prepared for them.'

'You could take that one of two ways,' Booth was whispering to Durant. The scientist hardly heard him now. His full attention was on the mysterious figure.

'Isolation leads inevitably to caution,' the voice was saying. 'No doubt you regarded the *Cygnus* with equal uncertainty. You must excuse my perhaps extremity of manners in greeting you. But remember that, though tiny, your ship is of a type unknown to me. I had no idea whether you were human or otherwise. When your origin became clear, I could not know what fanatical cults might have infected the politics of Earth since my departure. It behoved me to be careful. I have much entrusted to my keeping. I safeguard it to the best of my abilities.

'If I erred in welcoming you so brusquely, do remember that this vessel is ultimately my responsibility.' The figure rose, moved out of the shadows into the light.

'Welcome aboard the *Cygnus*, gentlemen, lady and machine. Please excuse Maximillian.' The tall, bearded figure gestured at the robot that still confronted them. It moved aside, well away but still close enough to make its intimidating presence felt. A fact which the speaker, Holland thought, surely realised.

'He is most solicitous of my health. Perhaps overly so But diplomacy has not been needed out here, and so I have not programmed it into him.'

It was Booth who verbally identified the figure they had by now all recognised. 'Dr Hans Reinhardt,' he murmured 'He always did have a flair for theatrical entrances.'

If *he's* alive, McCrae was telling herself frantically, then i was still possible . . .

'And for you a pen dipped in poison, Mr Booth.' Rein hardt regarded the reporter. 'I remember reading you

70

articles well before the *Cygnus* left Earth orbit. I trust your faculties have not dimmed since then? They say that the potency of certain acids increases with age.'

'I can still turn a phrase here and there, Doctor.'

'Your phrases were often sharp, Mr Booth. For a surgeon who employed words, you many times cut with surprising clumsiness, sir. You caused many of the subjects of your vivisecting articles to bleed rather profusely.'

'If I was doing any cutting,' Booth gave back, 'it was only out of a desire to expose the unhealthy or the dangerous. I left actual excision to others.'

Reinhardt only grunted at that. They could see him clearly now as he walked towards them. Booth and he were contemporaries. That was the only visible similarity between them.

Reinhardt was taller, with the build of an athlete. He had the look of a man fanatical about the care of both body and mind. Isolation had not bent him. He approached them groomed as faultlessly as the day he had addressed the international vision audience prior to the *Cygnus*' departure some twenty years ago.

Save for the preponderance of grey in beard and hair and the additional lines in the long face, he appeared little different than he had those many years ago. McCrae had her own memories of that day and of that farewell speech. She had romanticised Reinhardt then, for he had looked as much soldier as scientist, the epitome of the dashing, adventurous explorer, yet with intellect to match boldness.

She had never guessed how much soldier and scientist merged in the man's mind. Reinhardt regarded the mysteries of the universe not as indifferent questions of physics or chemistry, but as implacable, malicious foes. They were to be assaulted with science, vanquished at any cost, forced to yield their treasure-house of knowledge.

That belief still drove him. It was there in his attitude and especially in those piercing, slightly wild eyes. His gaze had always seemed to see a little farther into the universe than that of most men. It had fixed on reluctant bureaucrats and indecisive politicians and compelled them to appropriate the money to build and crew the *Cygnus*. Reinhardt had built the great ship. Other men had been his tools, and he had used them as roughly and mercilessly as he had used himself

71

Now those eyes focused on the helpless knot of visitors standing before him.

Holland and McCrae examined him in turn. They did not identify with Reinhardt as thoroughly as Durant. He was a fellow scientist, researcher, explorer of the unknown. But they did not have the same messianic zeal. Reinhardt's fanaticism set him apart from them. Apart from them and from the rest of mankind.

It did not trouble Reinhardt to see the distrust in their faces. He had lived with it all his life and fully expected it to accompany him to his grave. People would regard even his distrust with uncertainty. That personal isolation was corollary to his dedication. Long before most of the people now with him in the chamber had been born, he had realised the necessity of living apart from his fellow man. He'd accept it. He would do without close friends or family.

In place of them he accepted admirers – and there were many. Sycophants had proven useful. He'd used them as he had the bureaucrats to further his personal ends. If no one volunteered to read the obituary on his passing, it would not distress him. He would settle for having his accomplishments chiselled into his headstone. He smiled at the thought, and those watching him misinterpreted the smile.

It would require a very tall headstone.

Of all those now assembled before this bearded vision from the past, Booth was the least impressed. Many times in his long career he had interviewed or watched the great and the mighty. Maybe others reacted differently; but he, Harry Booth, had always paid attention and try as he had, not once had he ever seen air space between a great man's feet and the ground.

Reinhardt walked like any man.

'My network considered your *Cygnus* project,' Booth said bluntly, gesturing to take in the dome and ship around them, 'a waste of the taxpayers' money, Doctor. The administrators of the territories of India, Southeast Asia and South Africa all lost their posts because they supported you.'

'So the jackals of the press hounded the heels of government until the far-sighted among them were destroyed.' Reinhardt's voice was now as cold as the space outside the tower, and as impersonal. He had hereto been almost apologetically polite. Now he was seething.

'The men you speak of will be enshrined by the citizens of the future for their bravery in the face of ignorance and barbarism. The memories of those who slaughtered their careers will become dust, less than footnotes in the pages of history. They are the short-sighted fools who are always blind to the fact that some things can't be measured in monetary terms. All such primitives will eventually pass the way of the Neanderthal, weeded out of mankind by sensible social selection as were the racists of the dark centuries.

'Fortunately, the *Cygnus* was on her way and out of the system before those idiots could think to call her back.'

'Dr Reinhardt?' McCrae purposely made herself sound as helpless and child-like as possible. The man might be a blind visionary, but he was not insensitive. Procuring the funds for construction of the *Cygnus* had required understanding as well as force.

Her approach worked. His manner changed with startling abruptness as he turned to face her. The smile he bestowed on her verged on the paternal.

'My dear child, I know who you are as I know the identities of your companions. I can foresee your question. I'm sorry to have to dash your hopes, but your father is dead.'

McCrae sagged despite her belief that she had prepared herself for that answer. Holland comforted her as best he could. To imagine that her father might be alive was one thing. No amount of preparation had actually readied her to hear his actual fate from the lips of the one man in a position to know.

'Sorry, Kate.' Durant wished there was more he could say. He was as inept with words as Holland. They left that department to Booth and to the rambunctiously glib Pizer.

'A man to be proud of,' Reinhardt continued, trying to console her. 'It was a grave personal loss to me, though never as strong as it must be to you. He was a trusted and loyal friend.'

Diplomacy or no, Holland found he could no longer ignore the questions raised by the emptiness of the tower and the sections of the *Cygnus* they had already passed through.

'And the rest of the crew?' He watched the scientist closely.

'They didn't make it back, then?' Reinhardt appeared simultaneously hurt and surprised, as if he had expected

73

Holland's words but had hoped not to hear them.

'No. What do you mean, "make it back"? What . . . ?'

'Pity. A good crew, good people all. Dedicated to their mission.'

'Wait a minute,' said Booth sharply. 'I'm missing something here. We know that the mission was eventually recalled to Earth. Yet you and the ship are here, and you say the crew is . . . ?'

'Expenses again. Yes,' murmured Reinhardt.

'What happened after the recall was issued? You *did* receive it?' Would Reinhardt, Booth wondered, have a reasonable explanation for the mystery that had teased the people of Earth for twenty years?

The scientist took a deep breath, began without looking at them. 'I did as you would expect me to! – argued, pleaded, even threatened. But an order like that could not be ignored, though I would have done so if I could.

'But there were others aboard and I knew their sentiments. Also, we had been gone from Earth for many years. The feelings of many of the crew towards their mission had changed. Weakened, I would say, but they were all after all only human. The reaction was to be expected.'

He paused for a moment, waiting for comments. There were none.

'We turned about and set course for Earth to comply with the orders. Despite all our precautions, we ran into difficulty. We encountered a phenomenon none had expected, not those of us aboard ship nor the people who had designed the ship.

'While travelling at supra-light speeds we passed through a vast field of a unique variety of heavy particles. We were through the field before its effects or even its presence could be predicted. There our drive was permanently disabled, despite the best efforts of our repair technical staff. All our communications facilities were likewise damaged, beyond any hope of calling for aid.

'There was one remaining option – abandoning the ship and utilising two of our three auxiliary survey craft to return directly to Earth. As their drive systems had been quiescent during the particle field storm, they proved to be undamaged.

Booth started to say something, but Holland put a restraining hand on his arm.

Reinhardt looked at the reporter, then continued hi

story. 'I knew this was the choice the crew preferred,' he said, 'and so I made it easy for them by ordering them to abandon ship and return home as directed. I told them I would attempt to put the *Cygnus* on the same course to return . . . at sublight velocity.' He smiled.

'Everyone knew that travelling from our position at the time would take me some three hundred years to make Earth orbit. Perhaps it was another of what you term my theatrical gestures, Mr Booth, but I chose to remain behind, aboard my ship.' He gestured, a wide sweep that took in the interior of the tower and by inference the whole of the ship.

'I fought too hard and too long for the *Cygnus* to leave her, certainly not to return to Earth and admit failure. I thought it proper to uphold the ancient tradition of the captain going down with his ship.' His expression mocked them.

'You have experienced the gravitational power of the wonderfully complex stellar object nearby and know that the *Cygnus* and I may yet pursue the analogy of the sinking ship with considerable fidelity.' His tone softened as he again regarded McCrae.

'Your father believed. He chose to remain with me. We never learned what happened to the others, those who left on the two survey craft. But when years passed and no rescue ship came to find us, we could guess. I am saddened to learn for certain that they did not make it home.'

Booth looked thoughtful. 'Odd that two separate ships failed to make it back or even make contact with Earth or a navigation beacon,' he ventured.

'Not so,' Reinhardt responded. 'Neither vessel was equipped with the deep-ranging communications equipment of the *Cygnus*, nor with her highly sophisticated and complex navigation system. That both ships should be lost is, while sad, not unnatural or unexpected.'

'Then if the chances for them were so slim, why did everyone else except you and Frank McCrae choose to go?'

Reinhardt stared pityingly at the reporter. 'What would you have done, Mr Booth? Taken the chance of making it back to Earth in a less efficient ship, or chanced living the three hundred years necessary to make the journey at sublight speeds?'

Durant was more interested in the living legend addressing them than in people they could no longer help. 'You've lived out here for all the years since the others left . . . by yourself?'

'Not exactly by myself, Doctor. Until his death, I had the good company and companionship of a man of similar dedication, Frank McCrae. After his passing . . . I knew enough crude psychology to realise that even I needed some form of companionship if I was to remain sane. So I created companions . . . of a sort. There were the *Cygnus'* surviving mechanicals still aboard. With their aid, I re-populated the ship with tougher, less emotional assistants.' He gestured at the rows of silent figures manning the consoles behind them.

'I made them as human as I possibly could.'

'But they don't seem able to talk,' McCrae observed.

'When I can make them sound as human as I, I will finish that aspect of their construction, dear lady.'

The elevator door opened suddenly. They turned.

Charlie Pizer was standing framed in the doorway. He was surrounded by a cluster of efficient-looking mechanicals. The downcast Pizer immediately brightened at the sight of his companions. His normal insouciance returned.

'Hi, folks.' He indicated his escort. 'Have you met the goon squad yet?'

'I am sorry for the humourlessness of your company, Mr Pizer.' Reinhardt retained his grin. 'Again, my friends, I confess that manners are not the strong points of my machines. Please join us, Mr Pizer.'

The first officer stepped out of the elevator, carefully watching the machines that had accompanied him. They did not follow.

'Dismissed,' Reinhardt spoke sharply to the guards. The elevator door closed in front of them. It was an indication of instant, unquestioning obedience, which Holland noted for future reference.

'They reflect the manners of whoever programmed them,' Pizer said, ignoring a warning look from Holland. 'They took my pistol. I'd like it back.'

'What for? To shoot me, maybe?' Reinhardt expressed astonishment. 'You were disarmed for your own safety. Maximillian and my other robots are programmed not only to react against aggression, but to prevent it.'

'I assure you,' said Durant hastily, 'nothing of the sort was intended.'

'I still don't see why, once you saw who we were, you directed the automatic guards in reception to disarm us,' Holland said.

'Captain Holland, I have already explained that I saw what you were but not who you were. Your state of mind could not be scanned. For all I knew you were a punitive expedition sent out specifically on the word of surviving malcontents among the *Cygnus'* crew to kill me.

'Nonetheless, I did not *direct* the sentry machines in reception to disarm you. You yourself just said they were automatic, and so they are. They responded, I believe, to your brandishing of weapons.'

'That's a normal reaction for a group entering a strange, non-communicative vessel.'

'And disarmament was the reception room's normal re-action to your display of guns. Both you and the reception area brain reacted, if you'll pardon the analogy, to similar programming. I have often said that the differences between man and machine are superficial.'

'I'd still like my pistol back,' Pizer repeated, unmollified.

'Your property will be returned to you in good time, Mr Pizer. Until then I must insist for your own safety that it remain secured. Lest you lose your apparently considerable temper and induce some slow-thinking mechanical to violence.

'As to your boarding with weapons showing, were I a military man I would be most suspicious. However, I am a scientist, so I understand.' He finished with an expansive smile. 'Rest assured you are not prisoners. You're my guests, the first it has been my pleasure to entertain in quite a few years.'

As Reinhardt turned to speak to McCrae, Pizer moved next to Holland and leaned over to whisper to him. 'There's a whole army of those things on board,' he declared, with a gesture back at the elevator, 'and nobody told *them* we're guests.'

'Take it easy, Charlie. Everything Reinhardt's said about the way we've been treated so far is reasonable. Not nice, but reasonable. Let's give the old boy the benefit of the doubt unless he gives us stronger reasons to believe he's something other than what he claims to be. Besides, we haven't any choice.'

Reinhardt was still talking mostly to McCrae when Holland interrupted him. 'We won't impose on your hospitality, Doctor. We'll require some minor spare parts. Our trouble's with our atmospheric regeneration system. If you can help us out, we can manage the repairs ourselves.'

'And then we can offer you the means of returning to Earth, Doctor.' Durant eyed him respectfully. 'In something less than three hundred years. As to your reception, I wouldn't be concerned. In the years you've spent out here you must have learned much that is new. You'll be warmly greeted on your return, sir.'

'That is a matter of difference between you and your friend Mr Booth,' Reinhardt replied, matter-of-factly. 'What makes you think I want to return, Dr Durant?'

SIX

AFTER a long moment of stunned silence, Durant spoke again, trying not to sound patronising. 'Sir, I understand your feelings about the *Cygnus* and the possibility of an, ah, ambivalent reception back on Earth. Believe me, I sympathise. You seem to have made your peace with the universe out here.' He indicated the dim silhouettes working steadily at the far consoles, then the hovering mass of the robot Maximillian.

'You also seem to have forged a workable relationship with your companions, who all will outlive you. But surely you realise that no matter how comfortable you have managed to make yourself, the *Cygnus* is in constant danger of being swallowed up and destroyed by *that*.' He pointed to the magnificent image of the black hole on the main viewscreen off to one side.

Reinhardt seemed less than sombre. In fact, he appeared amused by Durant's concern. 'Ah, yes, your captain was worried about that, too. There is no cause for alarm.

'As you have already discovered, the *Cygnus* and the section of space immediately surrounding it are immune from such danger. I developed, after many years of research and experimentation, a system-field which enables us to resist gravity even of the strength we are exposed to here.

'There were three auxiliary survey ships attached to the *Cygnus*. The crew used two in their apparently ill-fated attempt to return to Earth. The third has served me as an experimental vessel with which to explore such ideas as the gravity-field nullifier.'

'You can negate gravity, then?' Durant was gaping at him.

'No, Dr Durant, not at all. That accomplishment involves aspects of field theory too esoteric even for me. Someday, perhaps . . . but not yet. For now, anti-gravity is an impossibility according to the laws of known physics. I cannot negate gravity, but I can nullify its effect by influencing the gravity waves.' He paused for a moment to let the sense of what he had just said sink in.

'They are "bent" . . . that is an over-simplification, but will do for now . . . around the *Cygnus* and around any vessel or other solid object within the zone of field influence. Occasionally, outside forces and conditions may temporarily cause the field to narrow or expand. This field fluctuation is what nearly caused your destruction.'

Durant was rubbing his lower lip with a forefinger. 'That explains the calm around your ship. How powerful a gravity well can you defy?'

'That is the question, isn't it, Doctor?' Reinhardt replied cryptically. 'So far, theory and experiment seem to indicate that the greater the gravity, the narrower the field collapses around the *Cygnus*. But as the field narrows, it intensifies. I do not fully understand the mechanics behind this wave compression. Only that it exists.

'At some point it would seem that the gravity must overwhelm the field and destroy the ship hiding behind it. Calculations indicate that beyond a certain point the field can no longer be compressed. It becomes an invulnerable, inflexible barrier to the gravity surging around it.

'At this point the field influences the very fabric of space tangential to it. Exactly how that influence manifests itself I am not yet certain, but I have reason and equations to believe that it results in an incredible increase in the velocity of anything inside the field. If you apply increasing pressure with two fingers to a bean, one of two things happens. The bean's protective skin – its "field", if you will – collapses under the pressure and the bean is smashed. But if the skin-field is strong enough . . .'

'The bean squirts forward free of your fingers,' Durant concluded.

'Exactly.' Reinhardt looked pleased with himself. 'And that, my friends, is what I postulate will happen when the field is compressed to its maximum. It will cause whatever it envelops to burst forward to escape the immense gravitational pressure, providing it with a remarkable and sudden increase in speed.'

'Interesting theory.' Holland spoke pragmatically, his emphasis on the word 'theory'. 'We were broadcasting to you from the time we identified this ship as the *Cygnus*. If you were monitoring us constantly, as you say, you must have received our signals. I'm not sure I accept your statement about caution in the face of unexpected visitors as sufficient reason for ignoring us. If you were monitoring us closely enough to learn our names, you must have learned that our intentions were only friendly. Why didn't you at least respond to our calls?'

'There was my aforementioned fear of deception, Captain.' Reinhardt sounded irritated, possibly because Holland had not reacted as expected to the glory of the gravity-field nullifier. 'Also, while my receiving instrumentation is mostly repaired, I have not yet been able to conclude final restoration of the *Cygnus*' broadcast facilities.

'You will recall that I told you the particle storm destroyed all such on-board equipment. Yes, I was able to monitor your approach quite thoroughly. It was most frustrating being unable to reply.'

Pizer did not bother to conceal his suspicion of this explanation, and was upset that Holland appeared to swallow it.

'I wish to prove my good faith. Particularly to you, Mr Pizer.' The first officer looked startled. Apparently Reinhardt could interpret particle counts and expressions with equal alacrity.

'You've indicated you're in a hurry to depart and not to impose on me. Very well. Though your presence is surely no imposition, I want to help you in whatever way I can. Maximillian will take you to ship's stores. You may requisition whatever you need to repair your ship, Captain.'

Holland didn't try to conceal his delight. 'That's very generous of you.'

Reinhardt shrugged, sounded modest. 'I do not own the *Cygnus* or her contents, Captain Holland. I am only her commander. The ship itself and its contents are the property of the ESRC. You have as much right to her store of material as anyone. I believe you mentioned that your difficulties lay with your regeneration system?'

Holland nodded.

'You should find everything you need, though I fear some of the modular instrumentation and smartparts are twenty years or so out of date.'

'Thanks. We'll manage.'

'I'm certain you will.' He looked over at Durant. 'Meanwhile, I think I can assure you and Dr McCrae enough information to make your mission one of historic importance. When I said I did not plan to return to Earth, I had no intention of reserving what I have learned over the past two decades to myself. You shall have the honour of bearing news of my discoveries home and confronting the surviving critics of the *Cygnus*' mission with them. It will do my soul good to know that such knowledge will be transported by friendly hands.'

Durant was thirsting for revelations from the hand of the master. Though initially depressed by Reinhardt's confirmation of her father's death, McCrae too was growing interested. Although they had not located intelligent alien life, the new information they had gathered in eighteen months, if coupled with the twenty years of research the *Cygnus* had carried out, would be more than enough to make their journey a grand success. Furthermore, she could lay some of the credit at her father's feet. Surely Reinhardt would not refuse his old friend a share of the glory he himself seemed determined not to accept in person.

Reinhardt, pleased with their reaction, began giving instructions to the giant mechanical. 'Take them back to Maintenance, Maximillian. See that they are issued whatever they require from stores. Except weapons.' He smiled at Pizer. 'Your own will be returned to you, or replaced, when you are ready to depart.'

They started for the elevator. There was a grinding noise and Holland turned sharply.

V.I.N.Cent had moved slowly to leave, and in doing so had inadvertantly crossed Maximillian's path. The huge bulk had nudged the smaller machine off balance. V.I.N.Cent stopped, sent a stream of lights flickering in challenge. Maximillian leaned on him, and again Holland heard the abrasive sound of metal scraping metal.

'Back off, V.I.N.Cent,' Pizer ordered the robot. 'What's the point? We have to get to Maintenance. Back off, now.'

'Not until he does.'

'You're not programmed for adolescent behaviour,' the exasperated Pizer continued, eying Maximillian with concern. He wondered exactly how much control Reinhardt did exercise over the monolithic construction. 'When you're nose to nose with a trash compactor, you cool it.'

V.I.N.Cent didn't budge. Maximillian leaned, bringing his weight to bear. V.I.N.Cent's servos began to whine in protest over the load.

Holland didn't intend to permit the situation to go any farther. 'Call him off, Reinhardt.'

The commander of the *Cygnus* appeared amused by the confrontation. He seemed content to let the conflict play itself out. 'A classic confrontation: David and Goliath. Except this time, David is overmatched.'

'I said, call him off.' Holland did not find the situation amusing at all.

'On my ship, you *ask*, Captain.' Reinhardt said it without anger.

Maximillian moved forward slightly, crowding the smaller machine towards the elevator wall. Reinhardt abruptly tired of the game.

'That's enough, Maximillian. Remember, these are our guests, be they organic or otherwise.'

With apparent reluctance the giant moved slowly aside. He turned to enter the lift. Holland wondered what other bits of bellicose programming had been entered into the robot's memory.

He whispered hurriedly to McCrae, 'Communications problems aside and allowing for reasonable suspicion on his part, I still think he waited a long time to show any lights.' Then, louder, 'Take care while we're gone.'

Kate smiled thinly, as if to say she took care *all* the time, then moved to join Durant and Reinhardt in conversation. Holland heard her asking something about hypothetical curvatures of natural gravity waves versus artificial inducements as she moved away from him.

Pizer was waiting for them near the elevator door. It opened for them as Holland arrived. 'Those other robots, the smaller ones that escorted me up here? They aren't any more friendly than Dr Frankenstein's monster.' He gestured at Maximillian.

'They were only doing the job they'd been programmed for,' Holland pointed out. His voice turned angry. 'By the way, what were you doing off the *Palomino*? I thought I ordered you to . . .'

'One of them came up to the lock and said you'd asked me to join you. Since by that time I couldn't get through to you . . .'

'Funny. We tried to call you without any luck, either.'

'Yeah. Well, this thin hunk o' junk rumbled up and explained real polite that you'd met Dr Reinhardt and my presence was also requested. So I added everything up and decided to go see for myself. Then his buddies appeared and packed me upstairs to this place.'

'Don't worry.' V.I.N.Cent had assumed a cocky air. 'One or a hundred, I can handle them. They're badly outmoded. I'm a much more efficient model.'

Pizer's eyes appealed to heaven, which above the transparent dome of the elevator shaft seemed not so very distant. Lights flickered across Maximillian's chest in a sequence that hinted he had clearly understood V.I.N.Cent's words – and had filed them for future reference.

'Smile when you say that, V.I.N.Cent.' Holland was watching Maximillian.

V.I.N.Cent hesitated, but the look in Holland's eyes did not at all match his superficially benign expression. Reluctantly, the robot gave a polite twinkle of his own lights. If Maximillian accepted the gesture, or even understood it, he offered no sign in return.

The elevator descended in silence.

Reinhardt escorted his three guests slowly around the circumference of the command tower, explaining the function of each console and station, interpreting read-outs that puzzled them, patiently answering every one of their questions including those his expression indicated he thought foolish.

To Durant the most impressive thing about the tower was not the plethora of instrumentation, with backups for backups, nor the steady flow of information being correlated and stored by the *Cygnus*' research banks. It was the speed and efficiency with which every function was being carried out. Nor did he espy a single unit, screen or gauge out of order. Everything functioned smoothly after twenty years in space. To him that was far more impressive than what they were functioning for.

'This doesn't appear to be the crippled ship you described to us, Doctor. For one that supposedly suffered such extensive damage . . .'

'We repaired it, and it became operable again,' Reinhardt told him firmly. 'Much of the work was accomplished before the decision was made by the rest of the crew to try and return to Earth in the survey craft. The final difficulties with the engines defeated them.

'Subsequent repair and maintenance has been performed by my mechanical companions under my supervision. A ship like the *Cygnus* must necessarily carry a large contingent of repair robots. My assistance is needed only on rare occasions now, to interpret highly unorthodox problems. I had time to do nothing but work on the problems with the engines, you must remember.

'By now the *Cygnus* and her machines run themselves quite nicely, repairing one another, caring for one another, maintaining one another.'

'But always subject to your directives.'

Reinhardt executed a slight bow. 'I sometimes feel that I am only another cog in the *Cygnus* machine, Dr Durant. I am the repair unit of last recourse, the one who interprets what cannot be predicted. In that respect, the mechanicals flatter me. They are programmed to serve the crew. As I am the sole surviving member of that crew, they obey me. The fact that I am the ship's commander enhances that obedience. I do not command them. They serve me. There is a difference.'

Gallantly taking McCrae's arm, he turned and led the three of them towards another elevator.

'So you repaired the destruction as best you could, including your receiving and monitoring equipment but not your broadcast facilities.' Booth was speaking as much for the benefit of his recorder as for himself. 'But you never acknowledged any of the subsequent orders to return to Earth.'

'The crew made that choice. As to myself . . . be fair now, Mr Booth. It was the *Cygnus* the authorities wanted back. Not me. As I've said, the *Cygnus* was incapable of returning.'

'But she isn't anymore? You spoke about your work on her engines.'

'It's hard to say. The machines have managed to repair much of the damage caused by the particle storm, thanks to new discoveries we've made subsequent to the departure of the crew. Frank McCrae was largely responsible for many of them.' He smiled pleasantly at McCrae.

'Assuming I could return the *Cygnus* to Earth in a

reasonable time, Mr Booth, there are considerations that prevent me from doing so. Other worlds are yet to be explored. There are life dreams unrealised.'

'If this ship is now able to make it back to Earth and you refuse to obey orders by not making every effort to comply,' Booth hesitated only an instant, 'the authorities would consider that an act of piracy, Doctor.'

The reporter had a way of breaking through Reinhardt's spartan exterior. One hand clenched convulsively, relaxed only slightly as the doctor spoke.

'You do have a way with words, Mr Booth. I had thought I was immune to such petty criticisms and response-active words. Years of solitude have apparently weakened my armour. You should be proud of your talents.'

'Thanks,' said Booth drily. 'They usually enable me to dig out the truth.'

'One day you may dig too deep, Mr Booth. You run the risk of cave-in.'

'I'll take my chances. What about my analysis?'

'Certain short-sighted individuals have often interpreted the pursuit of great discoveries as piracy. I am about to prove to you that the ends of science justify the means of science. To be what we are, to become what we are capable of becoming, is the only end in life. I am risking only my own life to prove that. Without purpose this great craft is nothing, a free-floating junkyard, reworked metal ores and as purposeless as the ores still wasting away in the ground. *With* purpose it becomes an instrument of Man. With purpose, I can call myself a man. Those men unwilling to commit themselves to a high purpose are only shadows of men, as the ores are but hints of the refined metals they may one day become.'

Durant nodded knowingly at this little speech, his attitude that of an acolyte preparatory to being ordained. McCrae acted noncommital.

This is a dangerous man, Harry Booth thought to himself. He knew well that throughout history any human being who had ever adhered publicly to the principle that 'the end justified the means' had proven himself dangerous. It was a law as immutable as the energy-mass equations, and about as explosive.

*

The elevator had carried Holland, Pizer and V.I.N.Cent below the level of the cross-ship air car corridor that had brought them to the command tower. Now they were in the depths of the vast city-ship, travelling on foot down a much narrower passageway.

Looking around, Holland saw transparent ports and cylinders, part of the superstructure of the great ship. He recalled many years ago the appellation some eager reporter had hung on the *Cygnus*: the bridge of glass. The bridge to the stars.

Mankind had since learned that small bridges would serve his designs as well as great ones. Reinhardt was right about one thing, though. They were not as pretty.

Holland shrugged. People had starved themselves before in order to honour properly their gods, had gone without food to decorate their temples. The *Cygnus* was monument to another god, a faster-than-light temple of another kind.

With Reinhardt, he mused, as the High Priest. Reinhardt would be remembered as master of two disciplines: science, and salesmanship. Holland was willing to regard him as a friend, assuming the commander of the *Cygnus* was telling the truth and would truly help them to repair the *Palomino*.

Despite the fact that Reinhardt seemed to be the only human aboard, the ports they passed showed evidence of considerable activity. Intership air cars and other transports raced back and forth, carrying robots of varying size and shape to unknown destinations for unrevealed purposes.

Ahead, a group of small maintenance robots appeared and sped by, clinging to a vehicle that itself possessed a simple mechanical brain.

Holland watched them vanish down the corridor behind them. The whine of their transport receded into the distance, echoing in their wake like the last drops of a fading spring shower.

Pizer noted all the activity too. He glanced up at the alloyed mastodon convoying them. 'Pretty busy around here, aren't you, Max? Awful lot of activity for a ship that doesn't seem to be going anywhere, and I know old Reinhardt doesn't require *this* much service. What are you gearing up for? Expecting some more company, maybe? Or afraid of it?'

Maximillian trundled onwards without responding. The

first officer looked away. 'Loquacious chap, ain't he, Dan? You know, they say that machines incapable of communicating via human speech are degraded, simple brain types, incapable of performing anything beyond the most menial functions.'

Still Maximillian did not react. Perhaps he was programmed against such provocations. Perhaps he felt beyond such pitiful attempts. More likely he was just adhering to his designer's orders that the new visitors be treated as guests.

'Don't bait him,' Holland ordered. 'Reinhardt's control over him may not be as absolute as he'd like us to believe.'

'Oh, I think it is.' Pizer looked back up at Maximillian. 'Max here's just the Doc's errand boy and number one footwiper, ain't you, Max?'

Still the colossus refused to respond. Pizer gave up trying to provoke it.

Before long they reached another bend in the corridor, turned right into it. Maximillian moved ahead of them, extended a limb to key a sealed doorway. It opened with a clang, incongruous compared to the smooth functioning of the other doors they had passed through.

This initial impression that they were entering a rarely visited area was magnified by the state of the interior of the chamber they entered. Rows and rows of shelving and compact crates and containers stared silently back at the visitors. There was nothing as plebian as a cobweb hanging about, and electrostatic repellers kept the dust off, but they still had the feeling they were the first people to enter the storage area in some time.

Stationed behind the desk was a robot. Its head was canted to one side in fair imitation of a human asleep on the job. For all they knew the mechanical might have been waiting there behind its desk in that identical, unvarying position for a dozen years. He looked much like V.I.N.Cent and gave the impression of having been used hard with minimal repair.

Maximillian moved forward and swung a thick arm, knocking the quiescent robot to the floor. Its lights blinked on. Slowly at first, then with the impetus of increasing awareness, it rose to an unsteady hover. Its optics took in Holland, Pizer, V.I.N.Cent, settled inevitably on the ominous maroon form of Maximillian. It started to back away

'V.I.N.Cent,' stated the human's mechanical associate quickly. 'Vital Information Necessary Centralised. Labour force, human interactive. The Three Ninety-Sixth. Latest model, new '89 biomechanical neuronics, floating synapses, heightened initiative-and-awareness circuitry.'

Maximillian glowered down at V.I.N.Cent as he concluded his terse introduction and self-description. But though the older machine behind the desk stared with interest at its visitors, it did not respond to V.I.N.Cent's sally with an identification of itself. The older machine did not acknowledge in any fashion.

At first V.I.N.Cent was hurt. That rapidly gave way to worry and concern. But he added nothing to his initial words, continued to eye the other machine with puzzlement.

'Tell you what, Charlie. I'll head back to the *Palomino* and start breaking down that busted regenerator. Looks like they'll have everything we need here.' Holland turned to leave. Maximillian immediately pivoted, preparatory to blocking the captain's exit.

'I'm sure our host will take good care of us,' said Pizer hastily, guessing what Holland was up to. 'After all, the good doctor indicated he wanted his guests properly treated.'

'Don't worry about me,' Holland spoke confidently to the threatening mass of Maximillian. 'I'll find my way. Be back soon, Charlie. Make sure you get everything we might need.'

'Will do.' Pizer reached up and boldly tugged at one of the giant's arms, an arm which could have lifted half a dozen men off the deck without effort. It did not move. Pizer didn't expect that it would, but Maximillian would note the gesture.

'We need primary and secondary demand oxygen pressure valves, with attached micoputer units. And a decent ECS proportion flow controller.'

Holland was out the door and turning up the corridor they'd come down, walking with the easy air of a man who had all the time in the world. But he was sweating.

Maximillian moved half a metre towards the door, then stopped, obviously confused as to how he should proceed.

'Max, Dr Reinhardt told you to requisition the parts for s. Let's get cracking. I'm as anxious as you are to get out of ere.'

Still moving uncertainly, the huge mechanical turned

away from the door. Extending a limb, he plugged himself into the inventory. Lights flashed on the arm. Corresponding lights began to blink on within the rows of shelving. A drawer popped open, then a second, each occurrence matched by a distinctive musical tone.

' 'Way to go, Max. 'Way to go.' Pizer managed to conceal his relief.

While Pizer busied Maximillian with the long lists of parts requests. V.I.N.Cent sidled off to one side, hovered near the desk. 'I see by your markings that you're from the old Two-Eight. General Services, right? Where do you originate from on Earth . . . Amsterdam? Kuala Lumpur? All the factory jobs from Lumpur called their serial run the "tin cans", and proud of it. How about you?'

It was as if the older robot simply didn't have audio reception capability. From its markings and body style V.I.N.Cent knew that was absurd. But it continued to act as if it were completely deaf. It whined away down the nearest aisle of shelving, attending to chores which doubtless included maintaining the room and its functions. Lights flashed erratically on V.I.N.Cent's torso, the nearest he could come to non-verbally expressing frustration.

What in the Unitary was wrong with the old cousin . . .?

SEVEN

THE air car had transported them rapidly down the length of the *Cygnus*, far past the dock where the *Palomino* lay berthed in emptiness.

They emerged into a corridor, left the car. Reinhardt led them into a large chamber filled with the most complex instrumentation McCrae had yet seen on the ship. A steady hum came from somewhere nearby, a whisper of great forces and energies held in check.

The consoles lining the walls were of peculiar design. In places Kate clearly recognised units that were outmoded on Earth now by the twenty years that had passed. Elsewhere were components and devices whose purpose she could not decipher. And then there were hybrid instruments that combined very old, discarded aspects of space-going technology with sophistication superior to anything she'd ever seen.

The entire room was a mixture of the outdated and the ultramodern. It looked like a witchdoctor's hut lined with masks and dead animals on one side and a unitised free-state diagnostic computer on the other.

'Once left to myself,' Reinhardt was telling them, 'I had a great deal of time to explore ideas that previous endeavours, such as overseeing the construction of the *Cygnus*, had forbidden me. My isolation provided the time and the *Cygnus* laboratories the means for much extensive research. So I became obsessed with repairing the engines because all the experts were convinced they could not be repaired, and was tremendously frustrated when I was forced eventually to agree with them.' He smiled meaningfully, his hands conducting his words.

'That is, they could not be made to function in the accepted sense, in the way they had been designed to function. So I was forced to experiment with concepts that had lain long dormant in the back of my mind.

'Frank McCrae helped, until he died. Then I worked on alone with the computers, with all the power of the *Cygnus*' vast mental resources to aid me. The result was the achievement of one of man's greatest dreams, a dream attainable only in free space. I have discovered how to isolate and draw usable power from the reaction of matter and anti-matter.'

Their expressions revealed their shock, and he was pleased.

'Yes, I know many scientists consider such an accomplishment beyond the power of our physics, consider it impossible. They were correct. It is impossible . . . without the assistance of a stabilising field analogous to the one that bends gravity around the *Cygnus* and keeps us from being sucked into the black hole. So we see at work again the marvellous serendipity of science, where one discovery leads to another far greater.'

He turned to face McCrae. 'It was in the mining of an asteroid for sufficient mass to power the new engines that your father was killed.'

He moved to a long viewport, halted there and gestured below it. They moved to look.

Below was the largest open area they'd yet encountered on the *Cygnus*. Four large, sealed, massive shapes glowed faintly with their individual auroras. They were the ship's supralight engines, but different now. They had been altered. Reinhardt's mechanical workers had done an admirable job.

'I could give you the output of those engines in ergs, or gigawatts, or any other set of measures you chose. I will simply tell you, without exaggeration or boastfulness, that there is enough energy capacity down there to supply all of Earth.'

His listeners seemed impressed, so he forged ahead. 'The seemingly insoluble problem with matter-anti-matter energy production on a practical scale was never in the releasing of the energy but in the finding of a means to contain the reaction safely so it would not spread. My null-gee field provided that. It was all very simple, really. First it demonstrated that such a field is possible. Then the engines are modified to generate a variation of said field. They produce enough initial power to maintain this field within themselves and contain the matter-anti-matter reaction. This new source of power in turn produces a far more powerful field which surrounds the ship and enables it to hold its position against the attractive force of the black hole. You see, one discovery thus complements the other.'

'This is the realisation of the dream,' McCrae murmured aloud. 'It's the breakthrough to colonising the galaxy. One such engine would power a colony ship three times the size of the *Cygnus*!'

Durant was almost beyond words. 'You'll . . . you'll go down as one of the greatest space scientists of all time, sir. No . . . as one of the greatest *scientists* of all time.'

'I have never doubted that.' Reinhardt's air of self-satisfaction filled the room.

'You said that you wanted us to carry your discoveries home to Earth,' Durant went on excitedly. 'Does that include your work on matter-anti-matter and gravity? Do you mean to turn this technology over to us?'

Reinhardt nodded. 'It's high time others learned of their mistakes and my triumphs. I will accept vindication *in absentia*. You, my friends, will serve as the instrument of that vindication. Now that I know who you are and what you stand for I can trust you to do what is right.'

Durant had turned away, was once more drinking in the unique modifications of the power complex below their station. 'You should come back with us and enjoy the fruits of your success. Doesn't it mean anything to you, the chance to confront your critics in person with your magnificent achievements?'

'I have already told you that such personal adoration is not necessary. You do not understand me at all, Dr Durant. For me, the accomplishment itself is glory enough. To win he race is the vital thing, not the broadcasting of it to the osers.'

'You've done plenty of broadcasting of your beliefs and ccomplishments in your time.'

Reinhardt looked sharply at Booth, then relaxed and miled. Now that he had been able to display his considerable chievements he was past being baited.

'All means to an end, Mr Booth. I said what I felt it was ecessary to say, performed the actions I felt were required, ll for the sake of getting this vessel built and on its way. uch gestures as I may have made to the media were only to ssist in realising that estimable scientific end. not for personal ego gratification.'

Exercising unusual restraint, or perhaps caution, the reporter offered no reply.

'There is too much at stake here for me to think of returning to Earth now,' the scientist continued. 'Even if I wished to accept your invitation, Dr Durant, I could not. I stand on the brink of my greatest achievement.' He pointed to the massive engines below.

'All this is but a means to a still greater end, Dr Durant. Once I thought this ship was the ultimate of my accomplishments. Then I believed that of my discoveries in energy generation and gravity-field mechanics. Now I find all are only steps, steps leading to another, unimaginable beginning.'

'The beginning of what?' Durant was gaping at him.

Reinhardt had pushed his visitors' curiosity to the limit. Just when they thought they had him sized and catalogued, he shocked them with some new revelation, with still further miracles. Durant was no wide-eyed student. He had a vivid scientific imagination and was well versed in theoretical as well as practical physical prognostication, but Reinhardt had long since exceeded his capacity for wonder.

What, he thought dazedly, could be more important or impressive than the gravity-field nullifier or the discovery of a means to power every home and factory on Earth? Of only one thing was he still certain: Hans Reinhardt was not exaggerating. If anything, he had chosen to understate the importance of the discoveries he had thus far revealed to them.

'You'll learn all that in due time, Doctor.' Reinhardt smiled condescendingly at his fellow scientist. 'Be patient. It is not good to learn too much at one time. The mind loses the ability to place things in proper perspective.'

'The gospel according to Saint Reinhardt,' Booth muttered.

'I indeed preach a new gospel, Mr Booth,' the scientist admitted proudly. 'The gospel of a new physics, which will offer man a new way to look at his universe. I am no mad prophet. I preach only what I have learned. My sermons are founded on hard facts that can be independently confirmed. There is no dealing in superstition here.'

Again it was McCrae, who forestalled a potentially violent

confrontation, stepping verbally between the two men. 'I'd like some proof of your power source. Something to show that what we're seeing is more than just some carefully gimmicked standard supradrive engines.'

'And so you shall, my dear. You will have all the proof you wish. All the computer storage banks are open to your perusal. So are the engines themselves. As you will see, the read-outs and monitoring instrumentation are practically unchanged. So you will know the figures they offer you are genuine.' He looked around the room with the attitude of a proud father.

'When you examine the output of a single engine you will be more amazed than you can imagine. Come along, and I'll explain as we walk. Please feel free to ask any questions you like. I enjoy being able to provide answers. That has been the driving force of my entire life, you see. To be the one in the position to provide the answers.' He glanced back at Durant.

'Perhaps as we walk, I will also explain the beginning I was referring to, the next question I have chosen to answer.'

Durant and McCrae flanked the scientist as they strolled off towards a bend in the room. Booth pretended to examine the master power console, watched as they moved further from his position.

'A new source of energy for mankind,' McCrae was saying speculatively. 'This could revolutionise much more than deep-space travel. It could free the peoples of Earth from dependence on conventional sources of power forever.'

'Precisely,' agreed the pleased Reinhardt. 'I call the process the *Cygnus Reaction*, after my ship.'

As the others moved on, Booth remained standing by the quietly humming instruments monitoring the engines below. His companions disappeared around the bend in the room.

Booth looked around. The mechanicals manning the instruments ignored him. He turned and hurried away, moving in the opposite direction from the one taken by his host and friends. At the moment he was not worried about Reinhardt missing him as much as he was at the possibility he might encounter some of the *Cygnus'* metal sentries. The good doctor was obviously absorbed in detailing the marvels of the ship and soaking up the compliments McCrae and Durant would be providing him in turn.

Booth had had enough of scientific wonders for a while. There were one or two things bothering him that he preferred to check on away from Reinhardt's scrutiny. The time had come for a little investigative reporting. And if it got him into trouble, well, his curiosity had placed him in awkward positions before. He had always somehow managed to extricate himself. So if explanations didn't work with Reinhardt he suspected that flattery, humility, or both, would. He'd been following his suspicions and hunches on a professional basis for thirty-five years and damned if he was going to stop now.

Holland had located an air-car terminal and had chosen one likely to transport him back towards the reception area and the waiting *Palomino*. It responded to his programming, carried him smoothly forward. If he'd guessed wrong, he could always backtrack and switch to another car.

An intersection loomed ahead, several corridors converging. He stared intently at the nearing nexus, trying to recall if they had passed this hub previously or if one of the side corridors seemed more familiar than the one he was travelling down now.

They did not, but the intersection itself suddenly grabbed his interest. Six of the humanoid, dark-cloaked mechanicals hove into view. That in itself was nothing unique; he had become familiar with the appearance and design of most of the robots aboard. But their movements and particularly the object they convoyed between them caused him to frown.

The flat platform resembled a hospital-style gurney, less festooned with instrumentation but definitely similar in construction. The analogy was enhanced by the covered, somewhat irregular shape lying on the platform. Its silhouette was exceptionally human, more so even than that of the six mechanicals surrounding it.

They crossed through the intersection and vanished up one of the corridors. Holland knew he had to act quickly before the vehicle carried him past the nexus. If he travelled too far before stopping he likely would not find the right corridor when he backtracked. His hands worked rapidly at the programming unit. The car slowed, came to a silent halt just beyond the intersection. Holland leaned back, stared. The odd procession was just turning a far corner.

Palomino crew in the Cygnus control centre.

Cygnus control panel.

Cygnus
A massive, mile-long space vessel. A technological wonderland of unimagined complexity under the command of the obsessed genius, Dr. Rheinhardt (Maximillian Schell).

Cygnus dining-room.

CYGNUS CREW

Dr. Hans Reinhardt
(Maximillian Schell)

Robot sentry.

Maximillian

Humanoid crew members.

Maximillian.

Maximillian confronts V.I.N.CENT.

Maximillian

he huge, monster robot. He's one
f the classic villains of all times.
rankenstein's monster, Dracula,
arth Vader, and now, Maximillian.

Palomino control room.

V.I.N.CENT
His name means—
Vital Information
Necessary,
Centralized. He
reacts to human
speech, and responds
in kind.

V.I.N.CENT

PALOMINO CREW

Capt. Dan Holland
(Robert Forster)

Dr. Kate McRae
(Yvette Mimieux)

**1st Officer
Charles Pizer**
(Joseph Bottoms)

Dr. Alex Durant
(Anthony Perkins)

V.I.N.CENT

Harry Booth
(Ernest Borgnine)

Old B.O.B.

Old B.O.B.
The oldtimer who is outdated in technology, but just might become the most heroic robot of all times.

Palomino crew with Old B.O.B.

He hesitated briefly. Reinhardt didn't know he was here, doubtless still believed he was back in Maintenance and Stores with Charlie and V.I.N.Cent, working to procure the necessary replacement parts for the *Palomino*'s regeneration system under the watchful optics of Maximillian. No sentry or other machine had challenged his progress thus far. It was reasonable to assume that Reinhardt's instructions regarding the treatment of the new visitors as guests had filtered through the ship's mechanical crew. It was therefore possible he could go anywhere he wished without being confronted.

No doubt he was wasting valuable time anyway. His fancies were running away with him. But the object on the platform had looked *so* manlike. So did the humanoid robots escorting it, but if the thing on the gurney was a non-functioning mechanical, then why the concealing cloth? And why six escorts when one or two would have been sufficient to guide the ailing, cloaked machine to repair?

Such imponderables gave rise to flighty speculations that no doubt were nothing more than that, but he wouldn't feel comfortable until he knew for certain.

Holland did his best to lock the controls of the little car so that it would remain where he left it, awaiting his return. Then he hurried after the departed group. He turned the corner around which they had disappeared and was confronted by a long, bare corridor. A single closed door was nearby.

Careful now, he told himself. He knew these machines of Reinhardt's were personally programmed by him and realised they may have been imbued with personalities akin to Maximillian's. *They haven't bothered you yet, but they may not appreciate being interrupted or spied upon, and Reinhardt's not around to countermand any violent impulses you might trigger. So . . . watch it.*

He tried the door, ready to run, fight or talk fast as the occasion demanded. It opened easily. The long room inside was deserted. That is, the people were absent but their memories lay thick.

'Crew quarters,' Holland muttered softly to himself as he walked through the room. Bunks were stacked three high. They had the appearance of having been moved and re-arranged. He wondered at the cramped space. On a ship the size of the *Cygnus* the crew living quarters should have been more spacious. Even the *Palomino* offered more privacy.

He couldn't recall such details from twenty years ago. Maybe the builders of the *Cygnus* had felt that this kind of dormitory-type existence would promote conviviality among the crew. Or perhaps after many years in free space the crew had chosen to make such alterations themselves, a small band of humanity drawing closer together for psychological warmth against the vast, impersonal coldness surrounding them.

There were other possible explanations, but he didn't dwell on them. Names from the past jumped out at him from where they appeared on lockers and cases. Occasional bits of individuality shown startlingly from the walls in the form of a pin-up or solido. Some of the old-fashioned pictures were printed on plastic.

The room ended in another door. This one opened reluctantly, cranky with an air of disuse. It reminded him of the atmosphere down in Maintenance and Stores. Inside were row on row of old, musty uniforms. All appeared to be in good condition. Now his supply of ready rationalisations started to run thin. If the crew had brought casual clothing on the journey with them, he guessed they might have grown tired of their official uniforms and had chosen to try to return to Earth in less formal garb. How could he imagine their collective state of mind preparatory to embarking on such a lonely attempt? It was conceivable that prior to departing they might have voted to leave behind anything that would remind them of the *Cygnus*, including uniforms.

But he was less sure of that reasoning than he'd been about the bunk arrangement.

Another door opened off the room from the far side. It opened as easily as the first, but he was less prepared for what it revealed.

Beyond stretched a vaulted chamber like a small cathedral. At the far end he could see the cluster of robots busy around the gurney. They removed the object from it and placed it, covering and all, into a tube-like canister. The canister was built into the skin of the ship. Holland still couldn't identify the object. Nor could he place the design or function of the otherwise empty room, but he recognised the purpose of the canister readily enough.

His identification was soon confirmed by a faint puffing sound. A surge of frustration went through him. The canister was a disposal lock. Now he'd never know what the object on the platform had been. It was outside the *Cygnus*. Soon it would pass beyond the protective field enveloping the ship, to be captured and dragged down to oblivion by the pull of the black hole.

While he could not assign specifics to everything he had observed so far, together they added up to a puzzle whose outline he was beginning to perceive. If anything, he was shying away from consideration of those outlines. They framed an ominous possibility . . .

The door behind him was jerked violently aside. Maximillian hovered there over him, threatening and intimidating even while motionless. Despite his carefully rehearsed excuses, the unexpected and sudden confrontation had left him momentarily speechless. He stared at the dull red machine. As near as he could tell, it was examining him with equal intentness.

His wits returned and with them, his voice. He smiled with difficulty. 'Must've made a wrong turn. Guess my sense of direction's not as sharp as I thought. I'll be able to find the ship now, though.'

Maximillian gave no sign that this explanation impressed him, that he believed it, or that anything save Reinhardt's explicit orders kept him from shredding Holland on the spot. The feeling it gave Holland was that this machine had been designed to distrust everyone and everything save its single human master.

He held the smile, though he'd seen nothing to indicate that Maximillian could perceive and interpret expressions, and edged past it. Fear chilled him as he touched both wall and machine while squeezing by.

Maximillian's gaze had shifted momentarily to the robots now filing out of the far end of the room. Then he turned to study Holland as the captain walked with a carefully measured stride back up towards the corridor. Holland forced himself not to look back. Behind him, the colossus slowly closed the door leading into the vaulted chamber . . .

The room was high-ceilinged and domed with some transcent material stronger than glass that had a refractive effect. It was a bubble within a far larger expanse. The larger, sealed-in section was a vast, diversified garden.

Vegetables and fruit trees grew within the enclosure.

Harry Booth wandered into this inner chamber, his gaze held by the greenery and ripening fruits. For an instant he was able to forget he was dozens of light-years from Earth. He was back in midwestern North America, doing a report for his network on the coming crop year.

Yet the plants and trees he was seeing were growing in artificial soil. Some grew in no soil at all. They were kept alive and flourishing by the carefully regulated influx of specialised nutrients and fertilisers. He had seen more extensive hydroponic gardens, and denser vegetation, but none so efficient.

Their extent did not surprise him. A crew the size of the *Cygnus*' would require corresponding food sources. The smaller the proportion of recycled or concentrated foods, the healthier the crew would be. As large as it was, this was probably only one of several such artificial farms on board the great ship.

One of the mirror-faced humanoid machines stood before the main console, patiently monitoring read-outs. Occasionally it would adjust a control. The trees and ranks of ripening vegetables growing outside the control bubble derived their nourishment from injections and modulated circulation of premixed chemicals. From the central console the watchful robot could alter their diet, their water supply, even their weather.

'Hello.' The mechanical did not respond. Not that Booth expected it would. That would have meant deviating from its programming. It might not, as its brethren in the control tower, be equipped to reply. But he was hoping it would speak.

Instead, an arm moved, fingers stiffly turning a dial. A buzzing sound caused Booth to turn, look back into the artificially maintained undergrowth.

A swarm of tiny machines was flitting through the plants. The buzzing sound came not from the beat of tiny wings but from miniature engines and navigation systems. Booth moved towards the transparent wall, stared at the minute robots in amazement. They travelled efficiently, accurately from one plant to the next. After a moment of delighted contemplation he turned back to the figure standing before the console.

'Quite a layout. More elaborate than necessary, but they had time for aesthetics in the old days. They have simpler methods of artificial pollination now, but none so . . . well, charming. Did Reinhardt design them also? If so, I like his pollinators a helluva lot better than that over-bearing body-guard of his.'

None of this appeared to interest the figure. Booth leaned close, fascinated and yet repelled by the reflective, featureless face of the mechanical. He wondered if it was equipped to perceive the world around it via less familiar senses. Sophisticated sonar scanning, maybe. Or perhaps the smooth metal egg-shaped face was a specialised polarising shield and the robot's true optics lay behind it, seeing the world on wavelengths different from Harry Booth's.

It continued at its tasks as if the reporter were not present, let alone less than a metre from its face.

'Not programmed to speak, huh? Well, I suppose speech would make you a little too human. But then Reinhardt's a man who enjoys playing God, isn't he? Maximillian and the sentries aren't human-looking enough. He said he wanted, needed companions, so he caused them to be built. I guess you and your kind are as close as he could come to making himself some human buddies.'

As anticipated, the mechanical did not respond. Its assignment apparently completed, it turned to leave the room.

Booth ignored it, disappointed at its lack of response. He started to return his attention to the quaint tableaux provided by the pollinating machines, when something about the robot's movements caught his eye. In disbelief and confusion he stared after it, waiting and watching to make certain he hadn't imagined it. Then he was positive. His eyes grew wide.

The robot limped.

'Hey . . . wait a minute . . .' Waving, trying to attract the receding figure's attention, he started around the console. 'You there, wait . . . !'

The door closed behind the robot. Booth was seconds behind. A moment of terrible frustration when the door refused to respond for him, then it was clear and he rushed out into an empty corridor.

His gaze swept up, then down the passage. Empty. No

distant sounds, nothing save a memory that tantalised and wouldn't leave him – that and a horrible thought or two.

V.I.N.Cent extended a third limb. One was already disassembling sections of the shattered regenerator feed line. The other was sizing the replacements brought back from the *Cygnus'* stores. Visual callipers built into his optical system measured the new unit to within a tenth of a millimetre. He decided that the slight divergence in diameter was not critical enough to prevent the replacement from being utilised. It could be adjusted to the necessary tolerance. The difference could be filled with judicious application of a thin film of liquid polymer.

While he concentrated on the task at hand, he let his aural receptors remain attuned to the conversation continuing nearby.

'Charlie, I know what I saw.' A more contemplative than usual Holland was helping his first officer reseal several of the line breaks.

Pizer sounded half-distressed, half-amused by this admission of gullibility on the part of his friend and superior. 'Dan, nobody buries a robot. If they're beyond repair, then they're cannibalised for spare parts, or deactivated and stored against the time when repair becomes possible. The only reason I can possibly think of for chucking one out into space would be if the ship needed the extra room. And no ship ever built had as much surplus space as the *Cygnus*. So that doesn't make sense either. You just don't bury robots.'

'I didn't say it was a robot. I said it could've been a robot. But I didn't get a good enough look at it to be able to say for sure, and now we never will.'

Pizer paused at his work. 'If it wasn't a mechanical, then what? It's plain silly, Dan.'

'I don't know what it was they shot out into space,' Holland said, 'but they did it with all the ceremony and reverence of a human funeral. A simple disposal operation wouldn't require the presence of six attendants. That's a waste of energy, whether it's being performed by man or machine. No machine is intentionally wasteful of energy. Neither, I'd bet, is Reinhardt.'

'Maybe Reinhardt lied.' Pizer grew thoughtful. Holland

had certainly witnessed *something*. And he was so positive. If anything, the captain of the *Palomino* tended to the unimaginative. He did not invent data to accord with his observations.

Then ... what had he seen?

'Maybe,' the first officer continued speculatively, 'there are other survivors on board. You could have stumbled onto the funeral of one of the last of them. If you did see a real funeral, then what's the reason for the secrecy on Reinhardt's part? What's he been up to? What's he trying to hide?'

Holland sealed a weld angrily. 'Wish I knew. I haven't a clue, Charlie. I wouldn't put much past him. I just can't figure the man. His dedication to his work is all-consuming, but he seems genuinely interested in expanding our knowledge of the universe and the physical forces that operate within it for the benefit of mankind. It's hard to condemn someone for zealous execution of his duty. Certainly we can't without more evidence than a few glimpses of some maybe-funeral for an unknown subject.'

'Well, whatever he's up to,' Pizer observed, 'he seems sincere enough about helping us repair our ship. If he was running something sinister here the best way to cover himself would be to prevent us from leaving.' He gestured at the large collection of spare parts they had hauled aboard.

'None of these are booby-trapped. Checked out every piece myself. Everything's functional.'

'Would that be the best way?' Holland wondered. 'Or would it be better for him if we left safely, to return to Earth to repeat only his version of the events of the last twenty years?'

'A wolf remains a wolf, even if it has not eaten your sheep.' V.I.N.Cent sounded disapproving.

'Who asked you, big ears?'

'V.I.N.Cent's right.' Holland was nodding in agreement. Just because Reinhardt hasn't tried anything yet doesn't mean he isn't thinking about it. One thing we can be pretty sure of: our appearance here was a genuine surprise to him. I don't care how much mechanical help you have, running a ship like this without additional human assistance is a round-the-clock task. He may be stalling for time, trying to decide just what he wants to do with us.

'The sooner we leave here, the better. It's not a good idea

to give a fanatic like Reinhardt too much time to think.'

Pizer could not agree to that totally. 'If you excuse our treatment on arrival, he's been polite enough so far.'

'So far. Courtesy would be instinctive in someone like our host. Careful manipulation of guests comes later, after he's had time to size us up.'

'Whatever you say.' Pizer shrugged. 'In any case, the sooner we finish this, the sooner our options will be increased. Let's snap it up, V.I.N.Cent.'

'A pint cannot hold a quart, Mr Pizer,' the robot replied. 'If it holds a pint, it's doing the best it can.'

Pizer scowled at the machine. 'Lay off the snide homilies. And don't think you can muddle me with archaic units of measurement. I know my ancient statistics as well as you.'

'The two of you will work faster,' said Holland sternly, 'if you'll quit sniping at each other . . .'

EIGHT

REINHARDT stared angrily at the read-out. He touched several controls and was not pleased with the results they provided him. 'Get that communication re-established at once.'

Maximillian extended a limb and plugged himself into a console. Man and machine studied the flat expanse of the control centre's main screen. Alive with the death of plasma and other matter, the black hole filled the screen. The projected hues coloured Reinhardt's face like a water-colour wash. His attention shifted from screen to instrumentation, switching rapidly from one to another. Both hands danced over controls, causing figures and complex word-trains to appear on multiple gauges. He would note these perfunctorily, adjust other instruments accordingly.

Maximillian hovered nearby, a sentient extension of the ship's instruments. Physically he became a part of the *Cygnus*. Spiritually he remained plugged into Reinhardt.

Durant and McCrae strolled over to watch. Their attention was divided between the image of the roiling black hole and the intense, rapid work of Reinhardt – both awesome forces of nature.

'Fascinating . . .' Durant's reverent appraisal left some doubt as to whether he was referring to the vision of the collapsar or its nearby human dissector.

'Only from a distance,' McCrae commented with equal ambivalence.

Reinhardt finished his immediate work, turned to face them. 'Are you interested in black holes, Dr Durant?'

Durant smiled. 'That's like asking a sculptor if he'd be challenged by attempting to chisel a portrait from the face of the moon. How could anyone, scientist or layman, not be fascinated by the deadliest force in the universe?

'I've studied collapsars all my life, Doctor. The most amazing thing about them is how little we've actually been able to learn about them since their discovery in the late twentieth century. Of course, the problem is the same now as it was then. How do you study something that swallows up your instrument probes as soon as they get near enough to learn anything new? It's like trying to study a man who's invisible and can destroy anything that comes within a light-year of him. Under such conditions, study is impossible and all attempts at scientific analysis are reduced to guesswork.'

'The long, dark tunnel to nowhere,' said McCrae dispassionately. 'That's what they are.'

'Or to somewhere.' Reinhardt spoke casually. 'Those are the possibilities yet to be explored. Here Dr Durant has just admirably elucidated why our knowledge of such stellar phenomena is so slim, and nonetheless you proceed to offer a conclusion on the basis of imagination rather than fact. Not a very professional judgment, Dr McCrae. I would expect better of you.'

'I was being poetic, not analytical.'

Durant spoke before Reinhardt could reply. By this time the younger man's admiration knew no limits. 'Yet you've defied the power of that black hole with your null-gee field, sir. A stunning achievement.'

Reinhardt acknowledged the compliment. 'Your praise is excessive, Doctor.'

Durant went on. 'Your discoveries must have compensated you for the loneliness you've endured these past years. I can't believe you haven't experienced loneliness, despite the company of robot associates.'

'What can a man know of loneliness when he has the whole universe to keep him company? I have had suns for neighbours. I have spent hundreds of happy hours conversing with the mysterious signals that churn the ether. I've spoken with wonders and listened to the hiss and crackle of worlds being born. Heavenly choirs of quasars sing to me from distances unimaginable with inconceivable power. I am suffused with the gossip of the cosmos. So I am not lonely, no.

'Besides, who was it who said, "It is only alone a man can achieve his full potential for greatness"?' He paused. They were all silent for a long moment, though for different reasons.

'I have made peace with myself and the universe,' Reinhardt finally went on. 'I am kept alive as well as sane by my

106

hunger to learn, by my thirst to root out the jealously guarded secrets of nature from their hidden places.' He turned, waved towards the enormous, glowing screen.

'This massive collapsar, for example. Nature's most secure, most inviolate hiding place. Who knows what discoveries it shields?' He stared hard at Durant, yet at the same time seemed almost to be pleading.

'I think, Dr Durant, that you are a man who longs for a sense of his own greatness but has not yet found his true direction. Such personal discoveries come rarely at best, and never for most men.'

Now McCrae's attention was concentrated on her companion and not on Reinhardt.

'Perhaps,' Durant murmured, smiling hopefully back at the elder scientist, 'I'd find that here if you're in no rush for us to leave. There are still so many things I'd like to ask you.'

'And many things I'd like to tell you.' Reinhardt sounded pleased. 'Isn't that what I said my purpose in life was? To be the one who answers the questions?

'But I suggest we discuss that matter over dinner. Your friends should have the opportunity to hear also. Meanwhile, there is still a great deal I can show you here, if you're not yet bored.'

'I'm honoured by your generosity, sir.'

'And I'm gratified by your persistent curiosity and your willingness to listen uncritically to what I have to say. The hallmarks of a true man of science.'

Reinhardt led him off towards a far bank of instruments. McCrae moved to follow them, hesitated. Her gaze travelled back to the vast expanse of the viewscreen, lingered on the seething hell of the black hole as she struggled to subdue the storm in her own mind . . .

Mesons and muons, meteors and more vanished down the gravity well of the black hole. As they were torn apart by immense gravitational forces they gave up energy in the form of radiation. Some of it was at once exquisite and visible, like a cruising white shark or dark tornado. Some of it was still more deadly though detectable only with instruments far more sensitive than the human eye. None of it made sense in the way human-generated radiation such as radio waves did. The collapsar was nature gone mad. Yet at the same time it possessed balance and beauty.

It is sometimes that way with certain men.

*

Holland, Pizer and V.I.N.Cent, having received Reinhardt's invitation to dinner, were walking down another of the *Cygnus'* seemingly endless corridors.

Holland was casually memorising everything distinctive. A marking on a door, the number of lights overhead; anything that would enable them if necessary to find their own way back through the maze of passageways to the corridor leading to the reception area outside the *Palomino*.

Pizer's attention was periodically distracted by the regular appearance of groups of sentry robots, the same variety whose attention and efficiency he'd earlier experienced. V.I.N.Cent drifted alongside the two men. In his fashion the robot was nervous, apprehensive and decidedly upset that his colleagues had accepted Reinhardt's invitation.

'There wasn't anything else we could do, V.I.N.Cent,' Holland was telling him. 'Except for our initial reception, he hasn't made a single hostile gesture towards us. We'd have been asking for a confrontation if we'd refused his invitation without reason. I wouldn't be surprised if something that slight could set him off. You've noted how volatile he is.'

'I still don't like it.'

Holland regarded the robot with exasperation. 'It's only dinner. What could possibly be dangerous about accepting an invitation to dinner?'

'Said the spider to the fly.' V.I.N.Cent was not being flippant. 'I should be with you.'

'What for?' asked Pizer. 'To wipe the soup from my chin?'

'Better than wiping your face off the floor,' the machine snapped back. 'If you will continue to refuse to take care of yourselves, I don't see why you keep me from doing so for you.'

'We'll be safer without you and Max trying to knock heads.' Pizer eyed a nearby sentry with distaste. 'I watched Reinhardt when we were first in the command centre and you and his toy squared off. He was enjoying the spectacle. Next time he might not interfere. Not that I care whether it melts you into a puddle of alloy, you understand, but it could escalate into something *really* dangerous.'

'Your concern touches me,' V.I.N.Cent said sarcastically 'but it is misplaced. It is your skin you should be worrying about.' He assumed a lofty attitude, rose a half a metre higher above the deck.

'As would be expected of a mere human you are impressed by the size and overabundance of heavy metals in the construction of that clumsy mechanism. Its circuitry is twenty years out of date and its higher facilities pitifully inadequate. I would put it on a par with basic-programmed heavy materials loaders, certainly nowhere near in mental ability to my own class.'

'It's not Max's mental faculties that concern me,' Pizer replied.

'You are afraid of simple mechanical force?'

'Yeah, I am. You bet your metallic backside! And you should be too, for your own sake.'

'I can handle that thing.'

'Far be it from you to admit there isn't anything you can't handle.' Semantically outflanked, Pizer was ready to give in. 'Far be it from you to admit that subtle debate and refined discussion won't cause it to fall apart at the seams, battered to scrap by your stentorian oratory, before it can make sheet metal out of you.'

'Mr Pizer, there are three basic types of machines as well as men: the wills, the won'ts and the can'ts. The wills accomplish everything. The won'ts oppose everything. The can'ts won't will themselves to try.'

'Very Socratic,' said Holland, finally injecting himself into the discussion, 'but I doubt that Maximillian would respond as intended. Do us all a favour and try to be a *can't*, at least where the monster is concerned. I've got enough to worry about without you and him playing another robotic version of chicken. We need you, V.I.N.Cent, not another corkscrew.'

'But I . . .'

'That's an order, V.I.N.Cent.'

'Acknowledged, sir.' The robot fell into an electronic sulk, unhappy with the situation but powerless to alter it.

Privately he was considering options, creating scenarios and preparing himself for the worst. He was not angry at the two humans, however. They were prisoners of themselves. Captain Holland and First Officer Pizer were delightful companions, pleasant shipmates. But in his entire existence V.I.N.Cent had encountered perhaps half a dozen humans whom he felt could actually think straight.

Unexpected sounds, clicking and whirring and staccato buzzes, reached them as they rounded another turn in the corridor. Underlying them was something that might have been electronic music.

Puzzled, they slowed, hunted for the source. V.I.N.Cent led them to a wide doorway down a side corridor. As they reached the doorway the sounds seemed to jump out at them. None of the scattered sentry robots moved to restrain or intercept them.

The room beyond was filled with light and less visible varieties of illumination. Holland blinked, had to squint. Some of the visual effects inside were disorienting, even painful. He was not startled by the sight, only surprised to see such an area on board as prosaic a vessel as the *Cygnus*. He had encountered such places before – a recreation area for mechanicals.

Long ago, the idea of such facilities was criticised as wasteful, if not downright bizarre. The proponents of such facilities were branded as loco and were classed with the very addled machines they sought to soothe. But as the mental circuitry and design of mankind's mechanical servants became increasingly sophisticated, odd forms of behaviour that could not be explained as purely engineering errors became more and more frequent. Machines believed completely dependable suddenly went berserk at their posts. Delicate circuits visible only through high-power microscopes showed inexplicable shifts in electron flow for no known reason.

The robot psychologist came into being. Initial laughter died when the unexplained incidents dropped off in the areas where such men and their attendant machinery started to work.

It was determined that the tremendously fragile mind-machinery with which the new robots were endowed required exercise and use other than that programmed for it – much as did man's. The first tentative prototypes of the room Holland and the others were now staring into were constructed. Eventually the machines themselves took a metal hand in designing the recreation facilities for factories and ships and service industries.

Some of the games and sights they chose were variations or direct adaptations of human forms of recreation. Others seemed nothing but random light and noise to men. Mankind felt at a loss knowing that there were certain types of entertainment that his metal offspring could enjoy and appreciate while he, restricted to his organic brain and body, never could.

The longer they stood motionless before the room, the more vulnerable they became to awkward questioning. Several of the nearby sentry robots were already eying V.I.N.Cent uncertainly. He was one of them, but not with them.

'Hey, V.I.N.Cent, you'll have the time of your life in there,' said Pizer enthusiastically. 'Better than hovering outside just waiting for us to finish eating.'

The robot replied cautiously. 'I don't mean to sound superior, but I hate the company of robots. And these are all ancient models. I don't know if we can even converse, certainly not to my edification.'

'Twenty years does not ancient make, V.I.N.Cent.' Holland was staring with interest at a machine generating three-dimensional abstract patterns between two robots. 'It'll take your mind off worrying so much. Relax, have fun. Remember what they say about all work and no play.'

V.I.N.Cent generated an electronic sigh. It would be better to agree than to be ordered. This way, if he went inside voluntarily he'd have no compunctions about slipping out later if he felt the need.

'All sunshine makes a desert, so the Arabs said . . . before the advent of cheap solar power. You'll alert me if you have any trouble, Captain? If there's even a hint of trouble? I will enjoy myself more if I know you remain cognisant of my usefulness.'

'V.I.N.Cent, I'm always cognisant of your usefulness. You're indispensable, old pot.' He smiled. 'There's nothing wrong with our communicators. If anything unexpected starts, you'll be the first to know.

'Now go on in there, try to take it easy, and have a good time. You deserve it, if only for the amount of work you put in on the regenerator system.'

'Merely doing my duty, Captain. I am not programmed to function on the service-reward system.'

'That should make the rewards all the more enjoyable when they come.' Holland patted the robot on the back. Surface receptors immediately noted the contact, converted t into a stream of electrical impulses which were transorted to the interpretive section of V.I.N.Cent's brain. There hey were identified, correlated with such additional related

111

elements as Holland's tone of voice, the context of the conversation and his facial expression.

Not so very different from the way a human would have processed identical stimuli.

V.I.N.Cent moved into the noisy room. Pizer had been keeping an eye on the sentries. Now that V.I.N.Cent had been allowed to enter the recreation area without challenge, Holland and he could continue on their way.

One sentry seemed to be singling out the first officer for special scrutiny.

Pizer flipped him a jaunty salute. 'As you were . . .'

The sentry did not respond, but continued to stare after him until the two men had disappeared around a bend in the main corridor. A simple-minded mechanical programmed for few functions, it had by then forgotten all about the non-Cygnian robot now cavorting in the recreation room with other members of the ship's mechanised crew.

V.I.N.Cent regarded the shifting metal assembly with apparent indifference. He wandered through the crowd, seemingly oblivious to the outright stares of some of the other robots. None ventured to engage him in conversation, however, and he didn't attempt yet to draw them out.

He was hunting for a subject likely to be inclined to garrulousness if properly motivated. But it was difficult to distinguish one robotic type from another. The lights made visual identification difficult, despite the acuity of his optics. Furthermore, Reinhardt's machines reflected his personal rather than a standard cybernetic vision. The presence of this large number of hybrids and modified types further confused the matter. It was for such reasons that the human crew-members of the *Palomino* seemed to regard Reinhardt as nothing if not a scientific genius, despite their suspicion of him.

V.I.N.Cent held a somewhat lower opinion of the commander of the *Cygnus*. To him, the perpetrator of these and who knew how many other forms of mechanical destandardisation was more a Dr Moreau than an Einstein.

Doubtless most of the mechanicals in the room held their master in high esteem. So V.I.N.Cent kept his critical opinions to himself. For the time being, anyway.

He was searching for a robot designed to interact closely with humans: a Calvin series twenty, if he was lucky. Such a machine could converse with subtlety and would be more likely to talk freely than other, less loquacious types. There were none in sight, however.

What he spotted instead was a machine he had already encountered. Likely he'd get nothing from it, as he had – or rather, hadn't – previously. But it was of the same general style as himself. It might empathise properly if he could break through its enforced reserve. And the inelegant monster Maximillian was not around to intimidate the other this time. So he floated over to the old-fashioned pool table, hovering for a moment in the background to watch.

The aged B.O.B. unit utilised a pressure-sensitive cue to match the adjustable arms of the more humanoid machines, but he still missed the shot badly. V.I.N.Cent analysed the miss automatically, calculating the pressure-to-distance ratio involved, and came to the conclusion that the older robot's internal velocity calculations module need tuning or replacement. Or else he was simply a lousy pool player.

The surrounding robots, more of Reinhardt's cybernetic mutants, appeared to enjoy the miss. It was unusual to see one robot taunting or deliberately conspiring to humiliate another, but apparently the old B.O.B. unit regularly received such abuse. V.I.N.Cent was disgusted; the machines were behaving in an almost human fashion.

He drifted forward, monitoring the sequencing of his external lights so as not to betray his true feelings, and opened cheerfully, 'It appears you are in need of some help.'

The B.O.B. unit did not respond, but V.I.N.Cent was not to be put off so quickly this time.

'V.I.N.Cent is my name,' he announced, 'pool is my game.' He took the power cue from B.O.B., inspected it with the air of a machine designed not to use such devices but to manufacture them. Extending a set of fine manipulators he began making adjustments to the cue's trigger-and-fire mechanism.

Other robots around the room paused in their activities to watch. Several tried without success to identify the electronic tune the V.I.N.Cent model was humming via his internal synthesiser. They failed, not having his human-interaction library.

Within the control tower all was silent save for the steady

blips and pops from the multitude of computer read-outs. Humanoid robots stood or sat at their posts, attending to individually assigned functions.

Maximillian hovered before the command console. Occasionally the massive head would shift to take in a distant screen or gauge. A tiny spot of light appeared on one screen. The massive mechanical turned to study it quietly. A dial was turned, contact controls carefully attuned. The spot of light grew brighter, defining itself against the intentionally muted background of the black hole and its swirling halo of captured, radiating mass.

The light continued to travel steadily *out* from the Pit . . .

The table was not an antique, though it had the look of one. So did the matching chairs, and the crystal chandelier above, and much of the silverware and other accoutrements of a graciously set table. All were reproductions. They had been carefully crafted in the *Cygnus'* repair shops to Reinhardt's specifications. Three-dimensional history tapes from the ship's library provided the models. Only the huge painting of the *Cygnus* itself which dominated one wall was not an echo of man's past, though the frame that held it was.

Tastefully aligned drapes framed the expansive window that dominated the opposite wall. The window had the appearance of those once used in old wooden homes, the glass criss-crossed with thin, hardwood braces. But the transparent material was far stronger than glass; the wood, decoration instead of support; and the view beyond, one only a few humans had ever set eyes upon. It looked out onto the illuminated length of the *Cygnus* and the gravity devil in the sky.

Holland and Pizer entered the room. The rest of the human crew of the *Palomino* was already present. The captain's attention was drawn now not by the distant maelstrom of the collapsar but by the table, set with *fresh* fruits, *fresh* vegetables, salads and covered silver dishes from which rose wonderfully aromatic steam. It was all very different from the fare they had lived on during their eighteen months on the *Palomino*.

Two humanoid robots served wine from a real bottle, another reproduction. It would have tasted the same if it had been poured from a modern decanter, but that would have spoiled the effect. Holland knew that the commander of the *Cygnus* was not one to spoil an effect.

The room and the lavish meal laid before them was shocking, not for its elaborateness but because it gave the impression of being exactly the opposite. There was nothing to indicate that any special preparations had been made for them, beyond cooking more food than normal. Holland had the feeling that Reinhardt dined like this all the time. For a few seconds he found himself envying his counterpart.

That instant of envy vanished quickly. Fresh asparagus was a poor substitute for human companionship, an orange no match for sympathy from a fellow creature. Despite the opulent display, Reinhardt was more to be pitied than envied.

There was no reason he should stint on his meals, not with the resources of a vessel designed to feed hundreds devoted to satisfying his needs alone. Holland decided that Reinhardt was entitled to any compensations he could muster.

But for some reason the setting still disturbed him.

Bookcases leaned against other walls. Some held books made with real paper. Antique star maps decorated real wood panelling. The room was a mixture of the old and the new, traits which seemed more and more to characterise Reinhardt himself.

The commander of the *Cygnus* had risen to greet them as they entered. He did not comment on the absence of V.I.N.Cent though Holland knew it had been noted. Instead, after greeting the newcomers, he turned his attention back to McCrae.

'What a pleasant experience to dine once more with a ovely woman. That is an effect quite beyond the most laborate programming.'

McCrae nodded ever so slightly. 'Thank you.'

Reinhardt now looked back at Holland, who had moved o stand alongside Harry Booth. 'A great many experiments re in progress aboard the *Cygnus*, gentlemen. Some of them angerous. In the interests of your own safety I suggest that here are no more unescorted excursions for the duration of our stay.'

Holland thought the gentle admonition was intended for imself and Pizer. As yet he knew nothing of Booth's solitary xploration of numerous corridors, nor of his singular en- unter with the peculiar robot in hydroponics. But since einhardt appeared willing to let the matter drop with the simple warning, he wasn't about to pursue it. Nor was attentive Booth.

Reinhardt indicated they should be seated, moved quickly to hold a chair for McCrae.

'Please . . .'

She accepted the seat. The physical proximity of the commander made her nervous for reasons she couldn't define. Durant took the chair opposite her and Reinhardt, as expected, sat at the head of the table between them.

Durant found himself eying the painting of the *Cygnus* that dominated one wall and wondering who had painted it. Reinhardt himself, or one of the since departed crew? Or had it been on the *Cygnus* originally? Maybe one of Reinhardt's machines had executed the work. He inspected the crystal goblet on the table near his plate. It was a replica of a nineteenth-century English glass. All the other table settings had been made by machines. Why not the painting also?

Why did it disturb him to think that?

'We begin with fresh mushroom soup. Prepared from my own personal garden.' Several of the humanoid robots were already dispensing the thick potage. They moved and worked with a fluidity unmatched by the average mechanical.

'Mushrooms grow especially well on the *Cygnus*,' Reinhardt continued. 'Considering the dark and cold of their immediate surroundings, it somehow seems appropriate that they should do so well.'

Pizer was already downing the soup from the silver bowl before him. 'This is the kind of Christmas dinner I've been dreaming about for months.' He spooned another mouthful, swallowed, his eyes closing from the sheer pleasure of it. 'Delicious.'

'Thank you. I am afraid the spices, the white pepper, and the butter substitute are from the *Cygnus*' store of preserved condiments, but the parsley you see is also fresh, as is the wine in the soup. I have enjoyed reprogramming and experimenting with the machines which do the cooking. I have had ample time to develop an interest in such hobbies without having to neglect my serious work.'

Booth had barely sampled his soup, was staring down at it with a peculiar expression. 'I remember writing about the extensive hydroponics system, back when everyone was doing features on the *Cygnus*' construction. Large enough to support the needs of the entire crew, wasn't it?'

Reinhardt nodded agreeably. 'These days it's tiny, only large enough to supply my personal needs. Most of the cultivated areas have been allowed to lie dormant.'

'Naturally. Be a waste of energy and material to maintain them for no reason at all.' A robot refilled the reporter's wine glass. Booth was disappointed that his carefully phrased appraisal had failed to provoke some kind of reaction from Reinhardt.

'Our spare parts and our wine are vintage, Captain. I hope they all prove satisfactory.' He savoured the bouquet from his own glass, sipped delicately.

'We're modifying a few of them, Doctor, but we should be able to make everything work.' Holland chewed his food, swallowed and spoke while slicing another portion of meat. 'The changes that have taken place in the past twenty years have been primarily in the fields of guidance and navigation, life-support maintenance and automatics.

'Atmospheric regeneration systemology has remained fairly basic over that period. There's only so much you can do with air. The replacements you've provided us with were machined a little differently, and some of the alloys are different. Nothing that can't be adjusted to work on the *Palomino*. We'll be finished with our repairs by tomorrow, and ready to leave.'

Durant took immediate exception to that. 'Speak for yourself, Dan. I, for one, still have a great deal to learn from Dr Reinhardt.'

'Our mission's finished, Alex. It's time for us to start home. All of us.'

Durant opened his mouth to reply, but their attention was diverted by the sudden entry of Maximillian. The machine was a brutal reminder of the realities which held sway beyond the fairy-tale ambiance of the dining room. Reinhardt listened sagely to the rapid-paced spew of electronics from the robot, clearly understanding everything. Whatever the content of the message, it produced an immediate change in the commander's attitude. His mood turned from merely pleasant to downright buoyant.

'Thank you, Maximillian. Inform me in time to congratulate him formally.'

A last series of beeps issued from the machine. Then it pivoted on its repeller units and departed. Reinhardt dwelled in some other dimension for an instant, then remembered his guests. Lifting his wine glass as he rose, he addressed them all. His particular attention was reserved for the expectant Durant.

'A toast to you and your companions, Dr Durant, on the occasion of your visit to the *Cygnus*. You are the only people of Earth to know of my continued existence, the only ones to know that I did not vanish with dreams unfulfilled.'

Durant lifted his own glass in reflexive response. 'And to you, sir, and your magnificent achievements. May they multiply and increase.'

'So they shall, so they shall.' Reinhardt sounded self-important. Not pompous. Never pompous. He was driven beyond that.

'Tonight, my friend, we stand on the brink of a feat un-paralleled in the history of spatial exploration.'

'And what might that be?' inquired the ever-sceptical Booth.

Reinhardt glanced at him. 'If the data on my returning probe ship matches my computerised calculations, it will mean I can proceed with the ultimate test of both the new energy source represented by the Cygnus Process and the null-gee field generator. I will travel where no man has dared to go.' He was staring past them now, out the port into space.

Durant hesitated, disbelieving, but Reinhardt's gaze and manner could only be indicative of one possible destination. 'Into the black hole . . . ?'

Stunned as they all were by the wonderful madness of such a thought, that was as much as any of them could say . . .

NINE

REINHARDT continued to gaze past them, past the parameters of his ship. His was the look of a man whose dedication was coupled with disregard for anything but achieving a particular end. Such a gaze belonged only to true visionaries.

Also true madmen.

'You strive to attain a most singular end, Doctor,' an awed Durant finally added.

Reinhardt replied without smiling. 'No, Dr Durant. To attain the end of a singularity.'

'That's crazy,' Booth chimed in, not caring now whether he might provoke Reinhardt to anger or not. 'Impossible! It's impossible to travel into a black hole, let alone through one.'

It was not the aspersion Booth indirectly cast on Reinhardt's sanity that upset the commander of the *Cygnus*, but rather the reporter's scientific absolutism and negativity.

'*Impossible?* Impossible is a word found only in the dictionary of fools.' He was barely holding his anger in check.

Pizer glanced at Holland. Reinhardt noted the look, saw that at least the captain was giving the proposal serious consideration. It calmed him some. Foolish to allow a popular demagogue like Booth to upset him!

'Mr Pizer,' he told the first officer, 'I was dreaming of this when you were still flying kites. If scientists habitually restricted their researches to what their colleagues considered "possible" we would still be living in caves, or on the Eurasian land mass because of fear of sailing off the edge of the Earth, or restricted to the Earth alone because exploration of the cosmos might not seem financially feasible.

'Such attitudes are characteristic of the Dark Ages. I am surprised that any of you,' and he looked around the table, 'would adhere to such deterministic nonsense.'

'Dreaming is one thing, the dangerous pursuit of dreams another,' Holland argued. 'People have dreamed for years about such an attempt, and failed every time. Drone ships have managed to get close, but eventually all are trapped by the collapsar's gravity and they vanish beyond the event horizon.'

'You disappoint me, Captain Holland. I expected more empathy for such a journey from someone like yourself. Have you no desire, no curiosity to know what may lie on the other side of a black hole?'

'There is no other side,' Booth insisted. 'Anything that enters a black hole is smashed down to nothingness by the strength of the gravity.'

'That's one theory,' Reinhardt readily admitted, unperturbed. 'There are others.'

'The scientific consensus today says there's nothing on the other side,' McCrae put in.

'Yet if there is another side, which is where Mr Booth and I disagree, then by definition there must be something there. As I've just pointed out, my dear, the scientific consensus once insisted the world was flat.'

'It's not possible,' Holland still spoke thoughtfully, his voice devoid of ridicule. 'Every leading scientist says it's not possible.'

'Except this one,' Reinhardt said loftily.

'Assuming the impossible for a moment,' Holland finally hypothesised, 'that your field functions as you believe it will and that you can also generate enough power to break through to this imaginary "other side" . . . how do you propose to return?'

Reinhardt surveyed him with the full pity the dedicated scientist reserves for the layman. 'My dear Captain Holland, I do not expect to return . . .'

By now the pool table was surrounded by mechanical spectators, all viewing the action through optics operating on everything from infra-red up through the ultra-violet. Mutters of amazement and admiration filled the air. As yet V.I.N.Cent's remarkable display of pool prowess had not engendered any apparent hostility, not even from the mechanical he was playing against.

Making the usual ultrarapid calculations involving distance, mass and energy, V.I.N.Cent lined up his next shot. Another ball tumbled neatly into the far pocket. Nearby, the old B.O.B. unit he had befriended looked on in astonishment. The tension-cue seemed to have become an extension of V.I.N.Cent's mind as well as his body.

V.I.N.Cent noticed the flicker of lights on the older machine flashing the admiration sequence. 'The only way to win. Never give the other fellow a shot. Run the table on him.' He tilted himself sideways in the air, lined up a ridiculously difficult shot, and banked it home. A chorus of incredulous buzzes and murmurs rose from the robotic audience he had attracted.

'Are there any more like us on board?' V.I.N.Cent set up his next shot, a tough three-ball combination. B.O.B. shook its head.

But something had finally convinced the old machine to talk. 'I'm the last. There were others, but our series was fairly new when the *Cygnus* was first outfitted. A lot of us revealed bugs. Every one except myself failed early in our journey.' He turned prideful, tried to correct the list to his hover.

'I must have been one of the first in the series to be properly composed. I'm still operative. These upstarts think I'm some old freak.'

V.I.N.Cent made the shot easily, moved to follow up as the cue ball glided to a halt. 'We're still the pride of the fleet back home.' He fired another ball in. 'There are units like you and me operating at every level of fleet command. Also in private commercial service. We're highly regarded and valued.

'You could be fixed up easily enough. Install some of the latest reaction circuitry and logic capacitors and you'd be good as new. No . . . better than new. How would you like to go back with us?'

The hum of conversation surrounding the table and players abruptly ceased. A couple of the machines near B.O.B. flashed warning lights.

V.I.N.Cent appraised the scene and the attitude of the other robots. All were Reinhardt-made or modified. None appeared sympathetic to his casual offer. He decided he'd find no allies among these mechanicals. With one possible exception.

'I think you'd be wise to drop the subject,' B.O.B. advised him.

After studying his audience a moment longer, V.I.N.Cent gave the equivalent of an electronic shrug. 'Forget it. I was just joking. We wouldn't have room for additional machines anyway.' Then he added as an idle afterthought, 'One of those parts Maximillian drew for us doesn't work. I'll be needing a replacement for a regenerator boost module number A-34.'

He turned back to the game as if nothing had happened, lined up another ball.

'That shot does not compute,' insisted one of the again fully absorbed onlookers.

'Don't bet on it,' V.I.N.Cent warned him, 'I have not yet begun to compute.' He made the shot, with extra English to spare. It catalysed the expected flurry of electronic oohs and ahhs.

It also allowed old B.O.B. to slip out of the recreation room without being noticed . . .

Booth had his recorder out and activated. He set it next to his plate. Reinhardt either did not notice it or else he had no objection to the reporter's recording his statements. The latter was the more likely.

Holland was the one currently talking. 'According to what you've told us, Doctor, the surviving lifeboat-survey ship has been converted to accept both your matter-anti-matter energy system and the gravity field distortion unit. But you say it has only travelled *to* the event horizon, not past it into the black hole itself.'

'I admit that being able to pass that close to oblivion and return successfully is a tremendous achievement.' Reinhardt didn't change his expression, accepting the compliment as his due. 'But it's akin to sailing a ship atop an ocean as opposed to diving to its bottom. When you begin travelling beneath the surface you have to deal with radically different natural forces. It's the same when you pass the event horizon.'

He tapped his plate idly with a fork. 'How do you expect the *Cygnus* to escape being crushed by the gravity in there? Most theories hold that the centre of a black hole no longer contains anything we'd recognise as mass. It's simply a self-sustaining gravity field of incalculable strength.'

'I would assume—' Durant interrupted, 'that Dr Rein

hardt has sufficient confidence in his field's ability to bend the damaging effects around his ship, to drive a hole through what we might call, for lack of better terms, "solid" gravity.'

'Indeed,' Reinhardt was clearly delighted to have Durant's support, 'I know that you're thinking that one slight error in navigation could be fatal, Captain. That is your field, and so I accept your criticism where that is concerned.

'But I know exactly what I am doing and how I shall proceed. I have worked on the requisite calculations for nearly two years. The course I've chosen will take the *Cygnus* into the Pit at the most acute angle possible. The incredible speed generated by the ship's engines will be augmented by the gradually increasing pull which will rise to a climax as we strike the event horizon.

'The combination should permit me to slingshot through the dimensional warp I believe exists at the centre of the singularity in an instant, long before the shielding null-gee field enveloping the *Cygnus* can be collapsed. I have no intention of waiting around inside the event horizon to test the ultimate limits of that field. It will be sufficient if it protects the *Cygnus* for several seconds.'

'You're going to encounter all kinds of secondary effects before you ever reach that point.' McCrae sounded as dubious as Holland. 'What about the intense radiation, the heat generated by the collapsing matter entering the hole?'

'My previous probings and all my studies have shown that if I remain exactly on course, the *Cygnus* will pass through unscathed. Furthermore, since the heat within the collapsar's accretion disk is gravity-related, much of it should be diverted around the *Cygnus* by the null-gee field.'

'*Fantastic!*' Durant was completely overwhelmed by the proposal. 'Both the notion itself and the physics involved are beyond my concepts of magnificence.' He shook his head slowly. His thoughts were a confused mixture of awe and disbelief. They were mirrored in his expression ...

Having disposed of his last opponent, V.I.N.Cent drifted away from the pool table. Most of the robots who had watched the contest remained there. Crowding around the table, they pushed and shoved one another for the chance to use the cues. With considerable frustration and little success, they were trying to imitate V.I.N.Cent's techniques.

The three-level pinball machine crackled and chimed satisfactorily as V.I.N.Cent operated the dozen flippers within. His mind was not on the game. It appeared he moved randomly from one machine to the next. All the while he was edging closer to the exit. At last he allowed a final ball to find its own noisy way through the labyrinth of the last machine and slipped out into the corridor.

The sentry robot who had been keeping watch on him turned away for but a moment. When his gaze returned it was in time to see V.I.N.Cent scudding down the corridor. He signalled to his companion, and both moved quickly to the doorway, looked out. One glanced up the corridor, the other down as they functioned in tandem.

V.I.N.Cent was just turning the far corner.

Moving on smoothly pumping metal legs, the two sentries rushed after him. V.I.N.Cent was not restricted to such anthropomorphic methods of locomotion. The instant he turned the corner he accelerated on his repellers and shot down the corridor, rounding another corner where two passageways intersected.

The sentries reached the same turn, peered around it. V.I.N.Cent was long gone. Their comparatively one-track minds struggled to account for his sudden disappearance, failed. Blinking in confusion, they hurried down the wrong corridor.

Durant's mind was working furiously, trying to make sense of unheard-of possibilities. In the light of so fantastic, so grand a proposition it was hard to consider things rationally It was a losing struggle to moderate his enthusiasm.

'So you want the *Palomino*,' he was mumbling, 'to stand by and monitor your journey? You want us to act a observers to record your passage?'

'To another place,' Reinhardt told them, 'and anothe time, where . . .'

Booth was making a show of adjusting his recorder. distracted Reinhardt, somewhat broke the mood of scientifi ebullience which had filled the dining room.

'What are you doing, Mr Booth?'

'Just changing the sequencing on my recorder.' He smile apologetically at the commander of the *Cygnus*. 'I wouldn want to miss anything.'

124

'Commendable of you,' said Reinhardt.

'Thanks. I think it's important we be sure and get your last words. For posterity. It'll serve as a more effective warning against this sort of insanity than anything I could make up.'

Reinhardt's momentary euphoria turned once more to anger. Durant he could manipulate with the promise of new wonders. He could tease McCrae with memories of her father. Holland and Pizer he could overawe with his knowledge. But Booth . . . Booth retained the maddening, smug, self-satisfaction of the ignorant man confident in his simple view of the universe.

'You're not the first to think me mad. Better men than you, Mr Booth, accused me of irrationality. I could dismiss that. Others laughed at me. That I could ignore, with justifiable contempt. Worst though, were those who conspired against me and what I was attempting to do. In such cases it was necessary to . . .'

He caught himself, looked down at his food. When he gazed at the reporter again he'd regained control of himself. 'Left to men like you, Mr Booth, we would still be living in the dark times of the second millennium. I promise you, I will be victorious.'

'For a man who likes to think of himself as an educator, you talk an awful lot of conquest,' Holland observed.

Reinhardt stared at him. 'You would accuse me of militancy, Captain Holland? Very well. I accept the label. But I am a soldier only in the cause of science. I do not think "victorious" too strong a claim for the triumph I shall experience. And when I have done what I say I shall do, others will try to follow.' There was no humour in his smile now, nor did he try to temper the edge in his voice. 'And if successful in such attempts, they will then have to deal with me.'

'And what role would such people play in this newly discovered universe of yours?' McCrae was watching him closely.

But Reinhardt no longer seemed to care about appearing tactful or diplomatic. The moment of triumph over his enemies and scoffers was at hand. There was no longer any need to hide his zealousness from these few visitors.

'Perhaps none. I have created on board this ship the

beginnings of an entirely self-sustaining mechanical civilisation which responds to my orders and discipline and which—'

Holland wanted to hear more about Reinhardt's plans for his machines, but the commander broke off his speech as Maximillian re-entered the room.

Again, only Reinhardt was able to interpret the series of electronic sounds and lights put forth by the huge mechanical. When Maximillian had finished, Reinhardt turned back to them. The interruption had sparked a by-now familiar transformation. Reinhardt again was at his gracious best.

'Good news?' Holland inquired.

'Indeed. See for yourselves.' He pointed to the viewport. An approaching brightness was now clearly visible against the farther stars: sunlight glinting off an incoming ship.

'The probe I have referred to is about to dock. There are things I must do. I will see you again soon.' He pushed back his chair, rose. 'Please, continue your meal.' He smiled tightly.

'There is nothing you can do to assist and the docking procedure is dull and familiar. Excuse me.' He followed Maximillian out of the room.

'Well, Doctor,' Booth said as Reinhardt was leaving, 'no matter how foolhardy I think you are; win, lose or draw it's one heckuva story.' The commander of the *Cygnus* disappeared without replying.

The door closed behind him. Holland had thoughts of trying the closed door to see if they'd been locked in. Reinhardt's cool warning about straying unescorted around the ship still burned in the captain's mind. But there was no reason yet to force anything. If the door was locked, there wasn't anything they could do about it.

Better to do as Reinhardt had suggested and enjoy the rest of the dinner. There was a chance their regular dining schedule might be interrupted in the near future.

Booth looked around the table, uncertain to what extent his companions shared his analysis of Reinhardt and the man's absurd proposal. Eventually his gaze came to rest on the first officer.

Pizer stared back at him for a long moment. Then the younger man spoke while glancing towards the now closed doorway. 'Cuckoo as a Swiss clock . . .' He turned to his own meal, downing food as if the devil himself were after him.

Holland's thoughts were on the problem that might be raised by disciples of another type. He was watching Durant worriedly. The *Palomino*'s elder scientist was not eating. He was standing by the viewport, staring silently at the approaching probe ship . . .

V.I.N.Cent touched a sensor plate. When the door obediently slid aside, he drifted into the dimly illuminated Maintenance room. As he had hoped, a familiar shape was waiting for him: the battered but still talkative pool player he'd substituted for.

'My name's B.O.B. Twenty-Six.'

'Of course it is,' said V.I.N.Cent agreeably. 'But since you're the only unit of your type aboard, you can leave off the series numbers.'

'I couldn't talk freely before. Those other machines, the ones built or altered by Reinhardt? They would've had me disassembled. I have a lot to tell you.' His ill-lubed repellers whining faintly, he moved to the door and carefully scanned the corridor.

'If Maximillian knew you were here, unescorted, it would be the end for both of us.'

V.I.N.Cent hoped his words sounded as contemptuous as he intended they should. 'You've no need to worry about that clumsy dirt-mover. I can't understand why you're all so intimidated by him. If you go well-prepared into the jungle, the drunken elephant can't fall on you.'

'What's an elephant?' B.O.B. asked.

'Never mind. We'll have your memory tripled when we get home.' He was hunting about the desk area, reasoning that the items they needed would be where the supervising robot could keep close watch on them. 'Do you have lasers?'

Old B.O.B. moved to a counter. A thin, irregular-shaped metal bar extended forward from one of his arms. It fitted neatly into a socket in the countertop. There was a click. Several drawers popped open.

V.I.N.Cent gave the weapons thus revealed a professional once-over. All were slightly archaic, but quite sufficiently lethal. Not that he had a choice.

He chose a pair, checked to make sure they were fully

charged, and turned to leave. B.O.B. called for him to wait.

'Listen . . . I don't know exactly what you have in mind, V.I.N.Cent, but I'm with you. I've had enough of serving as negative pole for every thersitical machine on this ship. And I don't like Reinhardt, though it's against my programming to do anything about it. Not that anyone could, with Maximillian always hovering around him. Whatever you're planning, I'd like to help in any way I can.'

'I was counting on that, B.O.B.' Again V.I.N.Cent moved to depart and once more he was held back. 'Something else?'

'There are a few other things you'd better know about this ship,' the robot began. 'Your friends could be in grave danger.'

'I have confidence in Captain Holland and First Officer Pizer,' V.I.N.Cent informed him. 'In my opinion they often err on the side of caution, but for humans they can move decisively when events require. I'm certain they are amply suspicious of Commander Reinhardt's intentions and will treat any suggestions of his with due care.'

'It involves more than suggestion, V.I.N.Cent. You don't know anything, and neither do they, This has to do with . . .'

The probe ship drifted towards the upper surface of the *Cygnus* and the waiting dock. It decelerated smoothly, showing no ill effects from its epoch-making journey.

Durant still stood staring out the viewport of the dining room. He wished Reinhardt had invited him to go along to greet the probe pilot, even if it was a mechanical. But the commander had not, and Durant had elected not to press the request. A genius like Reinhardt would divulge secrets and discoveries when he saw fit. That was his right.

Pizer sipped his wine and spoke to the introspective McCrae. 'What does your feminine intuition say, Kate?'

She blinked, sat up straighter and looked across at him. 'That hoary old superstition? I don't know about it, but logic and reason tell me that for all his apparent accomplishments, Dr Reinhardt is walking a tightrope between genius and insanity.'

'I opt for insanity,' mused Holland aloud.

That comment prompted Durant to turn away from the port. 'I'm sorry, Dan. I don't buy that. Dedication isn' madness. Maybe he's a little over-enthusiastic in his quest for answers, but many great scientists were. He has more reason than most to want to vindicate himself and his theories. Considering the length of time he's lived alone out here, devoid of human companionship, I'd say he's done a helluva job of hanging onto his stability.'

'Whatever else he may be,' ventured Booth conversationally, 'he's an out-and-out liar. I visited one of the main hydroponics stations.' He grinned at Holland's expression of surprise.

'You weren't the only one curious enough to go for a solitary stroll, Dan. That *tiny* one-man garden of his that he told us about over dinner? The one just big enough to supply his personal needs? It's big enough to feed an army.'

'Nothing so strange about that,' Durant defended the absent Reinhardt. 'A small portion of one station is devoted to the raising of foodstuffs, while the rest is kept cultivated to assist in purifying the air. Remember, the *Cygnus* wasn't equipped with anything as sensitive as our up-to-date synthesiser regeneration system. Those closed recycling systems will only serve a small-sized crew like our own anyhow. If he wants to move and work freely about the *Cygnus* he has to maintain full atmospheric pressure throughout the ship. So he's forced to maintain the greenery to help clean the air.'

Pizer looked unconvinced. 'For my money it'd take a lot more than a few trees to *purify* the air around here.' He glanced at Holland. 'Tell 'em about the funeral, Dan.'

'Funeral?' Now McCrae was intrigued.

'Yeah,' Pizer went on, 'a robot funeral, with robot pall-bearers. Almost human.'

Durant voiced the expected scepticism. 'A decade or more without any human contact might make the man a little eccentric, but you can't ask me to believe he's programmed his robots to act *that* human.'

'Exactly.' Holland was moodily eying his no-longer appetising meal. 'I know what I saw, though. It was a funeral, complete to shroud and solemn observance. I can't say what it was a funeral for. The outline under the shroud *looked* human, but it could've been anything. It was ejected from the ship before I had any chance to try for a closer look.'

'Why go to such elaborate lengths to dispose of a robot?'

Durant's tone mixed cynicism with amazement at Holland's seeming guilibility. 'Besides, such a procedure would be wasteful. No matter how badly incapacitated, any mechanical could be beneficially cannibalised for spare parts. Maybe the *Cygnus* has no need of such spares, but I don't think Reinhardt would be needlessly wasteful of anything. Especially material as valuable as the components of a sentient robot.'

'I told you, I didn't say it was a robot.'

'What's that supposed to mean?'

Holland looked hard at him. 'We have only Reinhardt's word for what happened to his crew.'

Durant grew angry. 'The sort of possibility you're hinting at is incredible. You're going to find yourself very embarrassed if you raise the subject with the commander. He'll skewer you with records, tapes . . . all sorts of indisputable independent corroboration of his statements.'

'I hope so.'

'Ship's coming in,' said McCrae, changing the subject.

They watched as the probe passed their viewport and settled into its dock. Holland was forced to admire the efficiency with which the secondary craft had been modified to accept Reinhardt's new propulsion system. Her silhouette looked unchanged. She was an impressive little vessel, as big as the *Palomino*.

Booth spoke as they observed the descent and linkup. 'Speaking of humanoid shapes and the funerals of we-don't-know-whats, I ran into something else a little too human in the hydroponics station.'

Holland was on him immediately. 'For instance?'

'For instance, the robot in charge of controlling the operations there. It was almost human, too . . . in its malfunction.'

'What makes you think so?'

Booth only shrugged.

But Durant wouldn't let it pass. 'Yes, what was there about another robot to spook you, Harry? Reinhardt can't be everywhere on the *Cygnus* simultaneously. Certain minor operations must have to take care of themselves.'

'This robot looked like it had been taking care of itself for quite a while. It had a limp.'

'And that's what spooked you?'

'I don't spook, Alex. I've dealt with about every kind of

mechanical the cyberneticists have created, from military police models down to broadcast independents with enough brains to translate ancient texts for you.

'What I'm telling you is that I had a gut feeling I was looking at some kind of . . . person. I've seen damaged robots in operation before. Even if it's a household luxury model, a damaged humanoid-type with a bad leg walks with a certain unmistakable stiffness. That includes those with flexlimbs made of polyethylenes. But this character moved differently. He walked more fluidly than any injured machine *I* ever saw.'

'What the devil are you suggesting?'

'That we get off this ship as soon as possible,' Holland finished for him. Both men turned to look at the captain. 'Politely if we can.'

Surprisingly, it was Booth, who objected. 'Hang on now, Dan. If Reinhardt's engines can generate enough power to hold him steady here, for we don't know how long, I figure he's got enough to pull away from this spot without any trouble at all.'

'So?' Pizer was watching Booth warily. The reporter was apt to go overboard if it could mean a better story. Such enthusiasm was commendable. It had also been known to get people dead.

'So why not,' Booth said excitedly, 'take this ship *and* Reinhardt back home?'

'Easier said than done.' But Holland couldn't help considering the thought.

'Not all that much easier.' Now that he'd broached the possibility, Booth rambled on as if he were proposing the most natural solution in the world.

'We've got two scientific whizzes to figure his computer setup and reprogramme the robots. The programming can't be all that complicated; it's twenty years behind the times. Alex and Kate are not. If Reinhardt's managed to arrange things so that he can run this ship all by himself, the five of us plus V.I.N.Cent ought to be able to do likewise without working up a mental sweat. And while Kate and Alex are working on navigation and cybernetics, three of us are left to take care of Reinhardt and his steel dog.'

He paused for breath, then rushed on. 'Think of it! Reinhardt won't mind in the long run. Not once he's been besieged for information on his new drive system and the null-gee field. He'll thank us for dragging him back home. The government will be delirious because they'll have the *Cygnus* back and can use it to recoup their colossal investment, even if they just make it into a museum. The established research institutes will have two decades of new data to pore through. See,' he concluded brightly, 'everybody eventually benefits. Even Reinhardt.'

'He'd disagree with you, Harry.'

Booth frowned at Durant. 'He would today, sure, but not once we're back on Earth. Not if he's been telling us the truth. And if he hasn't been, it's our duty to take him back. He can face acclamation or trial, it's all the same to me. We . . . we could be heroes.'

'We could also be dead,' Holland pointed out.

Durant turned away from them. 'I don't believe what I'm hearing. Leaving aside the fact that Reinhardt is considering the greatest experiment in the history of modern astrophysics, he'd never consent to relinquishing his authority over the *Cygnus*. Never.'

'You can believe you're hearing *this*, Alex,' Holland said firmly. 'My job is to get you all off this ship alive. That's my responsibility and that's what I intend to do – the greatest experiment in the history of modern astrophysics notwithstanding. Once we're safely away we'll see about monitoring any crazy schemes Reinhardt has in mind.' He turned to the reporter.

'As for your suggestion, Harry, I suggest you cool it. Don't bait the bull.'

'I've done that plenty of times,' Booth spoke proudly 'and I'm still hanging around.'

'We're all aware of your accomplishments and you heroic, investigating-reporter background,' Holland replied soothingly, 'but don't push that man. That's an order. You'r not operating alone now. I have to think of everyone. Yo ought to, too. I don't want to see any of us left behind.'

Booth glared at him momentarily. Then he seemed t think things through and relaxed, nodding agreement. The still had time, he told himself. He was certain that he coul eventually convince Holland that his, Harry Booth's, pla was best for all concerned.

If he could convince Holland, then Pizer would aut matically go along. McCrae could be persuaded. Durant .

Alex would be a problem. His judgment was blinded by Reinhardt's visions. But he was only one man and more inclined to fight with his intellect than a weapon. Weapons were likely to be important in the upcoming discussions, he knew.

Not only would they return as heroes, he would be reporting the greatest story in a hundred years.

GHOST SHIP *Cygnus* RETURNS! . . . reported by Harrison G. Booth. No . . . HARRISON G. BOOTH REPORTS . . . Return of the ghost ship *Cygnus*.

That sounded better. He returned his attention to the viewport, much pleased with himself.

Reinhardt entered the pressurised cylinder, Maximillian following close behind. Ahead, the probe ship could be seen locking into the *Cygnus*' reception terminal. *Soon it will all begin*, Reinhardt mused. *The culmination of my life's work. The answer to one of science's greatest mysteries will be revealed.*

The possibility he might die did not concern him. If it had he would have returned to Earth long ago. He feared only ignorance, not death. The latter he knew for what it was: a cessation of the flow of certain fluids, the degradation of internal electric impulses which conveyed stimuli, and the eventual dissolution of various organic molecular structures into dust.

Sadly he shook his head. He could not fathom other men's fear of dying. Why, how could they be so concerned with existing when for the most part their existence was a waste? They contributed nothing, achieved nothing, merely took up space. Everything they did, every action of their meagre lives was geared towards inefficient utilisation of their environment for petty personal ends. Yet they continued to insist their way of life constituted a civilisation.

The cylinder moved towards the probe terminal.

TEN

V.I.N.CENT drifted silently alongside B.O.B. Both machines travelled as slowly as possible so as to minimise the noise produced by their repellers. B.O.B.'s tended to grind from time to time.

V.I.N.Cent was going to see the evidence that would confirm B.O.B.'s incredible revelation. The older robot had insisted, so that no doubt would be left in the minds of V.I.N.Cent's human crewmates.

They slowed to a halt by a closed door. B.O.B. repeated the admonition for silence, then activated the door. It slid back soundlessly. They drifted into a large room. B.O.B. reclosed the door behind them.

They were gazing into a roughly circular chamber lit by many-coloured lights. Deeper lights, powerful precision lasers, were firing down at a cylindrical platform. The platform turned slowly as the lights played upon it. Several humanoid robots were working at nearby consoles or over the round table.

When they moved, V.I.N.Cent caught a glimpse of their stations, computer consoles of the most intricate design. As the platform-table continued to revolve, the watching robots had a clear view of what lay atop it.

Several humanoid shapes lay within indentations in the platform. Their heads were the same as those of the humanoids operating the instrumentation, but the bodies lying in the indentations were not. V.I.N.Cent's sensors informed him that they were not, as he hoped, superb replicas of human forms. They *were* human forms. What lay behind the mirrored faceplates that covered each skull he preferred not to speculate on.

Lasers flashed at regular intervals, and other devices functioned. All were conducted by the robed, face-plated

134

shapes at the consoles. It was a compact symphony of remote surgery, advanced cybernetics, and complete moral dessication.

'These poor creatures are what's left of the original human crew,' B.O.B. whispered as softly as he could. 'They are kept alive by a technique of Reinhardt's I don't pretend to understand.'

'They are humans, then?'

'More robot than human now, V.I.N.Cent.' The old robot sounded forlorn. 'There was nothing a mere B.O.B. unit like myself could have done. Reinhardt had constructed Maximillian as a therapeutic research project, or so he told the other humans. With his aid, he was able to take over the ship. He and Maximillian had secretly reprogrammed the other robots to help him. They were not responsible . . . he'd altered their circuitry and memories radically. This altered programming did not manifest itself until the time he'd chosen for the takeover, when their secret, special programming was keyed by a selected phrase spoken only by Reinhardt.

'Those humans who survived – you see what's left of them working around the ship. Occasionally some die despite the best efforts of Reinhardt's programmed surgeons. Some die from natural causes, I'm sure, but I believe others experience a flash of reality and kill themselves.'

'Only a flash? Couldn't some of them,' V.I.N.Cent asked hopefully, 'still retain enough to be returned to a normal state?'

'I doubt it,' said B.O.B. sadly. 'Their brains have been altered to do Reinhardt's bidding. They retain no individual will, react to nothing save the task they are assigned to. When I was able to isolate myself with one, I've tried to communicate. None has ever responded to me.'

'How come you weren't reprogrammed by Reinhardt along with all the other robots?'

'It was through no cleverness of my own. But for an accident of circumstance I would be as obedient as any you have encountered. You see, I was lying dormant in the back of the Maintenance area when Reinhardt reprogrammed the robots in my section of the ship. My task was originally performed by humans, so I may not have been on any of his lists. I was reactivated several days after the humans had been killed ... or brought here to be altered. By that time Reinhardt was in complete command of the *Cygnus*. He was too occupied with other tasks to consider that he might have missed one potentially uncooperative robot. I have taken care not to draw attention to my independent nature.

'Regardless, he would have been right not to be concerned. A single unreprogrammed mechanical or two could be no threat to him. Not with the sentries already under his command and Maximillian to do his bidding.'

There was no aura of vengeance to B.O.B.'s words. Such extreme memory-emotions were denied mechanicals. But V.I.N.Cent thought he could detect a certain dissatisfaction.

'There must be something ...' he began.

The door opened behind them. Two sentry robots stood there. A rapid display of lights raced across their external monitoring units as they reacted to the presence of V.I.N.Cent and B.O.B. in the restricted area.

'They must know I've told you,' said B.O.B. hurriedly. 'Your presence alongside me is enough. We're done for.'

'Get down.'

B.O.B. cut his repellers and fell almost to the deck as the sentries' weapons rose to firing position. Before either could shoot, V.I.N.Cent's own lasers flared several times. Both sentries were knocked back into the anteroom, clear of the surgery. They spewed droplets of liquid metal and sparking internal modules.

Oblivious to anything not directly affecting their designated task, the humanoid surgeons continued operating. V.I.N.Cent led B.O.B. through the now open door, closed it quickly behind them. They concealed the two punctured metal shapes as best they could, then started up the corridor.

Perhaps when this new information was laid before him, Captain Holland would initiate action somewhat more compelling than conversation ...

Durant paced the dining room, ignoring the food and the view outside. How to make them believe, he thought frantically? How to show them the importance of Reinhardt and what he proposed to attempt? So far Dan and Harry had offered nothing against the commander except groundless suspicions. He *had* to convince them!

'What's wrong with you people?' His frustration poured out. 'The man has given us our lives – or have you already forgotten that his generosity is enabling us to repair the *Palomino*? Or that once he was sure we meant him no harm,' and he glared accusingly at Booth, 'he's been a perfect host? More than that, he's offered to let us take back to Earth details of his fantastic accomplishments and discoveries, knowing he can never be certain we'll see he receives proper credit for them.'

Holland looked sympathetic, but still said what had to be said. 'That doesn't obviate the fact that he's technically a pirate operating a stolen ship, Alex.'

'We don't know that!' Durant slammed a fist on the table, rattling crystalware and spilling gravy on the immaculate imitation lace tablecloth. 'He says the others abandoned ship and tried to return home. They may still be on their way, if they had trouble with their supralight engines.'

'I think we have enough evidence to believe otherwise, Alex.'

'Circumstantial, Dan! Only circumstantial. I've seen no reason to think that . . .'

Holland interrupted him. 'I've seen enough to make me worry. Both about the actual fate of the missing crew and Reinhardt's state of mind.'

'Don't be so blasted superior. Men like Reinhardt are a special breed. They push back the frontiers of human knowledge. Sure, that can be a little unsettling at times.'

Holland gave him a long look. 'You mean, one set of rules for those pushing back the frontiers and another for those of us who simply want to live with them?'

'Don't put words in my mouth. Where would we be without men like Reinhardt?'

'Healthier,' said Pizer. 'I'm not anti-research, Alex. You know that. Only against uncontrolled research. Like uncontrolled fusion. You can get burned both ways.'

'Reinhardt says he's checked everything.'

'Charlie doesn't mean that,' Holland explained. 'Science needs a system of checks and balances just like law. Here, Reinhardt is both.' He shook his head slowly. 'In my book, hat's research without control. It's Reinhardt's other activities that worry me most, not this intended suicidal plunge nto the black hole.'

'Other activities?' Durant's brows drew together. 'What are you talking about, Dan ... ?'

Reinhardt waited expectantly, watching the doorway opposite. The probe ship, now docked, rested nearby.

The door leading from the umbilical passageway opened. Quietly, the humanoid pilot of the probe joined them. Reinhardt looked him over, then said impassively, 'Maximillian will take you to debriefing. I want to check out your ship's instrumentation and the information you recorded personally.'

He stepped past the pilot. The pilot did not acknowledge the movement. He waited somnolently until Maximillian closed the door leading to the ship. Together, the two machines began the passage by cylinder.

The two destroyed sentries could not be seen from the upper end of the corridor, V.I.N.Cent noted with relief. His careful snipping of circuitry and module links had rendered their communications' systems inoperative, should they regain mechanical consciousness somehow. B.O.B. now carried their weapons.

'How long before they start searching for those two?'

B.O.B. considered. 'That depends on their duty schedule. They function round the clock save for one fifteen-minute maintenance check-up per day.'

'What about periodic reporting in to some central security station?'

'I don't know.' B.O.B. sounded helpless. 'That's not the sort of information provided to a clerical robot. If they do send such reports, they could be due any time.'

'Then we have to move fast. I'd rather not risk provoking any more sentries, but we can't take the time to be diplomatic.' He gestured back at the bulky desk concealing the incapacitated robots. 'Those two may already have been missed ...'

'... and so if he neglected his duty to the bureaucracy it was to perform a higher duty,' Durant was arguing strenuously

'I ask you once more, do you have any facts to support your macabre speculations? Granted the man's an eccentric as well as a genius, but he's not the mad scientist of some second-rate horror play. He's willing and eager to share his knowledge with us.'

'So?' Holland continued to worry about Durant. His defence and praise of Reinhardt had turned from lavish to slavish.

'So I won't allow you to rush us off this ship, Dan.'

'And I won't give you any more time to see the light, Alex. We're leaving. All of us, together.'

Durant stared back at him. 'That's really up to Dr Reinhardt, isn't it?'

No one had noticed McCrae. She was standing more than silently off to one side of the table. She was not withdrawn, nor was she daydreaming. She was working. The others continued to debate with facts, argue without knowledge.

'Dan . . .'

Holland barely heard the ethereal murmur, but he recognised that tone of voice instantly. Recognised also the faraway look on her face. So did Pizer, and Booth, and Durant. Conversation ceased.

'What is it, Kate?'

'V.I.N.Cent wants you to meet him in the reception lounge near the *Palomino* right away. Also Mr Pizer.'

Holland was already heading for the dining room door. To his relief, he found it unlocked. 'Let's go, Charlie.'

Downing the last sip of wine in his goblet, Booth rose from his seat. 'I think I'll tag along, if you don't mind.'

They located the elevator leading downward. As he emerged into a familiar corridor, Holland put out a restraining arm, then edged back into the elevator cab to join his colleagues.

'What's the trouble?' Pizer whispered. By way of reply, Holland gestured with a nod down the corridor. At the far end, they could see Maximillian and the probe pilot disappearing around a far bend.

Booth took a step in their direction, but Holland moved out to block his path. 'Now, now, Harry. That's not our party.'

'But the probe pilot,' Booth protested. 'If he's been to the vent horizon and succeeded in returning it means . . '

139

'To us it means nothing. Not now. Let's move.' Booth hesitated an instant, then nodded. They hurried towards the cylindrical tubeway and the air cars that could carry them quickly to the *Palomino* ...

V.I.N.Cent was actually aware of the weight of the laser weapons in his hands, but he kept them down. The sentry robots searching the nearby rooms were now moving away instead of towards him.

'Let's hope they continue searching in the wrong direction,' he said to old B.O.B. Both robots moved out of the concealing alcove and jetted up the corridor.

Most of his audience had departed, but Durant was still full of words and arguments. McCrae had to bear the force of them alone.

'He stands to accomplish,' her wide-eyed colleague was saying as he stared out the viewport at the black hole, 'one of the final discoveries that has so far eluded mankind. Our knowledge of stellar physics has grown tremendously in the past couple of centuries, Kate. Yet we still know nothing about the processes at work inside the event horizon of a black hole. We know little more than the first discoverers of the phenomenon. Reinhardt stands to fill in that blank in our knowledge.'

'Or die in the attempt,' said McCrae drily. She paused a moment, regarded her friend with a mixture of concern and contempt. 'I'm beginning to think you really do want to go with him, Alex. Do you want to die that badly?'

'It's not a question of dying.'

'That's what Reinhardt kept saying. Alex, I like to think I'm as professional and curious as the next scientist. But when curiosity swamps your natural sense of self-preservation, there's something addled in your mental clock.'

Durant hardly seemed to hear her, enraptured as he was by the sight of the black hole and the vision of exploring its innermost secrets that Reinhardt had conjured up for them 'It could be the most fantastic achievement since the dawn o creation,' he muttered, with fine lack of perspective. 'Eric the Red, Columbus, Armstrong, Kinoyoshi ... we could eclips them all.'

The door opened and he broke off as Reinhardt entered. The commander of the *Cygnus* quickly surveyed the room, spoke to McCrae.

'Where are the others?'

She saw no reason to lie. He might already know, and be testing her. 'Called back to our ship.'

For an instant Reinhardt seemed confused. 'There was no means of communica . . . ah, yes. The esp-link you share with the robot. Extraordinary. A technique which was developed after I left Earth. It was only a matter of time before biophysics matched the strides made by its inorganic counterparts. What seems to be wrong, for your companions to be called away from their meal?'

She shook her head. V.I.N.Cent didn't spell it out. Something having to do with the repairs, I'd guess. When you're working on something as sensitive as the atmospheric regeneration system, using makeshift spare parts, you've got to expect some trouble. It's the kind of repair work that ought to be done in an orbital yard, by qualified technicians. I'm not surprised they're having difficulties.'

'Let's hope they're solved quickly,' Reinhardt said. 'We are almost ready to embark on mankind's greatest journey of exploration. I'd rather not be delayed.'

Greatest, perhaps, she thought. Riskiest for certain. She turned her gaze to the viewport.

Reinhardt noted the look. 'The danger is incidental when measured against the possibility of being the first to possess the great truths of the unknown. To learn perhaps the secret of mankind's oldest dream.'

'What truth are you pursuing inside the black hole, Doctor?' She frowned at him. 'You seem to have something specific in mind. Does the bear actually have some idea of what he hopes to find on the other side of the mountain?'

He smiled back at her. 'Beyond the mountains, my dear. Beyond is a new beginning . . . a universe that may be suspended in time, where long-cherished laws of nature do not apply.'

'You live by the laws of nature. What if these prove inhospitable?'

'I can learn to master new ones. I am prepared to cope with whatever I may discover. Especially if I find what I hope to find.'

'Which is?' asked Durant expectantly.

141

'Eternal life. You know that time slows the nearer one travels to the core of a black hole, that seconds inside the event horizon can equal years on Earth?'

'I see where you're leading, Doctor.' McCrae tried to give the fantastic theory dispassionate consideration. 'True, you could live forty years in the hole while a millennium passes on Earth, but the forty years would still be only forty years ... to you. It would not extend your real lifetime.'

'That is near the centre of the hole, my dear. Once through the hole I believe I may emerge into a universe indifferent to what we call normal time, where those forty years will extend indefinitely. They may become four hundred years, or four thousand. There may be no upper limit if the aging process is effectively arrested. Life forever.'

'With no possibility of death?'

'Doesn't that interest you?'

'I find the prospect appalling.'

Reinhardt chose not to reply to that and regarded her with what seemed a certain sadness.

Holland and his companions stood nervously in the reception room, listening while old B.O.B. poured out a longer version of the tale of deception and murder he had earlier related to V.I.N.Cent. Occasionally Pizer or Booth would interrupt the older machine's story with a question. For the most part they listened in horrified silence. V.I.N.Cent hovered nearby, his attention focused on the doorway leading back into the maze of corridors.

'. . . and the officer the men trusted most was Frank McCrae, because he was a ship's officer as well as a scientist,' B.O.B. was saying.

'Kate's father.' Pizer was fuming.

'They turned to him when Dr Reinhardt ignored the orders to return home. They were prepared to take control of the *Cygnus.* That was when Dr Reinhardt unleashed his carefully prepared own takeover, using the reprogrammed robots. He rationalised his actions by accusing the rest of the crew of planning to mutiny. A mutiny against science, he called it, science and Reinhardt having become one and the same to his own mind.

'Dr McCrae was killed early in the struggle. The sentr

robots operating solely at Dr Reinhardt's discretion quickly finished the others. The rebellion was soon over.'

Holland stood quietly with the others for a while, finally asked the question he was afraid he already knew the answer to, 'What became of the rest of the crew?'

'The survivors are still on board.'

'Where?' wondered Pizer. 'Are they being held prisoners somewhere? That funeral Dan saw . . .'

'No, Mr Pizer. At least, their bodies are not imprisoned. You have seen them yourself, in the command tower, running the power centres . . .

The first officer looked uncertain, unwilling to make the final mental connection.

'Robots, Mr Pizer,' V.I.N.Cent spoke brusquely, 'humanoid robots.'

'The most valuable thing in the universe, intelligent life, means nothing to Dr Reinhardt,' B.O.B. went on remorselessly. 'To him, intelligence proves itself worthwhile only when it subordinates other interests to those of the greater good. By greater good, he came to believe it meant his personal interests and desires.

'The *Cygnus* contains an elaborate surgery. Once it served to repair . . . to cure, sick humans. Now it has been modified to programme human beings to act like robots. They actually retain less individuality than such mechanicals as V.I.N.Cent and myself.

'Without their "wills", the crew became things Reinhardt could command. To me they are neither machine nor man anymore, and less than either.'

Pizer looked sick. Holland turned to face the attentive reporter. 'That explains the funeral I barged into and the limping robot you saw. I was right about the object I watched being ejected from the ship. It was human. But so were the robot pall-bearers.'

'You mean there's a human body in those things?' Booth looked stunned. 'I thought it was just that Reinhardt was trying to make his robots as human as possible. I didn't think, didn't imagine it was the other way around.'

'None of us did, Mr Booth,' said V.I.N.Cent. 'Yet old B.O.B. is telling only the truth. I myself saw the surgery in operation.'

Holland searched for something on which to vent his

anger, something to break. He was frustrated by the sight of only seamless metal and unbreakable plastics.

'We can't just take off and leave those poor devils behind.' He continued to eye the reporter. 'It looks like we'll have to try your plan to take over the *Cygnus* after all, Harry.'

It was comfortably cool in the reception area, but the reporter had suddenly begun to sweat. 'And risk ending up like the crew? If they couldn't pull it off, what chance do we have?'

'What about our being "heroes", Harry?' Pizer was taunting him. 'Changed your mind mighty fast.'

'Lay off, Charlie. I didn't think we'd have to fight a setup like this. I didn't know Reinhardt had managed to overcome the whole crew. I thought they'd abandoned ship, like he told us. Taking on one man and one robot, okay, but not a programmed army. Robots set to guard are one thing. Murder's another.'

'Captain,' B.O.B. said gently, 'you would not be doing them a favour by returning them to Earth. The damage to their minds is irreversible. From what I have been able to observe and comprehend of the surgical process it is possible their ability to respond individually might be restored, but they would be as mindless as new-born infants. Death is their only release.'

'For God's sake, Dan,' Booth protested, 'be sensible about this. We can't take on every robot on the ship. They already overcame a crew familiar with it. We wouldn't have a chance.' He shuddered. 'We might even be taken alive.'

'Regardless of results,' said V.I.N.Cent, 'events have been set in motion which require that we act quickly, no matter the course we finally decide upon.'

'What events, V.I.N.Cent?' Holland asked him.

'I was forced to destroy two of the sentry robots. They discovered us while we were inside the surgery. Their counterparts are possibly searching the ship now. If the two I destroyed are found . . . The humanoid surgeons did not react to our presence, but it seems unlikely they did not record our appearance. If it is learned that we, and therefore through us you, know of the surgery and its function . . .'

Holland interrupted the robot. He had heard enough. 'Reinhardt couldn't let us return to Earth. Charlie, get aboard the *Palomino* and prepare for liftoff. V.I.N.Cent, get in touch with Kate and tell her I want her and Alex back here, ready to leave, on the double.'

V.I.N.Cent's lights twinkled in a particular pattern as they hurried towards the *Palomino*, indications that the esp-link was being engaged. Pizer hurried on ahead of him. And Booth . . . Booth let out a relieved sigh that his initially daring but now obviously foolhardy plan had been rejected.

As a reporter he had had occasion to live the life of the people he'd been documenting. He did not, however, wish to sample the existence of a member of the *Cygnus*' altered crew.

Within the command tower, Durant and McCrae looked on as Reinhardt guided the mechanicals there through various preparatory tasks.

'Lock in navigation on pre-programmed final course. Commence auxiliary inspection, all systems.'

McCrae was standing before the vast screen on which the three-dimensional image of the black hole was being projected. The gravitational maelstrom teased her scientific self. Emotionally, it terrified her.

Meanwhile Durant had strolled over to stand closer to Reinhardt. 'You've achieved all this on your own, Dr Reinhardt. You'd have every right to reserve your coming expedition to yourself, to reject the request of a johnny-come-lately.'

'In quest of Eternal Youth, Alex?' It was hard to tell if the commander was mocking him, but by now Durant was so far gone with worshipful admiration that he wouldn't have cared anyway.

'Scientific truth, Doctor.'

'Alex . . .' Reinhardt had been about to respond when McCrae's voice drew their attention. She stared blankly past them. 'Dan wants us back on board. They're ready to lift off.'

The commander eyed her speculatively for a moment, then turned back to his mechanical servants. 'Prepare engines. Stand-by to build for maximum thrust. Commence maximum expansion of the null-gee field.' Then, more loudly, 'Maximillian!'

Instantly the huge mechanical joined them, floating out from nearby shadows.

*

Within the cockpit of the *Palomino*, V.I.N.Cent and Pizer finished checking out the ship's systems. Holland and Booth soon joined them.

'How are your readings?' Pizer asked his companion.

'All systems are go,' the robot replied. 'Air regeneration is now working perfectly. Looks good.'

'Damn it, Dan,' Booth was arguing as they entered the cockpit, 'if we wait for Alex we may be too late. I've seen the look in his eyes before, believe me. He's been hypnotised by that man. He's not one of us anymore. He's become an acolyte.'

Holland considered, then spoke to the robot. 'V.I.N.Cent, tell Kate I want her back here fast . . . with or without Alex.'

'What if she objects, sir?'

Holland's teeth were clenched as he spoke. 'Then tell her *why* I want her back . . .'

ELEVEN

McCRAE continued to remonstrate with Durant. 'Alex, you can't throw your life away. 'You're a respected scientist, a good research man. You've got discoveries of your own ahead of you. Discoveries that will mean something, because you'll be alive to expound on them.' She was pleading desperately with him now. 'Don't throw all that away. Let him go if he wants to, but you . . .'

'He can do it, Kate,' Durant countered excitedly, blindly. 'I know he can. There's a whole new universe beyond the black hole. A point where time and space as we know it no longer exist. We'll be the first to experience it, see it . . . the first to explore it.' He turned away from her, his attention going back to the shifting images on multiple screens, smothered by the feeling that Great Things were about to happen.

It didn't matter. Kate was no longer listening to him anyway. A look of utter horror transformed her visage as V.I.N.Cent's hurried but graphic description of his own little discovery resounded in her brain.

'Initiate Cygnus Process,' Reinhardt was saying. 'Commence generation sequence . . .'

At the far end of the ship the order was received by humanoid technicians. Adjustments were made to controls and instrumentation. Eight enormous, drastically modified engines began to glow softly, taming the annihilation beginning within. The aura that appeared around each engine was a radiant side effect of the Cygnus Process. The halo of power.

Aboard the *Palomino* they could neither hear Reinhardt's commands nor witness his directives being carried out, but they could feel the results. A subtle vibration shook the cockpit, communicated from the skin of the *Cygnus*.

There was a moment's silence as each man absorbed the import of that vibration as their bodies absorbed the actuality of it. Then Booth began looking around wildly, like a man seeking some miraculous trans-temporal means of escape.

'He's going to do it! The crazy fool really means to do it. He'll kill us all if you don't get us out of here now, Dan. We've got to pull clear while there's still . . .'

'Take it easy, Harry,' Holland ordered tautly. 'He wants us free to monitor his flight into the hole. We've still got time.'

'He may have changed his mind. He may want to take us all down with him, to prove just how insane he is. You're gambling with our lives, and the odds are going up every second you hesitate.'

'Harry . . . shut up.'

Someone besides the men on the *Palomino* was aware that the time for discussion had ended. The time for decision-making had arrived, and was passing all too quickly.

Kate McCrae emerged from the fog of mind-to-machine contact. She blinked twice, then spoke with quiet finality to the man who was no longer her colleague. 'Alex, we've got to get back to the ship. Now. They're preparing to leave. Dan can't wait for us much longer.'

'I'm staying.' Durant's tone left no room for argument.

She still held one weapon she hadn't used. She employed it now. 'You don't understand, Alex. Reinhardt's a murderer . . . and worse. Those . . . creatures over there, the one monitoring all the instruments and flight consoles, the aren't humanoid. They're human. Or they were once.'

A crack appeared in Durant's surety. 'I don't follow you Kate.'

'Use your head, Alex. I know you've got one. They' what's left of the original human crew. They've been su gically altered on Reinhardt's orders to obey only his cor mands. Their wills, their humanity, have been destroyed.'

'I . . . I don't believe . . .'

McCrae pressed her attack. 'It's true, Alex,' she continue trying to keep an eye on Reinhardt at the same tin V.I.N.Cent and an old supply roboclerk saw the surgery. Y remember Dan's story about the funeral, and Harry's about the robot with the limp?'

'No ... I ...' Durant spun away from her, gods and decisions crumbling around him in the face of the unbelievable.

Could V.I.N.Cent be mistaken? Booth, sure. Dan, maybe. But a mechanical as reliable as V.I.N.Cent, one trained to observe and report only facts? V.I.N.Cent disliked Reinhardt. Could that be enough reason for a machine as facile and advanced as V.I.N.Cent deliberately to fabricate ...?

It couldn't be true. It couldn't!

Reinhardt must have noticed something amiss because he was walking towards them now, his gaze trained not on Durant but on McCrae.

'What's wrong, Dr McCrae?' He was staring intently at her. 'You look ill.'

Durant was fighting to organise his thoughts, to make sense from chaos. I need time, he thought frantically. Time to think this through. But there is no time.

'Kate's upset that I've elected to go with you,' he said hurriedly, covering for her.

'I'm afraid she's also going to join us,' Reinhardt informed them calmly.

'*No!*' She took a step away from them both.

Reinhardt regarded her with a mixture of compassion and an icy resolution his previous declamations had only hinted at.

'The optimum conditions for entering the black hole exist *now*. Everything is functioning perfectly. With your presence a new opportunity presents itself. You see, my dear, your esp-link will insure that news of our success gets back to the *Palomino* via the robot you are in mind contact with, and thence to the world. You will be helping to complete the mission your father gave his life for. A rare honour.

'Your friends will leave shortly, to save their own lives, not realising they are following my plan for them.'

'What you say about my father's not true!' she burst out.

Reinhardt sighed. There was much to do. He had no time for this. Silly woman. Like all the rest of them she could see no further than the pitiful span of her own life. She didn't realise that measured against the opportunity of unlocking the secrets of the universe a life was nothing. Nothing! It seemed that she and her friends had learned everything.

There was no longer any reason for the masquerade he'd been conducting.

Durant began edging unobtrusively towards the nearest console. The figures there ignored him, intent on their respective duties.

'My father was a loyal and honourable man,' McCrae was saying, refusing to be intimidated. 'He would never have condoned the abandonment of this ship so long as her life-support systems functioned.'

'I say he did.'

Durant now stood poised next to a humanoid operating a portion of the complex drive-to-direction instrumentation. Still the figure ignored him. Durant put a hand over the reflective, parabolic face shield, waited for the mechanical to object. It did not. He pulled the shield off.

A face that had once been human continued to take no notice of him, continued to stare only at the controls it had been programmed to watch. Eyes that were smaller versions of the face mask itself stared dully out at a barely perceived world. They hinted only at the void behind them.

Durant's mouth dropped open and he began backing away, gaping in disgust at the thing that had once been a man, a man with hopes and loves and hates just like himself. A man who had been drained of his humanness as thoroughly as a bottle is drained of its contents. Only the empty shell remained behind, refilled with the dank, noisome syrup of blind obeisance to Reinhardt.

'You might as well let me go join my friends.' McCrae continued to speak with more confidence than she felt. 'I won't send any messages for you, whether you're successful or not.'

'I'm sorry to hear you say that, my dear, but I have no time to argue with you. I would have preferred your co-operation. Perhaps it's better we work another way.' He glanced to his right, spoke with regret. 'Maximillian, see that the young lady receives appropriate medical treatment immediately.'

There was a hum that rose above the susurration of power flowing through the ship as the massive robot moved towards McCrae. She looked in disbelief at the nearing machine, realising instantly what was in store for her.

'No . . . you can't . . .' Don't stand there pleading like an idiot child, she told herself frantically. He's already altered – the word came hard in the face of her personal involvement – most of the ship's crew. Why should he hesitate to stop at you?

'Let her go!' Durant made a sudden, wild charge for Reinhardt. He never reached him. A burst of bright, deadly light from one of Maximillian's lasers drilled him as neatly as any knife.

Reinhardt allowed himself a disappointed glance at the scientist's prone form. 'I'm sorry for you, Dr Durant. I had hopes for a while that you might . . . but I expected too much of you. A pity you could not rise above your primitive self. I would have enjoyed your companionship.'

'If there's any justice at all,' McCrae said viciously, 'that black hole will be your grave, Reinhardt.'

'We are dealing here only with the laws of physics, my dear. Not with the arbitrary social contracts *man* calls law. If I perish it will be only a matter of physics, not the other. And you will die with me . . .'

Holland's hand paused, hovered over a control as Reinhardt's voice suddenly issued from the console speaker.

'You are cleared for liftoff, Captain Holland. I will allow you ample time to clear the *Cygnus*' null-gee field, but you must aim to achieve sufficient escape velocity immediately. Doctors Durant and McCrae have elected to remain on the *Cygnus* to participate in the great experiment. They wish you and your friends well.'

'I told you,' Booth said knowingly. 'Alex has bought Reinhardt's theory completely. He's as thoroughly under that madman's control as if he'd been surgically fixed like the others.'

'Maybe he has,' Holland countered, 'but Kate wouldn't.' Of one mind, they all turned to V.I.N.Cent.

'Dr Durant's opinions are no longer of concern. He is dead. Maximillian killed him as he was rushing at Dr Reinhardt. They're taking Dr Kate to the hospital.'

Holland was on his feet instantly. Reinhardt's intentions were as clear to him and the others as they'd been to McCrae herself.

'Get Old B.O.B. to show us the fastest way there. Harry, you stay here and watch the ship. Don't let anything aboard until we get back.' Booth nodded, seemed about to say something, but decided not to.

Pizer made a move to leave. 'Sorry, Charlie,' said Holland. 'You're staying too.'

'What?' Pizer looked back at him in confusion. 'You'll need all the firepower you can get.'

'We may have enough time to reach her. And we may not. It's important to let the people back home know what's happened out here. Harry can't pilot the ship. Don't wait too long, Charlie. Get her off before the gravity outside the *Cygnus*' field becomes too strong.'

'But Dan...'

'That's an order.'

'I wish you a safe voyage home, Mr Pizer.' V.I.N.Cent swivelled to leave the cockpit.

'Just make sure you get back aboard and in one piece, Heart of Steel. Then we can wish each other a safe voyage home.'

Holland followed the two robots back through the *Palomino* towards the tube connecting them with the *Cygnus*.

In the power centre, humanoid figures waited patiently at their stations. They had no need of a superior officer to direct them, as one had in the early days of the ship. All responded now only to one man's orders, and they responded in unison, extensions of his own hands and mind. The glow from the engines in the huge chamber below them intensified. It gleamed from their polished, featureless faces.

'Engage thrusters,' came Reinhardt's command, 'slow at first. Constant monitor on delivery systems.'

The crew of almost-men responded smoothly, efficiently. Outside, the section of space astern of the *Cygnus* assumed the aspect of a small sun. The expanding rush of intense light only hinted at the application of power to come.

Slowly the *Cygnus* began to move, distorting space around her in ways Einstein only hinted at, for a purpose he could not have imagined.

The reception area was deserted when Holland and the robots reached it. By keeping their weapons out of sight they avoided activating the hidden defence system that had disarmed them on their first venture into the great vessel. Old Bob, his repellers whining in protest, started off at high speed for the nearest elevator.

Meanwhile, McCrae was fighting not to think of what awaited her as the compact air car transported her and her silent mechanical escort down the corridor. She tried instead to console herself with the knowledge that Dan and the others would probably escape. She tried very hard, but she still wanted very much to scream.

The air car hissed to a halt and the sentries motioned her out. They walked down several corridors, turned a number of corners. As they entered a small anteroom that might once have been a reception area she noticed several other sentries dragging bits and pieces of two no-longer-intact robots out from behind a desk. One of the guards moved to a wall communicator, pushed the button located there.

The alarm irritated Reinhardt. All his life he'd been bothered by the instrusion of trivia. So he would not allow himself to become concerned even after he saw the two destroyed sentries. The thought of a rescue directed towards McCrae had seemed out of the question. That was changed, now that it appeared the others knew the location of the only operative surgery.

Until now he'd known only that the others were aware of his manipulation of the crew. The fact that they knew where the manipulations were carried out might induce them to try something foolish. Interference at this stage was intolerable, could not be permitted. He required the use of a compliant Dr McCrae immediately. It would be best to take precautions.

'The time has come to liquidate our guests, except for their robot and Dr McCrae. If they succeed in boarding the *Cygnus*, the others are to be eliminated. Do not damage their ship.'

Maximillian turned obediently and started for the near console, composing the orders he would issue to the sentries.

Buzzers sounded and echoed down every passageway. The little knot of machines and man slowed.

'Could Reinhardt know we're on board already?' Holland mused aloud.

'I do not think so.' V.I.N.Cent was searching attentively both ahead and behind them. 'But he has evidently decided we may try to rescue Dr Kate.'

Nearby, Old B.O.B. fluttered unsteadily on his repellers. They sounded dangerously close to grid failure. 'I knew we should have dragged those sentries you shot and hidden them somewhere else.'

'If you recall,' V.I.N.Cent reminded him, 'we did not have the time. The two of us dragging a pair of exploded mechanicals around with us would also likely have drawn more attention than we did.'

He looked back at Holland. 'It seems indisputable that Reinhardt now knows we are aware of the location of his abattoir.'

'And suspects we'll head there. He's right, but we've no time for subtlety.' Holland led them up the corridor.

Six sentries rushed down a passage. None save one thought to glance into the narrow service accessway leading off to one side, and he sensed only shadows within.

When they had vanished around the far turn, V.I.N.Cent leaned out, checked both directions.

'Clear,' he informed his companions. Holland followed him as they dashed across the corridor, making for another which Old B.O.B. insisted interconnected with the one leading to the surgery.

After a while Holland slowed, waited for Old B.O.B. to catch up. He had fallen behind twice already, his internal engines inadequate to the demands of continued speed. 'I wish he could move a little faster,' he murmured sympathetically. 'I know he's doing his best, but . . .'

'We have to wait for him.' V.I.N.Cent turned small circles impatiently. 'I could retrace my original path to the surgery, but that would take us through heavily travelled sections of the ship. The fact that we have encountered and had to avoid only a single party of sentries so far is indication enough that Bob can lead us there not only more quickly but with less danger of confrontation with Reinhardt's stooges.'

'I know, I know.' Holland suddenly frowned, eyed his mechanical associate curiously. 'You're not addressing him as *Dr* Reinhardt anymore?'

'He doesn't deserve the title anymore,' replied V.I.N.Cent matter-of-factly

B.O.B. finally rejoined them. They hurried on, matching their pace to his with as much patience as they could.

It seemed as if the *Cygnus'* instruments themselves ha

acquired an eerie form of electronic sentience. Everything on the bridge was aglow as if aware of what they were about to encounter. Their humanoid operators showed no hint of excitement.

Reinhardt's attention was fixed on the image of the rotating black hole. Maximillian had finished issuing orders to the sentries, now stood at his regular place before the command console.

'Bring us about, Maximillian. Line us up with navigation. Engine room, I want reaction-stability reports on each engine every sixty seconds.'

Slowly the great ship began to pivot, aligning itself with the distant maelstrom. Gravity twisted around it, and its engines commenced to toy with the fabric of space.

As the *Cygnus* turned, the *Palomino* shifted. Booth instinctively put out both hands to steady himself. 'We're moving. That madman's taking her into the hole for sure.' He looked to Pizer. 'What do we do?'

'We wait.' The first officer's gaze was focused on the external optical monitor currently peering down the umbilical connecting them to the *Cygnus*. Only the dim circle of light from the distant reception room showed on the screen.

The sentries handled McCrae forcefully but with care as they pushed her towards the circular operating platform. Apparently Reinhardt's instructions had been explicit: control her, but don't hurt her. *Don't damage the goods*, she thought furiously. Her anger helped moderate the terror that threatened to overcome her.

She tried to analyse the operating theatre as the machines efficiently strapped her into one of the moulded recesses. The multihued lighting felt harsh on her eyes. Probably it did not trouble the surgeons that were not-men. Two of them stood silently nearby, waiting for their next subject to be properly secured.

Surely they would apply some form of anesthesia before they began work. Surely.

Overhead she recognised the fairly standard assortment of narrow-beam, high-intensity lasers. They were capable of cutting flesh or bone to within microscopic tolerances. Nearby were lengths of thin tubing for supplying or draining organic fluids, as might be required, and other instruments for inserting various artificial devices.

She was so familiar with the arrangement because she had lain on a similar table once before. Idly she wondered if the size of the module to be inserted into her brain was larger or smaller than the esp-link already there. She also wondered how much of herself would have to be removed. Or disconnected.

At least she no longer worried about screaming. She was too frightened.

'We're coming, Dr Kate,' a familiar voice said comfortingly inside her head.

'V.I.N.Cent . . . hurry . . . please . . .' She could not allow herself the luxury of lapsing into hysteria. That would foil esp-link communication.

Lights came on in the instrument-laden dome overhead. Anesthesia, she thought frantically. Please . . . I'm still conscious! She was being rotated towards the deceptively dull cluster of lights.

Please . . .

The lights vanished, subsumed in a series of far more intense flares. She turned her head away as cooling but still hot bits of metal and plastic rained down around her. Looking back the other way she saw Holland. He was standing in the doorway, flanked by two hovering machines. A crazy-quilt of energy beams flashed from their weapons. An occasional opposing beam scored walls or floor around them.

'B.O.B., stop that thing and get her out of here! We'll cover you.'

Holland ran right, V.I.N.Cent the other way, firing at anything that moved and trying to dodge the counter shots of the surprised sentries in the room. Pieces of wall and machinery were flying in all directions. The noise from exploding components and torn alloy was deafening.

Still waiting for their instrumentation to respond to their instructions, the two humanoid surgeons stood dully nearby. Then one turned and reached to activate the nearby wall communicator. Holland and V.I.N.Cent noticed the movement at the same time. Two beams struck the surgeon in tandem. What was left of him tumbled into another sentry, throwing it off-balance and knocking it backwards; it fell beneath several of the now malfunctioning surgical lasers towards which McCrae was still drifting.

'Stand aside, Bob.' Holland took careful aim at the dangerously erratic mechanism and fired several times, making sure it was rendered completely inoperative. Bob then hurried to free McCrae, but sensed nearby motion of a belligerent nature and called out.

'Behind you, Mr Holland!'

The captain whirled as three sentry robots crashed through the doorway recently vacated by the invaders. Before Holland could fire, V.I.N.Cent popped up unexpectedly from behind a bulky storage cylinder blocking the path inwards. Three arms extended piston-like. Partially decapitated, the three sentries collapsed on the deck.

Holland turned his attention to McCrae. B.O.B. was helping her off the platform. 'You all right?'

She nodded, managed a sickly smile. 'I'll be better when we're back aboard the *Palomino*.' Wordlessly, he handed her a weapon and considered what to do next. It was unthinkable that Reinhardt would permit them to return to their ship with McCrae. He wanted her too much.

Aboard the *Palomino* Pizer was wishing he had a certain neck under his fingers when the console buzzed for attention. 'Dan . . . that you?'

'You're receiving us?'

'Loud and clear. What's happened?'

'Kate's okay. We're on our way back.'

'What about pursuit?'

'Scrap behind us, so far nothing in front of us. Hope it stays that way. Out.'

'*Palomino* out.' He leaned back in his seat, relieved.

Booth was not. He was worriedly studying his wrist chronometer. 'They're cutting it close. We're running out of time. Reinhardt's going to have to engage his primary drive pretty soon. Then it'll be too late for us to break clear.'

'He wants us, and V.I.N.Cent, free to monitor his dive. Remember?'

'We've caused him a lot of trouble, Charlie. I know his type. Before long he's going to decide Kate's not worth the trouble. Then we'll all be dragged in.'

Several sentry robots arrived and cautiously entered the smoking operating theatre. A door opened and a pair of humanoids appeared, started out past the sentries. The guards ignored them, moved to open another closed door.

Whirling, the larger humanoid blasted the guards with a concealed laser. As soon as the sentries were downed, B.O.B. and V.I.N.Cent emerged from the room about to be searched. They hurried after their disguised companions.

Unfortunately, the section of corridor they were retreating down was one of those covered by remote optical monitors. Having watched the previous action dispassionately, Reinhardt now addressed the huge machine hovering alongside him with equal unconcern.

'Maximillian, tell the sentries to fire on any humanoids between Medical Station and the *Palomino*. Instruct them to aim for the lower limbs. I still want the woman alive, if possible.'

Maximillian hummed a response, communicated with the patrolling sentries far more rapidly and efficiently than Reinhardt could.

Holland and the others entered a main corridor. Waiting sentries immediately opened fire from a far catwalk. The beams just missed the startled Holland. He ducked back into a side passage and joined his companions in returning the fire.

'They're on to us.'

Headgear was removed. McCrae shook hair from her face. 'Well, the costume got us this far.' She threw the reflective face-plate out into the corridor. It drew several shots before it was incinerated. The distraction enabled her to knock one guard off his elevated perch.

Her attention was instantly drawn from the remaining metal figures on the catwalk to movement far behind them. More sentries could be seen entering the distant end of the side passageway.

'Dan, they're behind us.'

Holland took a fast look, made a quick decision as he fired back at the new threat. 'The catwalk. Hop to it. We can't stay here.'

While he and the robots covered, she ran forward, twisting and dodging in an attempt to stay just clear of the sentries' fire. They could react rapidly, but they could not predict. She was careful to keep her movements random.

With the hovering V.I.N.Cent and B.O.B. forcing the sentries to fight a multi-level battle, Holland and McCrae fought their way up the main corridor along the catwalk.

Only their constant movement kept the sentries off-balance, Holland knew. They were functional but not terribly sophisticated machines. As long as Kate and he could keep from being pinned down where the mechanicals' superior firepower could be brought to bear, they had a chance.

V.I.N.Cent and B.O.B. dodged through the air, thoroughly confusing the sentries. Whenever one tried to concentrate on the unpredictable humans, one of the two flying robots would swoop down to destroy it. If they devoted the better part of their fire towards the robots, Holland and McCrae pressed forwards to obliterate them.

The sentries' slowness to make up their minds was further demonstrated when two tried to sight on the wildly diving B.O.B. unit He dodged between them and they promptly shot each other before their circuitry could cancel the directive to fire.

But one managed to singe B.O.B.

McCrae was first to notice the damage. 'V.I.N.Cent! B.O.B.'s hit!' She couldn't devote time herself to make sure the robot was still functional. The sentries kept her too busy.

Then there were no more sentries.

B.O.B.'s flight had become noticeably erratic. V.I.N.Cent drifted over, helped the injured machine slip smoothly towards the floor. There the load on his weakened repellers would be lessened.

Holland made a quick, thorough inspection of the damage. He wished he knew more cybernetics than the minimum that was necessary to command and perform a few basic repairs. Machines as sophisticated as V.I.N.Cent and B.O.B. were supposed to diagnose and direct their own repairs, if not able to perform them themselves.

'How badly are you hurt?' V.I.N.Cent inquired.

'First fighting I've done in thirty years, since I was run through post-manufacture testing. I only wish it had been Reinhardt and Maximillian out there.'

'That's the spirit.' McCrae led the way up the catwalk, Holland right behind. The two robots flanked them. B.O.B. continued to fight to retain his stability.

Within the command tower, a voiceless but clearly angry Maximillian reacted to the failure of the sentries. As if aware they were being monitored, V.I.N.Cent raised an arm and executed a snappy victory signal.

Despite his wishes, Reinhardt found his attention drawn

by the confrontation. He was furious both at the failure to recapture Kate McCrae and at the time he was being forced to devote to so petty a matter.

'Your crack unit outwitted and outfought by some mass-produced Earth model and that antique from storage.' Maximillian pulsed crimson, the strongest form of personal expression permitted him. Reinhardt had taken care not to gift his powerful servant with too much sentience.

He looked back to the image of the black hole, up to scan several read-outs. 'It's a pity about McCrae. But I will not leave them free to spread lies about me. I can't endanger the *Cygnus* by exploding their ship *too* soon. If they succeed in returning to their vessel with Dr McCrae, we'll give them some distance before destroying them.'

They were rushing ahead when Holland suddenly grabbed McCrae and pulled her down. 'Hit the deck! V.I.N.Cent, B.O.B. . . . watch yourselves. More of 'em up ahead.'

Bright arcs of destruction lanced over their heads, flashed around the evasive robots. There was a crude barricade before them. Sentry robots lined its crest, firing inaccurately but threateningly from behind the makeshift bulwark.

Their poor shooting was a comfort, but the one thing Holland had feared most had come to pass – they were prevented from reaching the reception area. It was just beyond the barrier, tantalisingly near.

The sentries' fire might not scorch them, he thought desperately as they rolled for cover, but if they couldn't break through they'd soon be trapped by others coming up from behind. Eventually Reinhardt would concentrate enough firepower to kill them no matter how unsteady the aim of his mechanicals.

He knew they couldn't afford the time to take the long way around. There might not even be a long way around. They *had* to break through ahead.

Somehow . . .

TWELVE

NO one was more aware of the frantic passage of time than the two men who waited nervously in the cockpit of the little research ship.

Booth again checked his chronometer, asked in frustration, 'How much longer are we going to wait? If they can't make it, they can't make it. There's no reason for us to die, too.'

'There's still time, Harry. I'm sure . . .'

Distorted by the nearby crackle of energy weapons, Holland's voice sounded over the console speaker. 'Charlie, do you read me?'

Pizer hurried to reply. 'Loud and clear, Dan,' he lied. The captain had enough to worry about. Pizer could understand him well enough.

'Time's up.' Holland spoke calmly, resignedly. 'Take her clear.'

Pizer thought a moment. 'Where are you?'

'Side corridor,' came the laboured reply. 'Near reception. They've got the passage blocked, though. We can't get through. They've got us pinned down.

'Lift off, Mr Pizer! You know your orders. I haven't got time to argue with you.' A hissing shriek drowned out his final words as a laser beam passed frighteningly close to the communicator grid.

Pizer had known what he would do if such a situation arose. He had known before they'd separated earlier, on the ship. Maybe Holland knew too, he thought. He told himself that was the case, rationalising his incipient actions as fast as possible.

His shipmates were close by. Too close for him to obey orders. He wouldn't mind a court-martial. Not if Holland and V.I.N.Cent were around to give evidence against him. If that was his destiny, why then, he was doomed no matter what he chose to do. So why worry?

Such are the convoluted justifications of the truly brave.

Booth stepped as if to block his way. 'You heard the captain. Orders are to lift clear.'

'You're pretty big on talking heroics, Harry, and on reporting 'em. Let's see some.' Leaving Booth to consider those words, Pizer pushed past the older man. With a muffled curse, the reporter raced after him.

Pizer was out into the reception area before any of the sentries, concentrating on the battle for the passageway, reacted to his unexpected appearance. He leaped to one side and fired as the single guard there brought up his weapons. The machine blew apart as Booth dove for the cover of a desk.

The first officer quickly regained his feet. He was trying to orient himself when the groans reached him.

'Damn...'

'Harry? You hit?' He hunted for the reporter, saw his boots sticking out from behind the desk.

'My leg . . .' Booth was holding it gingerly. He sat up slowly, grimacing with the pain.

'How bad?' asked Pizer, concerned.

'I think it's broken.'

'From laser fire? I didn't think that sentry got off a shot.' As he spoke he was anxiously scanning the large room. The single mechanical had been alone, however.

'No, from idiocy. I took a dive for cover that I shouldn't have.' He touched his lower leg and winced. 'When I was thirty I would've bounced. I'm afraid I'm not as flexible as I used to be, Charlie.'

'Can you walk?' Pizer knew he couldn't help the reporter and the others at the same time.

With Pizer's help Booth got to his feet, put a little weight on the leg. 'The real pain won't hit for a few minutes yet. I can limp, I think.'

'All right. Get back to the ship and take up a good defensive position near the lock. We'll be counting on you to make sure none of 'em get aboard, Harry.'

'Right. Don't worry about that. I'll make sure nothing boards.'

Pizer hurried off towards the nearby scene of action.

directed by the noise of fighting. He rounded a bend, skidded to a halt. Ahead was the barricade and its platoon of shielded mechanicals.

'I'm behind them, Dan,' he whispered into his communicator. 'What's your advice?'

'My advice was to lift clear, Charlie,' came the reply, 'but since you've more guts than brains, use your own judgment. I'm the one who was fool enough to get himself pinned down here.'

Pizer hesitated, thinking, planning. On the other hand, he abruptly decided, long-range planning had never been one of his strong points. From what he'd observed of Reinhardt's sentries, it certainly wasn't among theirs, either.

Confuse them. Don't give them time to react, he told himself.

Jumping out into clear view he charged the barricade. More concerned with creating a diversion than destruction, he fired as rapidly as he could. So closely packed were the sentries behind the wall, however, that his firing was more effective than he'd hoped. It was up to Dan and Kate to realise what was happening and fire carefully in his direction.

At the sound of Pizer's berserker yelp, the robots turned to confront their unexpected new assailant. Holland, McCrae and the two hovering robots charged the barricade simultaneously. Caught in a mental as well as strategic dilemma, the sentries were soon reduced to scrap.

Ignoring the occasional hot sparks that flew from isolated sections of mechanical, Pizer stepped over the heaps of steaming metal. Now that the immediate danger was over, he was a little appalled at his audacity. A good thing that he *hadn't* taken the time to think his actions through.

Holland and the others were already hurrying past him. McCrae grabbed at his arm. 'Come on, Charlie.'

Partway down the access passage they were halted by a call from behind. Old B.O.B. fluttered near a wall. The whine from his repellers was higher now, intermittent.

'You go ahead,' the damaged machine told them. 'I'll stay here and cover you against any fresh pursuit. I can't travel fast enough, and you can't spare the seconds.'

V.I.N.Cent looked to his human companions. 'Captain . . . Mr Pizer?'

Both men holstered their weapons, retracted their steps.

Holland examined the robot, shook his head in frustration. 'We can't carry him . . . he's too heavy for the three of us.'

'That isn't necessary, sir,' said V.I.N.Cent. 'If you and Mr Pizer can give him some support, he can redirect power from his stabiliser repellers to those providing forward drive.'

'Please . . . it's not necess—'

'Shut up,' Holland ordered him. 'If it weren't for you we'd probably all be dead by now.'

Pizer moved to the other side of the hovering machine. Each man slipped his arms beneath B.O.B.'s own, carefully avoiding the repeller grids beneath. They appeared to be carrying him as they started back down the corridor with McCrae and V.I.N.Cent alert for sentries.

Booth's injured leg had apparently undergone healing nothing short of miraculous. Running without any hint of damage he'd rushed back up the umbilical and into the *Palomino*. A quick jab closed the lock door behind him.

The command cockpit was a maze of instrumentation. But most of it was automatic and after eighteen months of spare time he'd managed to thoroughly study the basic controls. They would now provide more than amusement.

As he studied the pilot's console, he fought to recall the answers to the many frivolously asked questions he'd put to Holland. He hesitated only briefly before commencing to programme the ship's systems. A thin smile of satisfaction creased his face when the engines came on. Several critical gauges on the overhead console lit up. He had power. Now all the ship needed was direction, velocity, and its freedom.

Holland and the others staggered into reception. As they reached the open space the two men let go of B.O.B. and moved in opposite directions, to present smaller targets to the anticipated welcoming party of sentries. But reception was deserted. The only sentry present was the one Pizer had obliterated on his emergence from the umbilical.

'Stands to reason,' McCrae was saying, breathing heavily 'Reinhardt can only have so many sentry machines. Some o them would have to be deployed elsewhere on the ship, t insure we couldn't make mischief with, say, the engines Then something made her frown.

Her companions also heard it: the sound of distar engines, louder than those of the *Cygnus*. They rushed t wards the connector passageway.

'What's that idiot trying to do?' Pizer voice reflected his outrage and dismay.

Holland grabbed him, slowed him down. 'It's too late.' He pointed out the nearby port. The umbilical had already disconnected from the *Palomino*, was shrinking in on itself like a worm wriggling back into its hole. They were cut off from their ship.

A moment later the *Palomino* was drifting silently away from them, the sound of its familiar engines having ceased as soon as the umbilical had been dropped. They stood quietly by the port and watched, each lost in his or her private thoughts.

'What a fool I was,' McCrae was muttering. 'If I'd just done what Reinhardt wanted, you'd all be aboard and safely on your way.'

'We're not all Harry Booths, Kate.' Holland smiled thinly at her. 'I'd still have come after you.'

She smiled back, met his questioning stare.

The reverie was interrupted by a shout of surprise from Pizer. 'Look!' They turned from each other, temporarily putting aside but not forgetting, no, never forgetting, the unspoken bond that had formed between them. Time enough for elaboration of that nonverbal exchange later. Time enough . . . if they lived.

The *Palomino* had been climbing steadily away from the *Cygnus*. Now it was changing direction, no longer moving away. It had commenced to arc slowly back towards the *Cygnus*.

In the pilot's chair, Booth fought frantically with the stubborn controls. Steering a sophisticated craft like the *Palomino* was not like driving a personal transport, no matter how many automatics it possessed. Hasty, panicky reactions were apt to be more counterproductive than helpful. Everything Booth did only seemed to exacerbate the problem.

Reinhardt was equally aware of the smaller ship's troubles. It was coming dangerously near the *Cygnus*. 'That ship's out of control. Blow it apart before it hits us. Fire! Quickly, now.' He stared anxiously at the smaller vessel, not caring any longer who might be aboard it.

Laser cannon tracked the tumbling research vessel uncaringly. Silent orders activated automatic rangers. The *Palomino* intersected a predicted point in space. Several

165

energy beams simultaneously struck that intersection. The *Palomino* disintegrated in a brilliant shower of molten metal and torn fragments of self.

One such large fragment was ejected at considerable speed towards the stern of the *Cygnus*. It happened to strike a particularly vulnerable section of the great ship, tearing through sensitive instrumentation. Internal doorlocks slammed shut, trying to isolate the region from which air was escaping. Former members of the *Cygnus*' crew who were caught in the sealed-off areas passed blissfully into death.

The fragment slashed through the port engine control station. Vast energies were left temporarily unbound. Automatic safeties locked down as fast as possible, but they could operate no faster than the electrons flowing through their circuitry.

There was a substantial explosion.

It rocked the whole structure of the *Cygnus*. In reception, everyone except the floating robots grabbed for something stable. Nothing met those requirements, but the ship soon steadied itself. Artificial gravity once again took firm hold of the ship's contents, including the now shipless crew of the vanished *Palomino*.

'Harry . . . oh my God,' McCrae was murmuring. She stared out the port at the rapidly dispersing particles of what had once been their ship – and Harry Booth.

'I shouldn've known he was all talk and no guts and locked him up.' Pizer was feeling somewhat less than regretful at the reporter's sudden, unexpected demise.

'Don't be too hard on him, Charlie.' Holland was trying to think on two matters at once. 'He had reason to think we were the crazy ones, not him. He panicked. Harry reported science, but I don't think he ever really enjoyed or understood it.

'Anyway, he may have done us a favour. Reinhardt might have intended to blow us up anyway. I'm certain he would have tried if we'd managed to get aboard with Kate. Thanks to Harry, we're still alive.'

'And where there's life . . .' V.I.N.Cent began.

Pizer cut him off bitterly. He was in no mood for the robot's humorous homilies. 'He was trying to save his own skin, Dan. Don't make him out to be some sort of martyr.'

'There's a saying, sir,' the unflappable robot went on, 'that you can't unscramble eggs.'

'A penny's worth of philosophy won't buy us out of this.'

'A good offence is the best defence.'

'V.I.N.Cent,' Pizer said in utter exasperation, 'maybe if you took your witticisms and . . .' He stopped, forced himself to consider seriously what the robot was saying. 'You mean, go after Reinhardt and turn the ship around?' He shook his head.

'We wouldn't have a chance. It's one thing to fight our way through corridors to here, but he'd never let us in the control tower. He'd seal himself in, first. By the time we could try something extreme, like donning suits and breaking through the dome, it'd be too late.'

'That was not what I had in mind, Mr Pizer. There is an alternative.'

'I don't follow you.'

Holland, who had also been devoting considerable thought to their seemingly hopeless situation, did.

'The probe ship! The one that's already returned from the event horizon! It's equipped with the same Cygnus Process drive and the same null-gee field. V.I.N.Cent, you're a genius.'

'Yes, sir,' the robot acknowledged modestly. 'It's part of my programming.'

Holland turned on the other waiting mechanical. 'B.O.B., what's the quickest way to the probe dock?'

'Internal air car,' he replied instantly. 'I can programme one to carry us directly to the dock.' He was already starting back up the corridor.

A gaping wound near her stern, the *Cygnus* plunged ahead, accelerating towards the lambent vortex of the black hole. Excited to fluorescence by the storm of radiation pouring out from the event horizon, glowing gases began to fill space around the ship. Angry auroras swarmed around the ports.

Reinhardt was studying the ship's progress when a buzzer demanded his attention. Switching to a rear-facing scanner he studied the view thus presented in silence. Magnification was increased. A swarm of irregular-shaped objects was cutting the course of the ship. Hasty calculations indicated they would overtake the *Cygnus*.

167

'*Meteorites overtaking us. I knew there'd be a lot of cosmic debris sucked in with us but I'd hoped* . . . Maximillian! Bring up the output on the starboard power centre. We still have partial power from two of the four engines on the port side. Double the output on the others. We have to increase our speed.'

Lights flashed across the huge mechanical's chest in a sequence indicating uncertainty and advising caution.

'Do as I say. We must seize the moment, Maximillian.' His eyes were wide, wild. 'Hold our course. We will outrun the debris or ride out any impact.'

Pursued by the soulless components of a planet that never was, the *Cygnus* thundered onward. But she did not gain enough velocity to outrace the tumbling matter that crossed her astern. One jagged chunk of nickel-iron ploughed lazily into the crest of the ship, completely destroying what had been the reception area.

The impact jarred the entire ship. Holland stumbled, struggled to regain his footing. The *whoosh* of escaping air that had sounded momentarily, terrifyingly in his ears was cut off as a lock door slammed tight behind them.

The air car terminus was nearby. They followed B.O.B. into the first of the little vehicles. Holland programmed it according to B.O.B.'s directions. All around the ship, meteorites disintegrated under the increasing gravitational forces, or succumbed to intense internal radiation, or collided with one another and silently exploded. Through the transparent walls of the air car cylinder tube they could view the external destruction and the increasingly disturbed radiation that coloured the vacuum.

Something singed Holland's hair. He looked ahead, to see another air car rushing directly for them. Still programmed to seek out and destroy the intruders, four sentry robots were firing across the rapidly shrinking distance between the two cars.

Under the increasing stress the cylinder itself began bucking and groaning. Holland recalled the flexibility of the null-gee field, wondered if the damage to the ship's engines or the meteorite that had just impacted or perhaps both had done anything to reduce the field's stability. If so, the ship might come apart around them any second.

V.I.N.Cent and B.O.B. returned the fire of the approaching sentries. Seeing that the onrushing vehicle was not about to slow, Holland assumed manual control of their car. He sent them sliding up in a high bank onto the side of the transport tube without reducing speed. The startled sentries raced on past below them.

With a final, sorrowful groan the transport tube buckled, broke. An internal lock slammed down instantly, shutting the tube off from the vacuum outside. The car carrying the sentries continued forward, flying out into space with its occupants still turning to fire.

There was damage ahead as they once more found themselves travelling through the ship. Holland brought the air car to a halt, looked for a break.

'We can't go any farther over this,' he decided. 'We'll have to try walking the main corridor.'

B.O.B. led them away from the car. The main corridor and its catwalks were still intact, but by now walking itself was difficult. It was clear that the null-gee field was oscillating dangerously. One moment the ship sailed calmly onwards, the next the *Cygnus* barely shook free of the increasing gravitational pull. The muffled rumble of distant collisions echoed through the passageway.

They had started down the corridor when a violent shock forced them to halt, struggling just to remain upright. Refugee from some distant corner of space, a flaming ball of matter broke through the ceiling. Its velocity reduced by passage through the *Cygnus*' null-gee field and several intervening decks, it did not continue its progress through the ship. Instead, it struck and bounced, tumbling at high speed towards the little group of temporarily paralysed onlookers.

There being no place to hide, everyone dropped to the deck. Not that it mattered. The glowing metal flew by overhead, annihilated the section of catwalk they'd already traversed, and vanished through a partition.

It was apparently intended by the fates that they should have no time in which to breathe freely before either escaping or perishing. Another laser beam passed close by Pizer. Exhausted, they turned to locate the new threat.

A single sentry was standing in a side corridor, firing at them while reporting into a wall communicator. Holland and the others concentrated their combined fire in its direction and the mechanical was soon shattered. Before or after he'd completed his report, Pizer wondered?

The reception on the screen was jumbled and indistinct,

but clear enough for a furious Reinhardt to see that his guests were still mobile. The picture was so poor he was unable to tell how many of them were left, but the presence of even one antagonist running free aboard the ship during the next critical minutes was not to be tolerated.

'I want them finished this time, Maximillian.' He turned back to his read-outs, cursing the accidental encounter that had reduced the *Cygnus*' power and rendered it vulnerable to the swarm of meteorites. But for them, even the loss of nearly half his power would not have been sufficient to threaten the great experiment.

If the ship suffered further damage to its engines, however, he would lose something far more important than mere speed. The null-gee field would be weakened to the degree that it might no longer be able to protect the *Cygnus* from the immense gravitational strength of the black hole.

Several shards of interstellar flotsam narrowly missed striking the command tower itself. One deep-range sensor antenna was completely torn away. Others struck and damaged the corridors leading to the ship's stern. Another impacted close by the docked probe ship. It leaned precariously, almost breaking free of its cojoining umbilical.

Reinhardt resolutely kept his ship on its predetermined course. In free space the *Cygnus* could have avoided the meteorite swarm easily, by a sharp change of direction. But within the gravitational vortex surrounding the collapsar that was not possible. Furthermore, they were continually being torn apart by the stress, the resultant fragments flying in unpredictable directions.

Holland and B.O.B. led the way as they stumbled into one of the hydroponic stations. Gathering sentries followed close behind, exchanging fire with their tiring quarry.

Pizer heard a ripping sound. There was the sudden *whoosh* of escaping atmosphere. A tiny hole had appeared at the apex of the dome overhead, enough to suck vast quantities of air out into space. Automatic pressure sensors immediately sent fresh air pouring into the area, but the circuitry which should have slammed shut inner doors surrounding the station to seal in the damaged area failed to function. Air continued to scream out into space. Despite the valiant efforts of the temperature compensators, the dome turned dangerously cold.

With the drop in pressure ice began to form in the room. Plates broke, sending frozen bits of plant and hydroponic tubing swirling through the dome, caught in the miniature hurricane pouring upwards through the ceiling puncture.

Old B.O.B. jetted over to McCrae. His repeller units fought to keep him from being drawn upwards.

'Hang onto me!' he yelled. Letting go of the stanchion she was clinging to, she carefully transferred herself to the machine. With B.O.B. battling the wind they drifted across the now frozen surface of the deck towards the far doorway, still jammed open by failed circuits.

Holland and Pizer were also trying to fight their way across. They grabbed at anything still secured to the deck. Frozen missiles that had been alive and green seconds ago whizzed dangerously around them. Only V.I.N.Cent's constant worrying of the pursuing robots enabled the two men to concentrate on making their way safely across the station.

It occurred to V.I.N.Cent that it might be time to take some of his own advice concerning caution. He was battling the oncoming sentries alone, a confrontation that eventually had to prove fatal. Turning, he jetted towards the centre of the dome. At least there he had more room to manoeuvre. The sentries single-mindedly continued their pursuit.

Dodging in random directions, V.I.N.Cent was a difficult target to concentrate on. As he was the only one still offering steady resistance, the sentries directed the majority of their fire at him.

McCrae could feel the strain in the machine carrying her. It would drop half a metre, then struggle back up to its former altitude. The whine from B.O.B.'s repellers grew steadily more erratic. They would plunge almost to nothing before picking up fitfully again.

The temperature in the room continued to fall, placing an added burden on the poorly maintained B.O.B. unit. But they were almost to the beckoning doorway.

She stared at the opening with a mixture of hope and horror. If its damaged emergency module suddenly actuated, the door would slam irrevocably shut. They would be trapped in the dome. She tried to will it to remain open.

Holland blinked against the wind-borne particles, tried to see overhead. The hole in the dome appeared to have widened slightly. The hurricane intensified around them. He could feel the dangerous pull increasing on his body. If he lost his hold he would be helplessly sucked up and out into the void. Radical decompression by exposure to vacuum was a rotten, messy way to die. Despite the growing numbness in his fingers he held tight to the railing, continued to pull himself towards the far doorway.

Pizer was ahead of him, nearly to safety. That left only V.I.N.Cent. The robot should be just behind him.

'V.I.N.Cent! Are you . . . ?'

He'd intended to ask if the mechanical was all right, but a quick glance backward was enough to show that it wasn't. He could see external parts beginning to freeze up. V.I.N.Cent could stand the ultimate cold of empty space, so the frost beginning to coat his shell made no sense. But it was there, no doubt about it.

V.I.N.Cent's evasive hovering slowed. The machine came up close to him, halted. Then the uprushing gale got hold of him, began to draw him up and back.

Holding on with one hand, Holland reached back with a convulsive swipe, barely secured a grip on one of the robot's outstretched arms. His muscles protesting, he pulled the hovering machine slowly down towards him. They started again for the doorway. If he lost his remaining hold on the rail they would both vanish through the hole in the dome before Pizer or McCrae knew they were gone.

Programmed only to follow and destroy, the sentries had begun to cross the open area of the dome station. They slowed. As if time had stopped for them, they began spiralling slowly upwards, helplessly, towards the roof.

Old B.O.B. and McCrae were already standing in the corridor past the lock door. Pizer was next through, having to fight past the wind rushing down the corridor into the dome.

Like a man swimming upstream, Holland somehow managed to get V.I.N.Cent and himself into the passageway. Old B.O.B. immediately fired at the control module housing. The door slammed down. The gale slowed, swirled directionlessly about them. They stamped their feet, tried to warm numbed hands. McCrae wondered about frostbite. She could not feel the tips of her fingers.

It was Pizer who started first down the corridor. 'We can't wait here. If those sentries manage to open that door we'll be blown back into the dome. I couldn't make that crossing again. We've got to get moving, Dan.'

Holland examined the panting, chilled group of humans and machines. V.I.N.Cent was slowly thawing, but the cold had penetrated his metal body deeply. He seemed unable to stagger more than a few centimetres forward before having to stop and rewarm.

'Take B.O.B. and Kate,' he told Pizer. 'We'll catch up.'

McCrae shook her head, spoke tersely. 'No way. We can help him along, take some of the load off his repellers the way we did with B.O.B. until his internal heating unit is back to strength.'

She put her arms around the robot, the cold metal momentarily taking her breath away. Holland did the same opposite her. Between them, they hurried him along.

Behind them, behind the now sealed door, the ceiling of the hydroponic dome finally burst under the pressure. The air rushed as a body out into space, carrying with it frozen bits of plants, shards of console, circuitry and the remnants of the pursuing sentry robots.

'What happened to you in there?' Holland asked the steadily warming robot.

'Had to . . . divert power from heating unit . . . to repellers, to avoid . . . opposing fire. Chill worse than . . . I thought.'

'That wasn't too bright.'

'All safe now . . . all alive, aren't . . . we?'

'We'll discuss it later,' Holland replied curtly. He was angry. Angry at V.I.N.Cent for almost getting himself frozen to electronic death, angry for taking risks that he, Holland, should have been taking.

With V.I.N.Cent's lights flickering unsteadily but with increasing strength the little party of survivors staggered down the passageway, fighting to keep their balance as the ship shuddered around them.

THIRTEEN

REINHARDT glowered helplessly at his instruments ar
ranted at the storm as the *Cygnus* strove to remain inta
under the barrage of meteorites, a great ungainly bin
assailed by a swarm of potentially deadly bees.

A glowing, globular wraith bore down on the commar
tower. Reinhardt saw it, stood transfixed by the inexorab
approach of mass destruction. It just missed the tower itsel
ripped into the superstructure nearby.

The impact sent humanoids tumbling against one anothe
Several fell from the upper level platform to lie still ar
twisted on the deck. Equipment fell from secured places o
the walls, instrumentation snapped loose or winked out.

'Alert all stations for emergency running. Maximillia:
programme the probe. We may have to use it.' He studie
the main screen. A tribute to its designers and builders,
still functioned enough though the concussion had knocke
it askew. Read-outs set alongside another, smaller scree
offered the only good news. The last of the meteorites ha
swept past the *Cygnus*. There would be no more collisions.

He tested various controls, demanded information. Th
four undamaged engines were still pulsing smoothly, as we
the two still partially functional. Most of the remainir
damage had been to the ship's midsection: heart-rendin
but not fatal. He still had ample power and a measure o
control. But the read-outs were full of warnings of section
so badly battered they might fail at any time.

It did not matter now. It was too late to change mind o
direction, even were he so inclined. Both he and the *Cygn*
were committed.

The sudden silence and comparative stability of the dec

underfoot was almost as frightening as the storm had been. The little group turned a corner. The corridor beyond was completely blocked by metal wreckage. Holland inspected it closely.

'Can't see through. No telling how dense it is. Even if we had the capability we don't have the time to burn our way through.'

McCrae was still waiting for the ceiling to come crashing down on them. 'It's over. The storm is over.'

'Is there another way out, B.O.B.? Another way that could take us around towards the probe's dock?'

The mechanical turned, moved to a sealed doorway and extended a portion of one arm. It fitted into a matching receptacle set alongside the door. The metal panel slid aside and they found themselves in an alcove directly over the damaged power centre.

There was atmosphere in the huge chamber. There had to have been or the door wouldn't have opened no matter how insistent Old B.O.B.'s electronic entreaties. No doubt Reinhardt's efficient machines had already repaired the outer hull where the large meteorite had entered, repressurised the chamber, and gone elsewhere to repair more of the extensive damage.

But the repairs had not been perfect. Mixed in with the stale air was another odour McCrae recognised immediately: augmented hydrogen.

'Dan, this entire complex could go up in flames at any minute.'

Holland had also noticed the leakage. He stepped out gingerly onto the maintenance catwalk crossing over the engines and the deck far below. It swayed dangerously under his weight and he moved off.

'Any other way around this, B.O.B.?'

'No, Captain,' came the reply, 'and we certainly can't go back through Agriculture.'

Holland considered a moment. 'Okay. Take Kate across.' She started to protest. 'Now.'

B.O.B. extended his arms. Deciding that time was now more important than principle, McCrae grabbed hold. B.O.B. started off across the open space.

'Charlie, you and V.I.N.Cent are next.'

Pizer shook his head. 'Too much weight.'

V.I.N.Cent already had his limbs extended. 'Nothing ventured, nothing gained, Mr Pizer. Besides, there is no significant difference in weight between you and the captain. I'll travel above the catwalk, just in case.'

Pizer looked unhappy, but took hold of the proffered metal limbs and they started across, following B.O.B. and McCrae. She looked over a shoulder, saw Holland receding behind her and called out to the other, nearing robot.

'Hurry, V.I.N.Cent, you've still got to get back for Dan.'

With the added burden of the humans, neither machine was making much speed. Holland realised he couldn't wait. A chance spark could ignite the drifting hydrogen mixture and turn the chamber into a short-lived but highly realistic little hell.

He started out onto the catwalk. It swayed as before. Moving cautiously forward, he concentrated on maintaining his balance.

'Hold tight, Mr Charlie,' V.I.N.Cent was admonishing his passenger. The first officer was shaking with coughs as the air in the engine chamber became saturated with leaking gases.

Old B.O.B. and McCrae reached the platform on the other side. She let go, stepped clear, and looked back worriedly.

Holland was halfway across when the catwalk finally gave way. Instinctively lurching forward, he clutched at the falling end and swung towards the far side. McCrae screamed.

He turned his back towards the wall, somehow hung on as he slammed into it. The gas was beginning to affect him as it had Pizer, and he started to cough. Reaching up, he tried climbing the broken walkway, slipped, used all his remaining strength just to hang on.

McCrae and Pizer were trying to see down over the edge of the platform through rising, darker gases. Neither had a thought of running for safety.

'Dan!' She shouted without looking across to Pizer. 'I can't see him anymore!' She bent over, coughed violently.

'Get 'em out of here, Charlie!' came Holland's muted order from somewhere below. Both ignored it.

V.I.N.Cent started downwards. 'I think B.O.B. and I can bring him up, Mr Charlie.'

'Go to it, V.I.N.Cent.'

The robots drifted down into the rising gas. McCrae and

176

Pizer managed to open the door leading into the next corridor. Fresh air gusted gently inwards, driving back some of the suffocating miasma.

Carrying the dazed Holland carefully between them, the two machines reappeared moments later. They all started up the corridor. Holland was limping, and blood trickled from the gash over his eyes. McCrae tried to support him, working on the wound at the same time. The wonder of it was that he hadn't broken every bone in his back when he'd slammed into the wall. But then, she reminded herself, he'd always been the resilient type.

Reinhardt had forgotten the damage caused by the meteorite storm, had forgotten the disturbing presence of his only human adversaries. He was standing before the main screen, staring at the burgeoning blackness that expanded to shove fierce radiation to the sides.

Soon they would pass beyond the event horizon. At that moment they would pass beyond the limits of human knowledge. They would then encounter oblivion, or a new universe. Or perhaps, something no man had yet imagined.

'They couldn't stop us,' he murmured aloud. 'We'll make it. To the universe beyond. To my universe . . . and everlasting life.'

But Reinhardt was only a genius. He had plotted and gauged, predicted and planned and anticipated as best as any mere genius could. The difficulty came from the fact that he no longer had the full strength of the *Cygnus* behind him – only slightly more than half.

As the calculations had insisted it would, the null-gee field compacted around the ship. Lacking full power, the field-generation system was weakened. The already incomprehensible gravity it was passing through began to produce noticeable effects.

Instrumentation was shaken. Read-outs grew uncertain. The command tower itself began to vibrate under the stress.

'Increase power,' he directed Maximillian. 'Override the safeties on the starboard engines. We're going to maintain full field strength around us. We're going through.'

Within the crippled starboard power centre, a bit of metal fell from the ceiling. It struck another below, and a slight spark resulted. Suddenly, the vast chamber was filled with flame.

One of the engines, already damaged and unable to cope with heat from without as well as within, imploded. There was a sudden disruption of the field inside the engine which kept the Cygnus Process under control. A minute quantity of matter reacted with an equally minuscule amount of anti-matter before the latter could be field-contained or dispersed spacewards. The resultant explosion blew out the rear section of the centre, jolting the entire ship. Material and gas gushed out into the void.

Elsewhere on the ship, B.O.B. and V.I.N.Cent reeled as the artificial gravity momentarily went berserk. Depending on their position, the three humans were thrown against floor or ceiling or wall. The lights in the corridor winked out.

'Emergency battery system up full.' Reinhardt gave the order as the extent of the damage began to appear on internal monitors.

Light returned to the command tower. It was hesitant, flickering. As the pull of the collapsar began to affect the most massive portion of the *Cygnus* where the field had weakened further, the ship started to drift sideways. This further complicated the efforts of the null-gee generation system to protect it.

Holland helped Pizer to his feet. They ran faster now in the half-light. The walls of the corridor groaned around them.

The first sections of the great ship to feel the intensified effects of the gravitational pull were those already weakened by contact with meteoric debris. Bits of loosened or torn superstructure shuddered, fell away from the exterior. This in turn unhinged the stability of the areas they were a part of.

Shivering dangerously, the command tower remained intact. More and more instrumentation winked out. The consoles themselves threatened to tear free of their wall mountings. Oblivious to the danger, humanoid robots continued to perform their designated tasks.

Reinhardt had come to a painful but irrevocable decision. 'Maximillian, prepare the probe ship. She's not going to hold under this kind of stress, not on half power.' The massive mechanical turned obediently, moved towards the elevator.

Reinhardt paused a moment before following. Slowly he

turned to take a last look at the heart of what had become his private empire of discovery and exploration. Twenty years of his life he had spent lobbying for the construction of the *Cygnus*, another twenty to bring it to this point in space. He would go on, but without it. He would not be cheated of his triumph. His entry into the new universe would only be a little less grand.

Turning, he moved to follow Maximillian. A violent ripping noise made him look up. The overhead screen had torn loose from its braces.

He'd run two steps before something drove a knife into his legs. The screen struck with a resounding *crash*, pinning him to the deck close by the transparent wall of the tower. A brief, exhausting struggle proved he was hopelessly pinioned beneath the edge of the heavy viewer.

'Maximillian, help me!' Another piece of instrumentation fell from above, shattered on the deck nearby. 'Maximillian!' Reinhardt twisted his upper body, looked for his servant.

The elevator door was closed. Maximillian had already departed.

He turned his eyes to the rows of busy humanoids. 'You there! Help me. I said, *help me*.'

Programmed only to serve their assigned stations, they ignored him even as those very stations broke down around them. A panicky Reinhardt turned away, found himself staring out the port. Though leaning dangerously, the probe ship still rested in its dock.

Reinhardt began to lose his monumental self-control. 'Fools! Listen to me! Somebody, listen, or we'll all perish!' There was no response from the humanoids. He had reprogrammed them too well.

Turning his attention back to the screen, he tried again to push himself free. Occasionally his gaze would travel to the still functioning main screen, to the view of the expanding blackness that would soon swallow the *Cygnus*.

Somehow Holland put aside consideration of the agony in his injured leg and kept pace with the others as they raced down the corridor.

As the ship fell still deeper into the gravity well it started break up. The corridor trembled around the gasping group of refugees. The view through a wall port provided a boost no amount of rest could have equalled. They were nearing the probe dock.

'This way!' shouted Holland. They turned a last bend and found themselves standing outside the lock leading to the connecting umbilical. But when Holland jabbed the stud to open the door, it remained unmoving.

A red warning light came on instead as a nearby read-out provided the explanation.

Holland looked around grimly. 'Connector's been severed.' They started searching.

McCrae found the hoped-for locker. A dozen suits were neatly arranged inside. They chose three with full tanks, helped each other dress as minutes ticked past. A brief check insured that each suit was tight, that its internal oxygen system was functioning, and that the communicators were operative.

Holland waved the others clear. Pizer and McCrae moved down the corridor, the two robots the other way.

'Ready?'

Everyone acknowledged by grabbing tight to a secured section of wall or railing. Wrapping one arm around a protruding tube, Holland leaned over and touched the three emergency studs in proper sequence. The explosive bolts blew the lock cover out into space. A brief but intense rush of air pulled hard at everyone. It faded as distant emergency doors shut tight, sealing them off from the rest of the ship.

'Well, old timer,' V.I.N.Cent was saying to B.O.B. as they turned to head for the exit, 'you're going home after all . . . and as a hero, too.'

'Had to uphold the honour of the old outfit, V.I.N.Cent.'

McCrae, standing by the exit, noticed something moving at the far end of the passageway. 'V.I.N.Cent, B.O.B. . . . look out!'

Maximillian had appeared immediately behind the two machines. B.O.B. reacted first, thus caught the full force of the large mechanical's lasers. Circuitry flared as he was thrown backwards, bounced off a wall and fell to the floor. Maximillian shifted to turn his weapons on V.I.N.Cent and the others.

The delay had given V.I.N.Cent enough time to turn and fire himself. Both precisely aligned shots melted the pistols in Maximillian's hands.

'Get to the ship!' he instructed his human companions. 'I'll handle this.'

Maximillian had not been rendered harmless, however. Two additional arms came up, tipped with whirling blades suitable for trimming metal. They were designed to repair. They could easily well dismember.

V.I.N.Cent hovered in his path, fired again. But the material of the larger robot's shell was considerably tougher than the thin alloy of the two obliterated lasers. V.I.N.Cent fired again. The bursts had no effect on the oncoming Maximillian.

'Hurry, Captain.' V.I.N.Cent backed away from the larger mechanical.

The three humans exited through the blown hatch. Maximillian hesitated then turned his full attention to the darting, distracting V.I.N.Cent. He rushed up at him. The smaller machine dodged, fired again, seeking a weak place in the armoured monolith and not finding one. He dipped down to fire from closer range, ducked as the high-speed blades cut over his head.

Maximillian shifted again, trying to corner his opponent against the wall. V.I.N.Cent ducked and bobbed, firing. The edge of one blade snicked against his shell, sent him tumbling off-balance into the wall. The impact appeared to have damaged his internal gyro-balance system more than the blade had his exterior and he fluttered in one place, experiencing the robotic equivalent of dizziness. Maximillian advanced on him.

Outside the ship now, the three suited figures struggled to make their way towards the probe, pulling themselves through the twisted ruin of the *Cygnus*' external superstructure.

Maximillian was on top of V.I.N.Cent. The smaller robot spun, fired several rapid bursts, and just escaped through the small hole he had made in the hull before those whizzing blades could cut through his back.

Devoid of lasers and Reinhardt's restraint, Maximillian used the incredibly tough blades to open the gap wider. He pursued V.I.N.Cent out into space.

There was more room to manoeuvre outside, but the torn surroundings were less predictable. Maximillian rushed forward. V.I.N.Cent dodged, but backed into a curled length of metal. There was no cry of triumph as his opponent became trapped, but Maximillian pulsed a slightly deeper crimson as he moved forward and embraced V.I.N.Cent in a hug capable of distorting the strongest metal alloys.

A small door opened in V.I.N.Cent's lower body. The

larger machine did not immediately notice the tiny but efficient cutter that emerged. It pierced the huge mechanical's midsection, played havoc with delicate internal circuitry.

Tiny flares of fire spat from the hole as Maximillian loosened his grasp and spun away. His hover controls had been severed. Unable to guide himself he tumbled away from the *Cygnus*, caught in the intensifying tug of the black hole.

V.I.N.Cent spared the rapidly shrinking shape only a momentary glance before jetting back into the ship. Old B.O.B. was still lying where he had struck the deck. Most of his lights were out.

'Maximillian's finished,' V.I.N.Cent reported to him.

'You did well.' The reply from the metal form was faint.

'Thanks to you, my friend. I'll get you aboard now.' He drifted over the quiescent machine, prepared to extend service arms to encompass the barrel-shaped body.

'No.' The word was barely understandable. 'I won't be going with you.'

V.I.N.Cent hesitated. Desire battled realisation inside him. He could not avoid analysing the damage Maximillian's lasers had done. One blast had melted the majority of B.O.B.'s logic and cognition modules. He had very little mind left. What had been destroyed could be replaced, but the B.O.B. unit would have a new personality, a new self. He would not be what he was now.

Humans talked a lot about an intangible they called the soul. In all the lengthy catalogue of several thousand replacement parts for a B.O.B. or V.I.N.Cent unit, there was not one that carried that label.

'There's no need for me to go home,' the fatally damaged robot was saying, perhaps trying to cheer his friend, perhaps only stating the obvious. 'I *am* home. Out here. The same for me as it is for you.'

The final lights began fading as power failed along with the intricate solid-state brain. 'You're still new, still fully functional. Carry on for all of us, V.I.N.Cent. The humans will remember and praise their lost associates from the crew of the *Cygnus*. Only you can remember for the machines.

'Go now . . . help your friends . . .'

The last set of lights became dark. The thing on the deck was no longer alive. It was merely another piece of scrap metal – such as the *Cygnus* was fast becoming.

The corridor was threatening to shake apart around V.I.N.Cent. His shipmates might be having trouble outside. The suits they'd donned were not equipped with free-space manoeuvring units

V.I.N.Cent turned and jetted for the open hatch.

Holland was working his way across the battered surface of the ship. The sound of the *Cygnus* tearing itself apart reached him as an eerie groaning through the substance of his suit.

He ducked beneath a great arch of bent metal, pulled himself weightlessly across an artificial abyss. McCrae was right behind him, Pizer behind her.

He reached back and grabbed her hand to help her across the dangerously open space. For an instant her body swung feet first out into space. Then he pulled her down to where she could obtain her own grip. The strength of the nearing black hole was beginning to overwhelm the failing artificial gravity of the *Cygnus*.

Pizer looked back towards the ship's bow. The distant command tower was bending, twisting like a drunken lighthouse. He moved forward. His hand reached out for Holland's as he started across the gap – and their gloved palms parted. Slowly, helplessly, he began drifting away from the *Cygnus*.

Another fragment of metal drifted near him. This one, however, was mobile. One metal arm extended to clutch a thrusting bit of superstructure. Then they were both once more alongside Holland and McCrae.

'Thanks,' Pizer told him. He was breathing hard from the narrowness of his escape. 'A friend in need is a friend indeed.'

V.I.N.Cent responded with a twinkle of lights. 'You're learning, Mr Charlie.'

Reinhardt saw the tiny figures reach the side of the probe, cursed them under his breath. He cursed the cosmos itself, the unpredictability of it and man. Was there nothing pure and perfect a true scientist could cling to in the madness of the universe?

He cursed them again. Not because they had reached the probe. Because he had not reached it with them.

There was a violent splintering sound, and the vibration beneath him changed. The viewport exploded inwards. Shards of transparent plastic shot past him. At the same time the tower was torn free from the rest of the ship. Reinhardt's eyes bulged from sudden, savage decompression as he and the tower were thrown off into space. From decompression of flesh, from decompression of dream.

Holland opened the lock. They entered the probe successfully and removed their suits. Soon they were crowding into the tiny cockpit. The probe had been designed to accommodate two humans. The four of them filled it tightly.

McCrae happened to glance out the right port at the right moment. She saw the control tower spiralling away towards the vortex.

'Command tower's torn loose.' She experienced a brief moment of sorrow for Reinhardt. The sentiment was quickly quashed by the memory of the mind-wiped crew, of blank featureless face-plates concealing equally blank minds.

The engines of the *Cygnus* were still functioning but she was now directionless. Completely out of control, she swung wildly in the downspiralling well. One thruster broke free of its stern mounting, was followed by a section of broken bow.

Similar forces clutched at the probe ship as Holland frantically fingered the instrumentation. The engines were activated, then the null-gee field. The shaking stopped.

But they were still attached to the *Cygnus*. 'We'd better get the hell off,' he muttered. 'The whole ship's breaking up.'

He touched one control, then another. *Thrust*, and the probe lifted clear of the *Cygnus*.

Operating the console manually, Holland took them away from the ship. He was trying to put distance between them and the dangerous chunks of metal flying off the larger vessel.

They were clear, and he rested a moment. But the probe accelerated anyway, commenced a wide arc towards the collapsar. Nearby, the *Cygnus* continued to destruct. No longer protected by a null-gee field it was breaking into smaller and smaller sections.

Everyone aboard had reacted to the sudden, unprogrammed increase in velocity. Holland frantically began examining the instrumentation, trying to recall the phase sequence of twenty-year-old circuitry. Nothing slowed the ship's acceleration nor altered its course.

'I don't understand.' His muscles were tight with tension, and a little fear. Even with the null-gee operating they could sense an occasional tremor running through the ship as increasing gravity tugged at it.

'The field's working as it should. But none of the other controls are responding.' His hands wove futile patterns over the instruments.

'It's no good. I can't turn her.'

'There's no question about it, Captain.' V.I.N.Cent had settled back from the console and his own efforts to influence their course. 'The ship has been pre-programmed. I don't have the necessary information to override. Only two individuals might.'

'Reinhardt and Maximillian.' McCrae was surprised at how fast she'd resigned herself to the inevitable. At least the end should be quick.

'We're locked in, then?' Pizer leaned back in his chair.

Holland nodded agreement. 'Navigation is sealed. Probably in case the pilot is incapacitated, to hold the ship on course. Reinhardt was determined to make his journey, even if unconscious.'

'So we're going into the black hole after all, in spite of everything.'

Holland glanced over at his first officer, his friend. 'Check.'

Now that their destination was unavoidable, McCrae found herself speaking quite calmly. 'Let's pray that he was the prophet he claimed to be.'

Holland looked at her, his expression conveying a multitude of emotions it was too late to put into words. At that point, words would have been inadequate anyway.

'He who hesitates gathers no moss, and a rolling stone is lost.' V.I.N.Cent had moved to the back of the cockpit. The thought of being abruptly reduced to the size of a sub-atomic particle was one he could comprehend better than any of them. It frightened him.

Pizer patted his side comfortingly.

Holland watched the instruments. There were many he recognised and a fair number he did not. Several were evidently designed to monitor events beyond mere human perception. The probe continued to accelerate.

Ahead of them a blackness was eating the sky.

V.I.N.Cent extended his arms, braced himself against the sides of the cockpit. Holland continued to gaze at McCrae and she back, both sorrowing for what might have been. Pizer watched them both as the ship began to rotate, ignoring the advice of her outraged stabilising systems.

Something was squeezing Holland's guts, pressing down on his head and up at his feet.

A read-out on the console was marked in increments of several thousands. It had by now crawled patiently halfway up its length.

Abruptly, simultaneous with the fading of light inside the probe, it flicked upwards and vanished. Much else disappeared with it. Light, time, a sense of being alive, the efficacy of existence. A thought tickled Holland's brain, and a thousand years passed on Earth.

He was dimly aware that they must have crossed the event horizon. The line where things vanished forever -- time and space together. He considered the rhyme. Then he considered something else.

He should not have been able to consider his considering.

Something else impossible happening. Light. Light should not happen within the confines of a collapsar. Matter should not happen either. Perhaps he was no longer matter. Was pure thought affected by gravity? Did he still possess a body? He thought he was looking down at himself, but there no longer seemed to be anything there. Only darkness and quiet and peace. He was alone, adrift in an irrational dimension.

Then he imagined there were other thoughts curling and entwining among his own, though he could not immediately identify them. Kate? Charlie? V.I.N.Cent? They remained infinitely distant, tantalisingly near. Only the light ahead grew clearer. He imagined it had to be ahead. His speculations turned to the possible existence of white holes, knife wounds into other universes. He wondered if Reinhard could sense him.

Then there was something familiar again, recognisable warm. *Come to me*, it was saying. *Come to me, Dan. It's the only way.*

Kate! And she responded. *You must join with me, Dan. And you, Charlie. And V.I.N.Cent . . . if you can, V.I.N.Cent. Only thoughts have a chance inside here. Physical materialities will be crushed down to nothing, but thought . . . the essences ourselves . . . I think we have a chance . . . that way.*

Holland could feel something warm and all-encompassing reaching out to envelop him. The fragmentation of himself that had begun halted. He remained He.

It's working . . . came the powerful thought. *It's the esp-link . . . my thought projection ability . . . it will keep us together . . . if we fight for it!*

They blended, flowed together, thought itself strained beyond its normal borders under the unimaginable force of the collapsar. Then they were through . . . and amazingly, still whole. Kate was Kate; Charlie, Charlie; and Dan Holland still Dan Holland. Even V.I.N.Cent was there. They were themselves . . . and yet something strange and new, a galactic sea change that produced all the above and a new unified mindthing that was KateCharlieDanV.I.N.Cent also.

Dimly they/it perceived the final annihilation of a miniscule agglutination of refined masses – the *Palomino*. It was gone, lost in an infinite brightness. They/it remained, content and infinite now as the white hole itself.

They had been compressed, compacted, but had passed beyond and through with their selves still intact. With the passage came peace, and time to contemplate.

On a beach was a grain of sand. The sand was part of a continent, the continent component of a world, the world a speck of substance in the sea of infinity. They were part of that world, part of every world, for in passing out the white hole their substance had become dispersed. An atom of Charlie to a nine-world system, a molecule of Kate to a 'ocal cluster of stars, a tiny diffuse section of Holland spread hinly over a dozen galaxies.

Yet they could still think, for thought does not respect the rifling limitations of time and space. They were still them nd this new thing they had become.

Their thoughts spanned infinity, as did their finely spread ubstance, and they now had an eternity in which to conemplate the universe they had become . . .

THE TAR-AIYM KRANG
by Alan Dean Foster

The Tar-Aiym had been dead for perhaps a million years
Once they had fought against and then ruled the galaxy. But
now they had vanished, leaving only the legend of their final
artifact — the lost Krang ,

Nobody knew what the Krang might be, but everyone wanted
it. Until it was found . . .

For the Krang had a purpose. The Krang had power and a will
of its own.

NEW ENGLISH LIBRARY

ORPHAN STAR
by Alan Dean Foster

All of his life Flinx had lived in the marketplace on Drallar with his foster mother, an ageing shopkeeper. But Flinx did not belong there and although he knew nothing of his true parents he was determined to find out about himself and the strange mental abilities that he had been endowed with.

His search was to lead him into the clutches of Challis, one of the most depraved and powerful men in the Commonwealth . . . on to Terra where the records of his birth were kept . . . and finally to Ulru-Ujurr where the priceless and mysterious Janus jewels came from and where a new civilization was about to be born.

NEW ENGLISH LIBRARY

STARSHIP TROOPERS
by Robert Heinlein

Robert Heinlein's Starship Troopers are the jet-propelled
infantrymen of the future. In a galactic war of untold violence
and destruction, they scour the metal-strewn emptiness of
space and hunt out The Enemy.

But neither the viciousness of their electronic armour nor the
bloodthirsty militarism of their training can save them from the
grip of loneliness and fear.

Heinlein is an acknowledged master of Science Fiction, a
genius who has become spokesman for a whole generation.
And his starship trooper John Rico, rising from boyhood
dreams to high command in the cosmos, is a hero of the first
dimension — and beyond.

NEW ENGLISH LIBRARY

NAIL DOWN THE STARS
by John Morressy

Starfarer and skillman, Jolon Gallamor has been on the run since his tenth birthday. Among the diverse races and worlds of the galaxy so vividly described in STARBRAT, Jolon's skills as playwright, actor and bard are his passport to privilege and acclaim, all too often to peril and banishment. With each new planet he reaches, Jolon finds himself taking on a new role, hiding his past and keeping one step ahead of the catastrophe which threatens him.

Trooper of the Sternverein, thief, slave and fugitive, Jolon the peaceable battles his way around the universe, until as Alladale Anthem-maker he defeats an army and wins a world without spilling a drop of blood.

NEW ENGLISH LIBRARY

NEL BESTSELLERS